THE AVENGING ANGEL

A JIM MALHAVEN MYSTERY: BOOK 2

HELEN WHISTBERRY

CONTENTS

OTHER WORKS BY HELEN WHISTBERRY

A very heartfelt thank you to:
Rebecca S.
K.A. Miltimore
Jacob Klop
The Twitter Community of Writers
and as always,
my beloved sister, Maready

It was the screaming that first got my attention. That and the terrified expressions on the faces of the kids and nuns running from the Sisters of Mercy orphan asylum like a pack of hellhounds was after them. I seen more than one of those nuns crossing themselves or clutching their rosary beads as they herded their charges ahead of them down the front steps. The pair of smiling stone angels carved above the double entry doors looked down, smirking at the riot taking place below them.

"Mr. Malhaven!"

It was Sister Honoria trying to flag me down. She's the boss of the outfit and the reason I was on the scene to begin with.

She'd surprised me that morning by telephoning to the Carsworth City Crier and asking me to swing by the orphanage. She wasn't the biggest fan of the sensational reporting I did for the paper, so I figured something big must be up for her to give me a ring. I'd wasted no time hopping into my trusty Studebaker Champion, or the Champ as I affectionately called it, and scooting on over only to be greeted with this scene straight out of bedlam.

Honoria was standing still as a rock in the middle of a storm, looking way more annoyed than frightened if I was reading that beautiful face right. She was quite the stunner, habit and all, but she didn't stand for any nonsense and it took a lot to shake her.

"What gives, Sister?" I sung out, doing my best to wade through the sea of screeching kiddies to reach her. "Is the joint on fire?"

"Hardly," she replied with a lemon-sour note in her voice that told me I was right about her state of mind. "There's really no call for all this," she added, waving her hands around impatiently, "but once a few of the teachers lost their heads, it was like trying to reign in the ocean. I shall have a talk with them later when order has been restored."

Seeing the way those big green eyes of hers were flashing, I was glad I wasn't one of those nuns. I wouldn't want to be in their shoes when Honoria started in to give them what for.

"At least it's a warm day," she continued. "Most of the children have come out without their coats."

She was right about the weather. We were having an unusually balmy day for March. I'd left my old trench coat back at the office and was thinking I might like to shed my suit jacket only it didn't feel right to do so. I was on the job after all. Gotta keep up appearances. I did loosen my tie a bit and whipped my fedora down from its perch so I could swipe the sweat off my brow.

All the hard manual labor I'd been doing since the previous fall as part-time caretaker at Wynter's Hill Cemetery had gotten me in better shape than I'd been in since my Army days. But I was a big guy and rushing around to stories always made me work up a lather, especially when my bum legs started giving me trouble. I'd had a knife blade stuck in the left thigh and a bullet through the right one which might give you the idea I ain't always so popular. Comes with the territory of poking your nose in where it's not necessarily welcome.

I stuck my hat back on my melon, giving the brim a friendly tug. That topper had been a special gift from a special lady, one Mrs. Victoria Jankowski. The fedora had belonged to the late Mr. Jankowski. Now I had the care of it, I tried to always treat it right out of respect for his memory and as a sign of my boundless appreciation for his lovely widow.

"I don't think the kids will come to any harm in this weather," I reassured Sister Honoria as we watched the crowd milling around us.

We could tell the initial alarm was passing. The tots had started pushing and pulling one another, teasing, yelling, laughing even. There were only a few tear-stained faces here and there being comforted by teachers who were looking red in the face themselves. Like they knew they'd been caught out doing something kinda foolish. Whatever had given them all a scare must be inside that big mausoleum they called home, 'cause they seemed calmer now that everyone was outside.

I glanced up at the imposing gray face of the three-story building. There were about twenty wide stone steps leading up to the oversized wooden double doors under those carved angels I mentioned earlier. The angels were swooping down and reaching toward each other. I guess it was someone's idea to add them to keep watch over the poor little mites inside, but they always gave me kind of a creepy feeling.

The asylum stretched out to the left and the right of the entrance, rows of big windows looking out blankly at the city streets. A grim-looking place, but Victoria Jankowski herself had been raised up at the Sisters of Mercy and had turned out more than A-OK. It still tugged at my heartstrings to think of all those orphans with no ma or pa to make a fuss over them. Of course, my pa had been nothing to write home about so maybe they weren't missing so much after all. Having parents was no guarantee of a happy childhood. I'd seen more than enough evidence of that.

Deciding it was past time I started doing my job, I flashed a question at Sister Honoria. "What's the story? Why all the hubbub?"

"It's easier if I show you," she replied, tugging impatiently at my jacket sleeve and pulling me toward the entrance.

She steered me up the steps and into the grand front lobby, then down one of the side hallways to the big industrial kitchen. I'd had occasion to visit there once before, but it didn't look anything like I remembered. Everything had been clean and neat as a pin last time I saw it. Now? I rarely seen such a mess as was there. Pots and pans and every other cooking implement you can imagine were flung every which a way with all of it covered by the fine dust of what looked like it must have been an industrial-sized bag of flour.

I was so bumfuzzled by the disaster area, I almost didn't notice a familiar face lurking in one corner.

"Mr. Malhaven, I'm so glad you came. Maybe you can help us get to the bottom of this."

It was Marlene Sutherland, the sister of my pal and co-worker Marquis, better known as Q. Her smooth brown skin was marred by white handprints on her cheeks like she'd put her hands up to her face in dismay after touching the flour that coated every surface and was already settling on my old dark gray suit. At least it didn't show on her white nurse's uniform. Being responsible for the health of that many kids might have daunted some, but Marlene had graduated top of her class and was more than up for the task.

As a point of fact, as the flour started settling down a bit from where it had been riled up by our entrance, I noticed she had one hand on the shoulder of a small figure that was peering out from behind her skirt. A little girl, didn't look more than five or six years old maybe.

She was coated in flour from head to toe so it was hard to tell exactly what color her hair was, but her eyes were big and blue. Not a steely blue-gray like my Victoria's, but a pale, pale blue like the lightest color in the sky on a summer day when the sun is so bright, it almost hurts to look up. Between the pale eyes and the dusting of flour, she resembled nothing so much as a miniature ghost, peeking out at me.

"Hey there," I said to her, trying my best to look friendly. I've said already I'm a big guy, and I can add, in case you're interested, that I have auburn hair the color of a rusty gate and light gray eyes that ain't so bad, but I can't neglect to mention I have a hell of a scar running down one side of my face courtesy of the same goop that got me in the leg with the knife. It has a tendency to scare women and children, but this one didn't seem to mind. She just stared solemnly then gave me a small nod.

"What's your name?" I asked.

Marlene answered for her. "This is Lily."

Sister Honoria who was hovering close behind me leant forward and whispered in my ear. "Lily doesn't speak."

"Can't? Or won't?" I asked her sotto voce.

"We don't know. The doctor couldn't find anything obviously wrong physically, but she never speaks."

That was a shame, but she wasn't the first mute I'd met. Cornelius Cressley, former butler at the Wynter mansion out at the cemetery, and now man of the house thanks to his getting hitched to his former boss, Miss Livinia Wynter, can't speak neither, but he did have an obvious physical reason. Someone had cut his tongue out for him.

"What goes on here?" I asked, pointing at the mess.

"That's what we want to know. We've had a series of these pranks now and they are becoming more and more disruptive. It's why I called you. Marlene thought you could help us investigate, but while you were on your way over, this happened."

"And what's this?" I said, ever the keen reporter.

"The children were all in class when we heard a tremendous noise in here. A few of the sisters looked in to see what was going on, and they claim to have seen pots and pans flying through the air on their own. It sent them into a panic, and before I could stop them—well, you saw the results with your own eyes. A stampede from the building with all the children."

"Not all the children," Marlene objected, caressing Lily's shoulder.

"Yes, Lily was the only one in the kitchen when the teachers came to investigate." Honoria leant forward to whisper in my ear again. "Some of the teachers think Lily is to blame."

I looked at the catastrophe around us and then back at the small, quiet, white-shrouded figure.

"You mean to tell me she did all of this?" I said, pointing at the cabinets that reached up to the ceiling and had been emptied of all their contents. "She couldn't even get up there without a ladder."

"Of course not," said Marlene fiercely. "It's ridiculous."

I looked at Lily, and she stared back with those big, pale eyes. She didn't look frightened of me, even though I was towering over her like a giant, but I pulled off my hat and got down on one knee anyway so we could see eye to eye.

"Hey there, Lily. It's a real pleasure to meet you. My name is Jim, Jim Malhaven. I'm a reporter for the newspaper and it's my job to ask people questions. Would you mind if I asked you a few?"

She thought it over then gave me another nod.

"That's fine," I said, trying to be encouraging. "Now, you look like a good girl. You wouldn't ever cause this kind of trouble, would you?" I said, pointing to the chaos around us.

She shook her head in a slow, grave way that made her look wise beyond her years.

"That's what I thought. Bet you were just in the wrong place at the wrong time. But maybe you seen something. Did you see who did all this?"

Those big eyes got wider, and she looked more solemn than ever as she slowly nodded. This was progress, but I wasn't sure what to do next. How do you get a description from a witness who can't or won't talk? I had about decided I'd have to play a game of twenty questions —you know, male or female, tall or short, brunette or blonde—when she surprised me by suddenly laying down flat on the floor.

Both Marlene and Honoria started forward to make her get up, but I held out a warning hand to say, give it a minute.

The floor was thickly covered with the flour and sugar and whatever else had been spilled in the riot. Lily started making a movement with her arms and legs like the kids do in the snow when it's piled high. Then she jumped up and pointed to the shape left behind. This white stuff wasn't snow, but I recognized the shape just the same. An angel if I ever saw one.

CHAPTER TWO

"*A*n angel? An angel did all this?" I asked softly.

She nodded again, quickly and emphatically this time. She wanted to make sure there was no mistake about it.

Sister Honoria gave out with an impatient clucking noise behind me. I got the feeling she thought I was wasting my time, but I was getting somewhere now. Sure, it was unlikely a heavenly being had descended from on high for the sole purpose of making an unholy mess of the kitchen, but I had no doubt Lily had seen something.

"How did you know it was an angel? Could you see its wings?"

She shook her head and made a kind of pantomime with her hands, tucking them behind her neck and down the collar of the plain dress she wore.

"It had them tucked away?"

Another nod.

"Sounds smart. I always thought it must be quite the nuisance having to try and walk around with a big pair of wings knocking into everything," I said with a grin.

That earned me a shy smile.

"So, if you couldn't see its wings, what made you think it was an angel, I wonder?" I remarked, more to myself than her since I didn't expect an answer, but she slipped her small hand in one of my mitts and started tugging me toward the kitchen door. I lumbered to my feet and followed after her as she led me back down the hallway to the lobby.

There on the wall was a large painting with one of those brass signs indicating it had been given to the joint by some generous bigwig or other. It was probably a scene from the Bible, but I'll be the first to admit I ain't as familiar with that book as it might do me good to be. All I could tell is there was quite a crowd in the picture, but Lily pointed confidently to a figure on the edge of the group.

It was an angel in a flowing white dress with its long wings extended behind it who was trying to wedge its way into the mob. I wasn't sure what she was trying to tell me since she'd already said she hadn't seen any wings, but then she pointed from the angel to herself and back again.

It took me a minute but then I got it. They were both white—the angel in the picture shining with some kind of heavenly light in contrast to the dark crowd, and Lily covered in flour from head to toe. But what did it mean? Was the culprit dressed all in white? Had white skin? Maybe wearing a white dress—a woman then?

I was about to start the twenty questions routine again when Lily started an almighty sneezing fit that shook her small body from head to toe. Both Honoria and Marlene started clucking then, and Marlene whisked her away to get her cleaned up. My questions for Lily would have to wait, but I figured there was plenty more Honoria could tell me. She ushered me into her office. I flopped into one of the worn leather armchairs there while she settled herself behind the wooden desk.

"Give me details," I said, pulling out my notebook and pencil. "Sounds like this ain't the first little adventure you had here."

She gave me one of her serious looks. "I do hope, Mr. Malhaven, you can show some discretion. I understand you're a newspaper reporter and always on the hunt for a good story, but I only called you because Marlene said you were good at finding out things and I'd rather not involve the police if I can help it. I'm afraid they aren't always the most understanding, even when the offender is a child, you know."

Boy, did I. Juvenile delinquency they called it, and we'd run more than one story ourselves in the paper about wild teenagers, listening to fast songs, driving fast cars, and just in general, living life way too fast. In my view, kids in this year of our Lord 1951 weren't so different from when I was growing up. I even kinda liked a lot of that music they were all hot about, but it was one of those things that sold papers to the old folks who wanted to think everything was better back in their day.

I couldn't blame Sister Honoria for wanting to keep their troubles to themselves. My best friend, Joey Flanagan, was a cop. We'd grown up together, and he was the same as a brother to me, but I gotta admit, he comes down heavy as a sledgehammer on anyone he thinks is trying to get away with something they shouldn't. Sometimes, I think he takes his job too seriously, but then he's seen a lot of hard things on the streets. Makes a man cynical and hard himself.

Sister Honoria and my sweetheart, Victoria, were thick as thieves from the days when Victoria was still an inmate at the orphanage and Honoria was just starting out as a teacher there, so I forced myself to put aside my journalistic itch for the moment. I wouldn't ever do anything to upset the lovely lady who was the light of my life, and I knew she'd want me to help out her old friend without asking for anything in return.

I tucked my notebook and pencil back into my pocket and held up my empty hands as if to say, nothing to see here. "I gotcha. You wanna keep it on the down low. Any friend of Victoria's is a friend of mine automatically, so I'll do what I can for you. I promise not to write up anything for the paper without running it by you first, but I can't guarantee word won't get out anyway. That mob running screaming out the front doors a while ago might have attracted someone's attention besides mine, you know."

"Yes, I'm afraid you're right. We won't be able to keep a lid on this forever. We need to get to the bottom of it and quickly. It started several months ago. We hardly noticed at first, the incidents were so trivial. Things being misplaced here and there. We would think they were missing then they would show up later in an unusual spot. A vase of flowers found on the floor in one of the bathrooms, a ball from the playground left in an oven, that kind of thing. Barely annoying enough to worry about."

"Hm, yeah," I agreed. "Hardly criminal behavior."

"No. I didn't even make much of an effort to track down the culprit or culprits since the pranks were harmless enough. Children need to blow off steam sometimes. Create a little mischief. It's part of childhood."

"Wouldn't have thought the other nuns would feel that way, if you'll pardon my saying," I said apologetically.

Sister Honoria smiled, showing off her dimples. "I've gotten the feeling before you don't think highly of us, Mr. Malhaven."

I fiddled with my tie, feeling the heat. It was true I'd once thought of nuns as tough old birds, ill-tempered crows dressed all in black with a ruler glued to their hand, ready to hand out corporal punishment at the slightest excuse.

She laughed at me. Who says nuns ain't got a good sense of humor? "I can't speak for other institutions such as ours. But here, I encourage the teachers to balance discipline with compassion and understanding. After all, our children haven't gotten off to the best start in life. They deserve to have some fun as long as it doesn't get out of hand or interfere with their education."

"And I take it things are getting out of hand from what I seen today?"

"Yes, and this wasn't even the worst, I'm afraid. There was another, more serious incident. That's why I called you."

She hesitated. I could tell it was weighing on her mind, so I let the silence ride. I've found you get more info that way sometimes than if you rush in and try to talk it outta someone. Sure enough, she spilled the beans.

"Night before last, a couple of men knocked on the front doors to say they thought they had seen someone on our roof. It was very late, just before midnight. Our custodian leaves for the day at six, and there would be no reason for anyone else to go up onto the roof. The men offered to come with me and help search in case it was someone looking to break in, but I had a suspicion it was related to our recent pranks and wanted to shield any of the children who might be up to something. I told them I would take a look and asked them to take a turn around the grounds instead and look for a ladder or any other sign of someone climbing up to the roof."

"That was mighty brave of you, going up there all by yourself."

"Don't worry, I rallied the troops. Marlene lives here on the grounds with us, and I woke up Sister Martha and Sister Bertha as well. I don't believe you've met them yet, have you?"

I shook my head. "Don't ring a bell."

"When you do, you'll understand why I felt the four of us were capable of routing any invader we might encounter," she said with a smile.

"I'm sure you ladies were more than up to the task. What did you find?"

She lost her smile quick as though a bad memory had knocked it away. "Nothing, at first. The moon was out but was hidden behind a cloud, and we couldn't see far with our flashlights. Martha and Bertha started exploring along the top of the west wing, and Marlene and I walked down the east one. When we were getting close to the end of the building, the moon suddenly reappeared. That's when we saw her."

I moved forward to the edge of my seat, always eager for a thrilling tale, whether I can use it for the paper or not. "A her, you say. A dame?"

"Not exactly a 'dame,' as you call it, Mr. Malhaven, but it was a girl. A little girl. Lily, in fact." She grew ashen as she said it, like it pained her to remember.

"The girl from the kitchen? She keeps popping up, don't she? But she looks as innocent as a mouse. What was she up to?"

"She didn't look to be up to anything. She had her back to us. Marlene and I started walking quietly towards her. We didn't want to startle her as she was so close to the edge of the roof. It was a cool night and all she had on was her nightgown. I remember being afraid she would catch cold when suddenly—"

Sister Honoria clammed up as though it was too hard to say the next thing. I tried the silent treatment again, and after a moment, she gathered her courage to continue her tale.

"Suddenly, she spread her arms wide, like a bird, and before we could say anything or try to stop her…" Honoria trailed off.

It was the first time I'd ever seen her rattled about anything. She's a tough one, and it took a lot to shake her. I'm the same way. Battle-hardened from my Army days during the war and things I'd experienced and seen since. I don't flinch at every little thing that happens, but even I gotta admit it shook me what she said next with a catch in her voice.

"She jumped."

CHAPTER THREE

"Jumped!" I repeated, not sure I'd heard her right. "But I just saw her alive and kicking, didn't I? Hope you ain't gonna tell me that was a phantom wandering around. I've had enough of those to last me a lifetime and a half."

Sister Honoria's smile broke through at that. She was conversant with the ghost tale that had been the means of bringing me and Victoria together, but not without a few bumps in the road and chills in the night that still made me sweat to think of.

"No, she's as real as you or I. Fortunately, the men checking the grounds below had caught sight of her at the edge of the roof and were in position to catch her and save her from serious injury. God was watching out for her," she added, making the sign of the cross with a look heavenward. "But I've never been so frightened in my life as when I looked over the edge of the roof expecting to see her broken body below."

Couldn't blame her for that. I'd seen a lot of death and dying in my time. You get hardened to it. But I can't say I'd have glanced over the edge myself without a twinge of horror at the thought of what I might see. There's a difference between watching war-weary men struck down in the midst of a gun battle and seeing the life crushed out of an innocent child before they've hardly begun.

"It was a lucky break those guys catching her," I said. "What do you make of her jumping? Could you find out what made her do it?"

"No. As you've seen, she doesn't speak and she's very… strange, isn't quite the right word. Different, maybe. Different to the other children. So serious and solemn. She seems old beyond her years."

"What is she, five or six?"

"Maybe, or maybe even a bit older. We're not exactly sure. She was found six months ago wandering in the city park at night by the police. They tried to locate her parents, even advertising in the newspaper, but she had nothing on her that would identify her, and no one ever came forward to claim her."

"That's right. I remember now. Old Maudie Adams down at the Crier wrote up a tearjerker about it. She's first-class with the sob stuff. So, that's the girl in the story, huh?"

"Yes. We named her Lily White because she was so pale and thin when she came to us, a bit like Snow White when she was lost in the forest. We've done our best to fatten her up, as the witch did to Hansel and Gretel," Honoria said with a slight smile before sobering up again. "But she's never spoken, and we may never find out what happened to her before she came to us. I fear it was no fairy tale. She has an aura of sadness about her that is rare in so young a child."

"Are you saying you thought she was trying to… you know," I said, not wanting to say what I was thinking out loud. "When she jumped off the roof?"

"No, of course not," she denied, although the troubled look on her face made me think I wasn't the only one to have the identical thought. "Such an act is a mortal sin. Why would someone so young have any reason to think of it? No, the way her arms were outstretched, I think she wanted to fly. Children can be very fanciful. Particularly shy and quiet ones who tend to live in their imaginations. Lily's obsessed with this idea of angels. I'm afraid we do go on about them quite a bit here, and of course, the children see the carvings over the front door and the painting in the lobby."

Honoria rustled through the papers on her desk until she came up with a stack of sheets that she passed over to me.

"She makes these sketches all the time. We find them everywhere around the building."

The pencil drawings she gave me weren't bad. I'm not saying they were as good as a Norman Rockwell cover on the Saturday Evening Post, but they weren't the usual scribbles of a child. It was easy to see they were of angels, and not just any angel, but the same one in all of them. A lean figure. A man, or more like a youth, late teens, early twenties maybe, if an angel can be said to have an age. Weren't they supposed to be ageless?

Had to catch myself up there. What was I thinking? I didn't believe for a second Lily was seeing a genuine angel, but there was no doubt she had a definite idea or person in mind. All the drawings showed the same face, with enough details—a slightly crooked nose, the wide set eyes—to make me think it wasn't just something she was dreaming up.

I studied the face and thought Lily had caught something in the expression. A sadness to match her own? Or resignation. The kind of look someone might have if nothing good had ever happened to them, and they had the idea nothing good ever would. I kind of felt sorry for the guy, though maybe I shouldn't if he was behind all the mischief the nuns had been putting up with.

A thought struck me, and I shared it with Honoria. "She's no slouch with a pencil. Does she know how to read and write yet?"

"She does. In fact, she reads and writes at a very advanced level. Her spelling is perfect, and she is a voracious reader of anything and everything she picks up."

"There you go," I said leaning back in my chair in satisfaction, thinking for a minute like a dope that I had come up with a solution she hadn't been smart enough to think of. "Ask her about her past then and let her jot down her life story for you."

That earned me quite the look, and I can't say I didn't deserve it, but at least she didn't kick me out of her office then and there.

"We have tried doing that, naturally, Mr. Malhaven. Unfortunately, she either doesn't remember anything about her life before she came to us or doesn't choose to share it with us. As I said, Lily is different. Unusually private and reserved for a child. She has a kind of dignity about her, a grace. She had obviously received a good education before she came to us. I feel she must have come from a privileged background."

"Which makes it all the stranger she ended up here, don't it? Even if she wandered away from home, why didn't her family come around to claim her? There was plenty in the paper about it at the time, and I know for a fact from my pals on the force that they sent out bulletins across the country. If she came from money, it's possible she was even kidnapped and they let her loose or she got loose, but there would still be someone out there looking for her, wouldn't there?"

"You would certainly think so, but the police had reached a dead end in their investigations the last I was informed."

"It's a puzzler, ain't it? She must have been living somewhere with someone before she came to be found in the park. Unless she was raised by wolves or something."

"I don't believe so, Mr. Malhaven, unless the wolves were unusually literate," Sister Honoria said with a satirical look before sobering up again. "Someone obviously took the time to teach her to read and write. She was on the thin side and very pale when she came to us but otherwise looked well-cared for. She has excellent table manners and is always meticulous about her appearance. She didn't learn all of that living wild in the woods."

"Very mysterious, but you called the right guy," I said, leaning back in my chair again. "Marlene was right. Finding out things is my stock in trade, and I ain't so bad at it if I do say so myself. What do you want me to concentrate on first? The pranks or the girl?"

"I would suggest both, Mr. Malhaven. The pranks didn't start until Lily came under our care. Unfortunately, some of the sisters are superstitious and believe Lily is under a dark cloud, or even possessed by an evil spirit, if for no other reason than her continued silence and the air she has of holding herself apart from the others. Children, and even some adults I'm afraid, can be very intolerant of anyone who appears different from themselves. The incident today can only serve to increase their fear."

I was working up to say something very profound about human nature when I was forestalled by a knock at the door.

"Come in," Sister Honoria sang out. The door opened to reveal Marlene ushering in a newly spruced up Lily.

She looked different now that she wasn't coated head to toe in flour, but I recognized those unusual pale blue eyes right off. I could see she had hair that was out of the common way too, a blonde so light it looked silver, braided into two long pigtails that hung over her shoulders. I got why she might make people nervous. There was something unearthly looking about her, like she had dropped in on us from outer space. Combined with her silence, I had to admit, it was kind of eerie and gave me an uneasy feeling myself.

At least it did until she gave me a quick shy smile. I may look the toughest of tough guys on the outside, but as Victoria always reminds me, I'm one big ball of mush on the inside. My heart went out to that little girl, all alone in the world, and now the object of superstition on top of it. I guess Honoria would tell me God had a plan for Lily and was looking out for her, but from where I was sitting, I couldn't help but wonder.

"Look who cleans up nice. None the worse for wear, I see. You're looking better than me," I said ruefully, noticing my suit jacket was sporting a nice sprinkling of the white stuff.

Lily walked over and brushed gently at the flour on my sleeve as though she wanted to help me out. This wasn't the kind of reaction I usually inspired in the kiddies so I can't tell you what she saw in me, but I can report it made me want to protect her and make up to her for all she might have gone through in her short life.

"Did Sister Honoria tell you about what's been happening, Mr. Malhaven?" Marlene asked. "Are you going to look into it?"

"Sure. Should be a piece of cake for a top-notch reporter such as myself. Maybe I'll start by talking to our Mr. L. Get his take on the situation," I added with a wink, referencing the business manager of the organization, Mr. Samuel Leonard. I'd had a suspicion for some time he and Marlene might have had more than professional feelings for each other. She'd usually just roll her eyes and brush off my teasing about it. Not this time. This time she glared at me to give me the hint I'd put my big foot right in the middle of something nasty.

Sister Honoria spoke gently. "I'm afraid I had to let Mr. Leonard go. It was a difficult decision as he's been with us for so many years, however, some… irregularities came up in the bookkeeping that I could not ignore."

"Are we talking about the same Sam Leonard? He always acted like a straight shooter to me. A regular OK guy," I asked, puzzled at this unexpected turn of events.

Marlene jumped in on that. "He is! There's no one more honest than Sam! I mean, Mr. Leonard," she amended. "I'm sure it was all some kind of misunderstanding."

Sister Honoria's eyes started flashing and she looked like she was girding up for battle. I had the feeling this wasn't the first go round she and Marlene had had about this very subject but before she could get going, the door bust open and two linebackers stomped in. That is, they were built like linebackers, but as they both had on habits, I assumed they were actually nuns.

"Sister Martha! Sister Bertha! What is the meaning of this interruption?" Honoria asked in a tone so frigid, I'm surprised it didn't start in to snowing in that office.

The linebackers exchanged glances before one of them drew herself up to say, "We have all been talking and we've come to a decision. Things cannot go on in this way. It isn't good for the children."

She pointed one meaty finger in my general direction. I felt Lily pull herself closer to me as though she had an idea of what was coming next.

"We are all agreed. That child must go!"

CHAPTER FOUR

*I*f I thought Sister Honoria was looking frosty before this bombshell, it was nothing to what she looked like after. I'm kinda astounded Martha and Bertha didn't drop dead on the spot, but they were made of sterner stuff. They stood their ground with barely a flinch.

"Nurse, please wait outside with Lily." Honoria waited for her order to be carried out and the door to close before turning back to those other two. "What a thing to say, Sister Martha! And in front of the child. I've very disappointed in you both. Isn't our mission to look after all of God's poor lost children? How dare you suggest we cast one away."

"We must protect God's children, yes. But Sister Margaret and Sister Agnes know what they saw. That child was standing in the midst of the kitchen as pots and pans flew around her head. And she was smiling. That is not God's work, Sister Honoria. That is the Devil's work. And it is our duty to reject all things of the Devil."

Remembering the trust Lily had placed in me, I couldn't help but jump in. "Come now, ladies. You can't really think that slip of a girl was responsible for all that mess in the kitchen."

"And who might you be and what business is this of yours?" This was Bertha, deciding she better get in on the action.

"This is Mr. Malhaven," Honoria explained. "A reporter with the Crier. I asked him to come help us investigate what is happening."

"Oh, Mr. Malhaven," Sister Bertha chirped. "You of all people should agree with us. I remember those articles you wrote on the haunting out at the cemetery. You must be convinced evil forces exist."

Given that the trouble out at the boneyard turned out to have been the result of all-too-human agents, she was taking a lot for granted. Sure, there was one or two strange things I still couldn't explain from my adventures with a supposed ghost named Wally, but that hadn't turned me into a believer in spirits. Call me cynical, but I'd found plain old earthly greed, anger, and meanness were more than enough to explain most of the evil deeds that went on in the world.

"You'll have a hard time convincing me Lily is responsible," I said. "She looks and acts sweet as a kitten. Besides, whoever's behind this is probably trying to pull your leg more than cause any real harm. I don't think you exactly got another Hitler or Benito Mussolini on your hands here. I bet you'll find it's one or two of the boys in back of it. I know just such a young troublemaker myself."

I was thinking of a certain someone name of Mikey. He would fit the bill as mastermind behind these stunts if only he was an orphan and not one of the ever-multiplying mob belonging to a Mr. and Mrs. Cummings, who seemed more or less resigned to having a professional hooligan in their midst. As I always say, if you're gonna pop out that many kiddies, there's bound to be at least one clunker in the bunch. That's just the law of averages.

"We do not think this latest incident can be explained away as a mere prank. And don't forget," Martha said, "Lily jumped from the roof of this building. That is not the action of a normal child."

"And to survive such a fall with very little harm done," Bertha chimed in, crossing herself. "It's unnatural, and it's not only us who think so. The staff have talked of nothing else since it happened."

"It appears quite natural to me," said Sister Honoria. "If you cannot see the hand of God moving to protect Lily, maybe you need to spend more time on your knees at prayers and less time gossiping like a bunch of old hens with nothing better to do!"

I thought for sure that would set them back on their heels, but they weren't done yet. Martha had one more grenade to lob.

"We hoped it wouldn't come to this, Sister, but we are prepared to go to Father Michael with our concerns and even… even to the Bishop if need be."

I hadn't thought Honoria could go any redder in the face, but she looked ready to bust a gasket. Her fists balled up at her side, and I wouldn't have been surprised if she took a swift poke at those two ladies even if they were about twice her size. I didn't want to have to witness such godly women coming to blows. Besides, an idea had popped into my brain. That happens to me now and again.

"No need to go pulling rank on Sister Honoria here. I think I got a solution that'll work out for everybody. Why don't I take the girl to stay with Victoria Jankowski for a few days while I investigate all this? I'm sure we'll find out it's only a couple of the boys trying to stir up excitement. My pal Joey Flanagan and I used to get up to all kinda shenanigans together when we were at loose ends. But it might not be such a bad idea to get Lily away for a few days until we get it figured out. She might even enjoy the change of scenery. You said she's already a whiz at reading and writing, so it won't hurt her much to miss a few days of school. Give things a chance to settle down."

I wasn't sure my brainstorm even registered with Honoria at first, she was looking so hot and bothered by the stink of mutiny in the air, but then she turned to me with a grin. "We have come to a pretty pass, Mr. Malhaven, if you are suggesting Lily would be better off in a graveyard than under our care."

I grinned back at her. One thing I can appreciate is someone who keeps their sense of humor even in trying circumstances.

"You consider cemeteries holy ground, don't you? What better place for God to keep an eye on her?"

"I appreciate the offer, Mr. Malhaven, but Lily is such an imaginative child already. I'm not sure such surroundings would be suitable for her."

"Oh, it ain't so bad out there. Plenty of room in that big old house to rattle around in and lots of space to play outside. There's trees getting ready to bloom, and we planted hundreds of flower bulbs last fall that are popping up. We already got a bunch of the prettiest purple crocus and yellow daffodils around every corner, those first harbingers of spring."

"Why, Mr. Malhaven, that was positively poetic!"

I had to blush. Victoria never gets tired of teasing me about my fondness for blooming things. I guess it is funny to see a beefy, hard-looking guy leaning over to sniff a delicate rose, but I seen a lot of ugly things in my life. Gives you an appreciation for beauty wherever you can find it.

"Shouldn't you check with Victoria first? It is a serious responsibility looking after a child."

"She'll get a kick out of it," I asserted confidently, though I'll admit it gave me a twinge of doubt as to whether springing such a surprise on her was a good idea after all. Victoria had lost her only child, Karolina, when the infant girl was only a few months old. I wouldn't want to be responsible for raking up bad memories for her.

Before I could have a change of heart, though, Martha and Bertha, who'd been watching this debate in silence like spectators at a tennis match, crossed their arms in front of their substantial bosoms and announced, "It's settled then."

Sister Honoria got a stubborn look on her face. I could tell she was thinking about defying those two, but I knew she'd put the child's best interests ahead of her own need to show them who was boss. If there was this much bad feeling against the girl, she couldn't argue getting Lily stashed safely out of the way for a few days would be better than letting her become a target of superstition and gossip.

She walked to the door and opened it, calling for Marlene and Lily to come back in the office.

"Lily, dear," she said, leaning over and touching the girl gently on her shoulder. "What would you think about going away for a few days? Mr. Malhaven here knows a very nice lady who lives in a great big house, and they'd love to have you come and stay with them for a little while. Would you like that?"

"That's right," I added. "Whataya think about me and you breaking out of this joint?"

Lily considered the offer for a minute in that serious way she had before making her answer clear enough by coming over to me and looking up with another shy smile.

"That's the ticket," I said, sticking out a paw for her to take. "Why don't we wait out on the steps while they get your duds packed up?"

As noted, I'm all marshmallow on the inside, so the feel of that tiny hand in mine and her trailing along beside me with such blind faith set my heart to glowing more than a bit. Made me think I might have to revise my position on kids. Maybe they weren't so bad after all.

We didn't have long to wait before Marlene appeared with a small bundle in her hand. Lily accepted it somberly. I didn't know who this girl was or where she'd come from, but watching her standing there so polite, holding all her earthly possessions wrapped up in a package no bigger than a Sunday roast, I knew I was gonna make it my business to find out.

CHAPTER FIVE

I loaded Lily up in the Champ and drove off down the narrow city streets, navigating our way out to the edge of town. She looked smaller than ever on the big bench seat in the car. Scrunching herself up against the door and rolling the window down, she stuck her head out when we hit the wide-open country roads, letting the wind blow in her face and rattle her pigtails. Guess it made a nice change from being cooped up in the asylum. Maybe she'd never been out in the country before? I kept trying to make notes in my head of any hints that might paint a picture of what her life had been before she'd been abandoned.

We passed a field of dairy cows and I heard a gurgling sound. She looked over to me with a smile. I realized she was giggling and pointing at them.

"Moo-oo-oo," I said like a goof, but that made her laugh even harder, so it was worth playing the fool. She could make noises at least. Made me wonder if she might be coaxed into gabbing with some patience.

I thought she'd be feeling pretty low about being kicked out by the nuns, but she actually looked more light-hearted and less serious. Maybe I was right about the change of scenery doing her good after all.

Of course, the scenery in question being a boneyard, I guessed we'd have to wait and see.

Wynter's Hill Cemetery ain't too far out of town, so it wasn't long before we reached the big iron gates with the name of the cemetery written out in fancy script above. They were standing wide open the way they always do during the day to welcome visitors. The place was founded by a Mr. William Wallace Wynter, former bootlegger and all around not nice guy. He'd had three daughters, two of which had come to a nasty end the previous autumn, mostly due to their own evil deeds, but in my opinion, a lot of that could be laid at the door of their miserable father. Meanness is something kids can learn just the same as good manners and reading.

Made me think Lily had experienced some kind of good influence in her young life from what I'd seen so far. Although, as we'd only made each other's acquaintance a few hours previous, I told myself to keep an open mind until I got to know her better. I'd learned the hard way not to judge a book by its cover.

We wound up the long gravel drive toward the big house on the hill right in the middle of the graveyard. It was an imposing two-story mansion with a big double-door entrance and rows of picture windows. I always figured Mr. Wynter built it with an eye toward intimidating his visitors and impressing upon them how important he was. I was relieved to see Victoria's new Caddy convertible parked out front.

Maybe I should explain at this point that Victoria used to be the hired help at the cemetery but had found out during those aforementioned events about six months back that she was actually related to the ladies of the big house. In fact, one of the late and, sad to say, unlamented Wynter sisters had been her ma. Victoria had been given away to the orphanage by Mr. Wynter Senior, mostly, it seemed to me, out of pure meanness. Although it was true Victoria's mother was unwed and likely to stay so since Wynter had arranged to have his daughter's lover knocked off after framing him for murder.

But I digress. All you really need to know is Victoria lived in the big house now with her aunt, Miss Livinia Wynter, technically Mrs. Livinia Cressley since marrying the butler. I lived in the caretaker's cottage on the grounds to be closer to the light of my life and to help out with keeping up the cemetery when I had time.

I'd thought about quitting the paper and leading the quiet life out in the country, but part of me couldn't bear the idea of giving up on the fun of chasing down leads. Part of me wanted to maintain some independence, too. The paper didn't pay much, but ever since Victoria came into the Wynter family and all the money that went with the honor, I thought it was more important than ever to prove I could fend for myself.

I knew Victoria would gladly share her newfound fortune with me. In fact, she'd offered to buy me a new car to take the place of my old clunker, but I was too proud to accept that kind of help, so she'd bought herself a brand-new, candy apple red convertible instead as a treat. Like I said, I was glad to see it parked in the drive because it meant she was around the place somewhere. I figured the sooner I sprung my surprise on her the better. I'd never seen Victoria hesitate one second to lend someone a helping hand, but then I'd never given her such a test as bringing home an orphaned child before.

As Lily and I got out of the car, it didn't take long to figure out what direction to go 'cause I heard Victoria's rich alto voice. She often hummed or sang as she worked. Tried to get me to sing along sometimes, but as I couldn't carry a tune in a bucket, I always told her I'd rather sit back and get an earful of her dulcet tones instead.

I grabbed Lily by the hand and headed toward the sound of the melody, one of the popular love songs of the day. Coming around the corner, I saw Victoria in all her glory, swinging a pickaxe at the base of a large overgrown bush. One of the many things I love about her, she ain't afraid of a little hard work. She was concentrating on her task and didn't hear us until we were right up on her.

She turned around, that honey-blonde waterfall of hair and those eyes, blue-gray like a stormy sea, sending the usual thrill through me. It was a sight I'd never get tired of seeing after once thinking I'd never see it again.

"Jim! What on earth happened to you?" She abandoned the pickaxe and came over to brush at the mess on my suit. "You look like you rolled around in a dustpan. What have you been up to?"

"You know, a little of this, a little of that. I'll explain later, but first, introductions are in order," I said, pulling Lily out from where she had been hiding shyly behind my leg. "This is my new friend, Lily. Lily, this is my friend Victoria."

Victoria gave me a questioning look but quickly leaned over and took one of Lily's hands in both of hers for a friendly shake.

"I'm very pleased to meet you, Lily. I know any friend of Mr. Malhaven's will be a very good friend of mine."

Lily nodded a touch but hardly more than one of the statues in the cemetery might.

I seen a shadow moving low, a sleek black cat keeping his one good eye on us. "Look, Lily, another friend of mine. That there's Archie. He enjoys a good rubdown behind the ears. Wanna go make his acquaintance?" I asked.

I didn't have to ask twice. She ran over to the cemetery's resident mouser and sat down on one of the low tombs as Archie climbed onto her lap, purring loud enough for us to hear it all the way over to where Victoria and I stood watching.

"Who is she, Jim?"

"She's from Sisters of Mercy. I'll fill you in on the whole deal tonight, but I promised Sister Honoria we'd take care of her for a couple of days."

"We?"

"Well, I can pitch in some, but I ain't got that womanly touch."

"I see. So, you really mean you volunteered me then. You might have checked with me before promising Honoria such a thing, Jim. It's not a walk in the park, taking responsibility for a child."

"I know, but they got trouble over there and some of the inmates have taken against Lily through no fault of her own that I can see. I thought it was a bright idea to get her out of the way while I investigate. I should have asked you first, but one thing led to another and—"

She held up a hand. "I know, I know. That's what always happens with you, isn't it?" She still had a bit of fire in her eyes, but she paired it with one of those million-dollar smiles of hers, so I thought she'd forgive me. Victoria has a generous spirit that's never let me down yet. "Of course, she can stay with us as long as she needs to if things are as bad as you say. I'm not sure what Livinia or Mr. Cressley will have to say about it though."

"Lily and Cressley have something in common. Lily can't talk, either. Or won't talk," I amended. "The doc checked her out and wouldn't say she couldn't talk if she suddenly took a notion to."

"Poor child," Victoria said so soft and low, it felt like she'd gone very far away from me to a distant time or place, and those beautiful eyes filled with tears.

My heart ached to see her looking so sad. I wouldn't have hurt her for anything, not even the moon and the stars. "Is this okay? I could find somewhere else to stash her easy. Joey Flanagan and his wife, or Marlene and Q's mother."

"No, of course I'll look after her. It… it just struck me Karolina would have been about her age if she'd lived. Lukasz had very fair hair. I always wondered if Karolina would have taken after him. She might have looked rather similar to Lily."

Victoria shook her head, rattling away those sad memories of her husband and infant daughter. "I'll take her into the house and get her settled. There's a lovely sunny spare bedroom right next to mine. Can you fill me in on the details or do you need to head back to town?"

"I gotta run now. I want to start checking around. Sooner we get to the bottom of this trouble, the better for her, but I'll give you the full scoop this evening. Thanks for taking care of her. I think she's a sweet kid."

"Listen to you, Mr. Sentimental. I thought you didn't like children?"

"Maybe I'm finding out it depends on the kid," I whispered as Lily came back up to us after being abandoned by Archie when he spied a squirrel chittering and scolding in a nearby tree. The two animals were engaged in a comical standoff as I said my goodbyes to Lily.

She wasn't too happy at the idea I was abandoning her. She

grabbed on to one of my hands with an iron grip, not to mention a look on her face that threatened waterworks.

"Hey, it's okay. I'll be back before you know it, and Victoria will look after you real good," I said, patting her hands with my free one. I bent over and said to her all conspiratorial, "I'll let you in on a secret. I'm kinda sweet on Victoria. She's a very pretty lady, don't you think? And she's just as nice as she is pretty."

Lily stole a look over at Victoria who stood patiently, like she was gonna let Lily decide things for herself.

I grinned. "Maybe you could keep an eye on Victoria while I'm gone? Make sure she's not getting herself into any trouble when I'm not around. Whataya think?"

That earned me a smile and another one from Victoria. I don't often have such a way with persons of the feminine persuasion, so I had to pat myself on the back.

Victoria held out a hand to the girl. "Don't worry about Mr. Malhaven, Lily. We can't get rid of him. He has a way of always showing back up like a bad penny. I'm making a chocolate layer cake today. Do you want to help me? We can have it ready by the time he comes home for dinner."

"You see there," I said. "Now you know I'll be back. I wouldn't miss Victoria's seven-layer chocolate cake for any amount of money."

The girl looked doubtful, but she did let loose of me and walked shyly over to Victoria, taking her hand. They stood and waved at me as I got back in the Champ and drove away, Victoria so tall and lovely, and that little ghost beside her, lost but no longer alone, for a time at least.

CHAPTER SIX

I decided to start in on my investigation by stopping back by the office first. Q was always ready to sink his teeth in to any mystery that involved digging through the back issues. He'd been hired to put the Crier's files and old copies of the paper in order down in the morgue and had inherited quite a mess, so he still had a lot of work to do. At least, that's what he told me each and every time I paid him a visit.

Before heading to the basement to see him, I swung by the desk of old Maudie Adams. She was quite a character, but she was our character since she'd worked at the paper longer than anyone else there, including my editor, Morty. She had iron gray hair that must have reached down to her ankles when unpinned, but since no one had ever seen her when it wasn't wrapped around and around her head in a kind of turban style that was all her own invention, I guess we'll never know.

I'd also never seen her without an unlit cigarette hanging from one corner of her mouth. Never caught her with a lit one yet, but she always offered me a fresh one and a lighter when I stopped by. I lit up and took a drag as she made tut-tut noises at me and turned to root around in the junk that overflowed her desk drawers so much that she couldn't shut them.

"Where is it? Where is it? I know it's right here. There we are!" she exclaimed in as much triumph as if she was Stanley stumbling across Mr. Livingstone in the middle of the jungle. She fished out a clothes brush and leapt to her feet.

I was always amazed at how limber she was for someone who'd been around the block so many times. She did a jig around me, swatting with the brush so hard it was painful as she attacked the remaining flour on my suit. "Imagine going out in the world like that. If you had a good wife at home, she'd never let you leave the house looking that way, Jimmy."

"If I had a good wife at home, I'd never leave the house," I cracked and was rewarded with a sharp swat on the rump with the brush for my troubles.

Looking a lot more respectable after she got done with me, I pulled a chair up across the desk from her as she sat back down at her type-writer and started pounding at it a mile a minute.

"Gotta finish up my copy and get it to Morty so I can grab lunch. My stomach's roaring like an angry bear that's been poked with a stick, so make it quick if you got a question."

"I'm working on a story. Might be a follow-up to one you did about six months ago. That girl they found alone in the park."

"Little Janey Doe? I thought that was a good touch if I do say so myself. That was a choice story. Sob stuff. I can write that kind of thing with both eyes closed and one hand tied behind my back. What about little Janey? They never found the parents, did they? I think she ended up at, you know, whatchamacallit, with all the scarecrows."

"Sisters of Mercy. They renamed her Lily White."

Maudie snorted. "They'd have done better to stick with Janey Doe. Imagine being a dame stuck with the name Lily White your whole life. That's just the kind of name them nuns would think up. Comes of not seeing more of the world like me and you, right, Jimmy?"

Given Maudie had never been farther afield than an hour and a half bus ride to Chicago to take in a show, I wasn't sure I agreed with the comparison, but I sidestepped the question by filling her in on the goings-on at the orphanage.

"Sounds more in your line than mine, Jimmy. Ain't the spirit world your beat?" she cackled, leaning across the desk to give me a sharp jab of a boney finger in the shoulder.

Sighing at the reminder that I'd never live down my undeserved reputation as a ghost chaser, I pressed her for any details she could remember about the story.

"You best go and check with your buddy down in the morgue. There wasn't a whole lot to work with, so I doubt I left anything out of my stories for the paper. He can probably find 'em quick, too. Smart young lad, and it wasn't that long ago, was it? Right after the big scandal about those crazy Wynter sisters broke."

She kept typing as she talked, the ding of the typewriter as it neared the end of each line, the whir and crash as she slammed the return lever home, and the mechanical tap, tap, tap of the letters striking the paper forming a kind of punctuation to her words. She ripped the page she'd been working on out, picked up two other pages from random stacks on her overflowing desk, and thrust them at one of the copy boys running by on his way to Morty's office.

"Now I can finally get some eats. Say, Jimmy, got any nickels on you? All I got is a buck and that cashier, Wanda, at the Automat don't like me none."

"That so. Care to say why?"

"Let's just say we got into a disagreement one day, and in the heat of the moment, I might have accidentally knocked into a guy going by with a tray resulting in Wanda getting splatted with a cup of joe. You shoulda heard her screech. Had the nerve to say I was trying to scald her when you know as well as I do the coffee's never hot at that place."

"I'm surprised you weren't banned from the joint."

"No one can prove it was anything but an accident, and my money's as good as the next guy's. You got any nickels or not? I'd as soon get in and out of there without having to talk to Wanda until she's cooled down some."

"Why don't you just go to another place? The hamburger dive down on the corner ain't bad, and it's cheap as dirt."

"They don't got lemon cream pie like the Automat. Just like my ma used to make, that pie."

"Okay, okay." I knew better by now than to try to talk Maudie out of anything she had her mind set on doing. I rooted around in my pocket until I came up with enough nickels to buy her a feast. As I put the change in her palm, she got a look in her eye as though a lightbulb had gone off.

"Just remembered there was one thing I left outta the paper. They found some kinda coin on that girl. Something you don't see every day. It was the only real lead they had to go on when they found out she couldn't talk. All her clothes were homemade, no labels. Nothing else on her."

"What about shoes?"

"No shoes. She was barefoot. And no coat neither and it wasn't exactly balmy that night. Lucky someone found her when they did. Might have been a different story I was writing up."

"Who found her?"

"Cop. Anonymous tip on the phone, I think. That'll all be in the paper. The coin, though, one of the cops asked me not to mention it. There was something special about it. Thought they could use it to track down whoever dumped her there, but I guess they never did."

"I'm surprised you passed up such a juicy tidbit."

For the first time in my life, maybe for the first time in anyone's life, I was witness to Maudie blushing, and not just a bit but as red as an overripe tomato. "I owed the guy a favor."

"Huh," I said, my mind boggling on what a cop might have on her that would make her squash a big lead. "You remember his name? Maybe he can tell me more about the coin. I'm trying to help the girl out. She's in trouble."

"More trouble? Some folks're born under a dark star, ain't they? It was that cop friend of yours, the big Irishman."

"Flanagan?"

"That's right, but don't go needling him about what he has on me. That's between me and him and ain't none of your stinking business."

"Aw, c'mon, Maudie, you know you can trust me."

She gathered up an ancient black leather handbag from her desk and gave me a playful shove. "Look who fancies himself a comedian all the sudden. They should give you a regular spot on that Toast of the Town show."

"I didn't know you had a television set. What'd you hit, the jackpot?"

"No, Mr. Comedian. I go over to Mildred's on Sunday nights. She's my neighbor. Her son bought her one. Mr. Bigshot. Buys his ma fancy presents so everybody on the block knows it. Now get outta here. That lemon pie's calling my name." She stomped out of the newsroom without a glance back.

I was glad I'd caught her. The coin bit was a good lead. I wondered what it was about a coin would make it so special the cops wanted to keep it under wraps. I'd have to catch up with Flanagan and see what he knew about it and about the case. And if he happened to let drop what he had on old Maudie, well, that wouldn't be my fault, would it?

First, though, I hopped the elevator down to the basement to check in with Q. Wanted to give him a heads-up on our new case and see if he could dig out those back issues for me.

Deep in thought, at least by my standards, I stepped off the elevator when the doors opened and almost didn't notice the two gorillas waiting impatiently for me to get out of the way so they could go up until I heard a familiar voice.

"Mr. Malhaven!"

It was my pal, Q, but he wasn't looking his usual dapper self. His shirttail was hanging out beneath his sweater vest, blood was dripping from a nasty slice through the dark skin above one eye, and his big horn-rimmed glasses were nowhere to be seen. I'd never seen him once without them, so I knew something wasn't right. The blood was a good giveaway, too. Then I noticed those two galoots had a pretty firm grip on him, one on each arm, and were intent on muscling him into the elevator.

"Hey, whataya guys think you're doing?" was all I could think to say, so astonished was I.

"Nothing to see here, buddy," one of the toughs said, flashing a police badge in my face. "Just gettin' another creep off the streets."

The elevator doors slammed shut in my face.

$\mathcal{I}$ stood as still as one of those dummies in a store window display for a minute, staring at the elevator. The last thing I remembered seeing from before those doors shut was Q's face, looking out at me with a mixture of pleading and pride. Like he was ashamed to be asking me a favor but didn't know what else to do.

Shaking off my stupor, I looked down and saw his glasses lying at my feet. The frames were bent and one of the lenses had popped out. I picked 'em up anyway, stuffing them in my pocket and heading for the stairs, limping up them as fast as I could on my rickety pins. I was hoping to head the posse off in the lobby, but by the time I got there, it was empty. Pushing out the front doors, I saw a black coupe pulling away from the curb in the direction of the local precinct house.

I debated backtracking down the street to where I'd parked the Champ, but it was only a few blocks to the police station if that's where they were headed. It was faster to walk, even limping along. On the way there, I tried to imagine what could have happened. Q was about as upstanding a citizen as I knew. Never missed a day of work, good to his mother and sister, always with a helping hand for me or anyone else at the paper. "Creep" was the last word I'd use to describe him. What in the world was going on?

Entering through the beat-up wooden doors that led into the station, I couldn't see Q and his escorts anywhere and wondered if I'd mistaken their destination. My pal Joey Flanagan was standing around, jawing with the desk sergeant like he usually was when he didn't have a case to work on. He raised an eyebrow at me when he saw me standing there huffing and puffing and gave me the nod toward the door again, following me outside when I took the hint.

Flanagan lit up a cigarette and gave it to me, firing one up for himself, too.

"Jimmy, my boy, thought you'd be showing up before too long when I saw what Bryant and Williams dragged in. Wasn't that your boy from the paper? The one who helps you out sometimes?"

"If you are referring to Mr. Marquis Sutherland, a fellow employee at the Crier and a model citizen," I said, not liking Joey's attitude, "then, yeah. And whatever you picked him up for, you made a big mistake."

"That's quite a long limb you got yourself out on, especially for such a big guy as you are, Jimmy. Be careful it don't break and send you crashing down to the ground. You might at least wait until you heard what he done."

I set my mug in the expression Victoria calls my donkey look, 'cause she knows I'm about to be as obstinate as one and to settle in for a long fight.

Joey must've recognized the look, too. He held up a hand. "This Mr. Sutherland may be your next best friend to me, but I hope you don't ever catch me going around and stealing change purses from little girls."

I couldn't help it. I bust out laughing. The image of Q, in all his dignified glory, grabbing a purse from some kid and running off with it was more than my imagination could swallow.

"Now I know there's been a goof up."

"Not so fast. We got an eyewitness inside. The victim herself. She was on her way here to spout her tale to us when your Mr. Sutherland strolled by on his way to work, bold as you please. She recognized him right off the bat. She and her friend tailed him to the paper and then came back here to report. Williams and Bryant went and fetched him. End of story."

"You gotta be kidding me. You're taking her word for it? How old is this girl? Shouldn't she be in school right now? Sounds like a juvenile delinquent to me. And you and me both know how reliable witnesses are. I've interviewed seven different people after a bank robbery and gotten seven different descriptions of the bad guy."

"Why don't you park yourself out here and wait and cross-examine her to see how reliable she is? Should be coming out any time now. Probably be thrilled to bits to speak to such an esteemed member of the press as yourself."

Flanagan gave me the sympathetic eye. "I know you got a soft heart, Jimmy, but you gotta wake up to the fact there's some kinda people you can't trust. Don't let it eat at you. You still got me to rely on, pal," he added, with a punch on my shoulder, before disappearing back into the station leaving me behind, still steaming.

Joey and I may go all the way back to when we were both wearing diapers, but that don't mean we see eye to eye on everything. Might have once, raised up the way we were, but during the War, my men and I got thrown into plenty of hairy situations right alongside all kinds of other platoons. When you're playing hide and seek with the enemy in a humid jungle on an island farther from home than you'd ever thought you'd be in your life, you stop worrying so much about the color of the skin of the guy next to you as long as he knows how to shoot a rifle and he's on your side.

I wouldn't have made it out alive without some of those guys and wouldn't ever forget it, but Joey hadn't the benefit of such hard-earned wisdom. In fact, most of the cops I knew were apt to come down all the harder on a perp the darker his skin was. Not fair, but that's the way it was.

Taking Joey's suggestion, I cooled my heels on the sidewalk to see if I could get a word with this so-called witness. I'd finished my smoke and was checking my pockets for another when she came out. She wasn't as young as I'd been led to believe. Looked thirteen or fourteen. Not yet a woman, but old enough to be careful about her dress and blonde hair, like she already had the opposite sex on the brain and was practicing how to catch somebody's eye.

Her companion was less flashy. Hair that mousy color that's no color in particular and with a carelessness about her dress that indicated to me she had more important things to think about. It took me a sec, because I hadn't seen her since the thrilling events of the previous fall, but it came back to me.

"Mabel Cummings, ain't it?"

Our paths had last crossed because her big sister Margo was a witness to that ghost I'd been hunting, and her little brother Mikey, hooligan in training, was almost helpful despite himself in helping me crack the case. But there had been no question to me that of all that large Cummings gang, Mabel was the one that won the brains lottery. I had a feeling she'd be able to help me set things straight for Q if anyone could.

"Mr. Malhaven," Mabel said. "I'm glad to see you. There's been a mistake."

"Sounds like the understatement of the year to me. Who's your pal here?"

"Lorna Hamilton, what's it to you, scar face?" cracked the blonde, giving me the evil eye.

Luckily, I got a tough hide, so I didn't take it personal. I been called worse. "Ain't you a riot. You the one fingered Marquis Sutherland for robbery?"

"So what?"

Didn't take a genius to figure I was interviewing a hostile witness.

"So, I believe, as Miss Cummings has so sagely observed, there's been a mistake, that's what."

"Says who?"

These are the moments that try a man's soul, but I'd dealt with enough hard cases to keep my head up and soldier on.

"Says me, but then I'm just a reporter with the Crier. I'd love to hear your side of the story and so would my readers." I'd found ninety-nine times out of a hundred, folks can't resist the idea of being in the paper. Most have a thirst for fame they may not even realize they have until I show up at their door.

"Oh, is that right? Mabel, why didn't you say something?" Lorna replied in a suddenly oh-so-cultured voice, fluffing the ends of her hair in case I had a camera hidden behind my back that I was gonna whip out to capture her for posterity. "I'm terribly sorry, Mr.—"

"Malhaven."

"Of course. Mr. Malhaven. You must forgive my rudeness. I've had a most harrowing morning. I'm really not myself at all."

A loud snort shot out of Mabel's nose which I guess Lorna decided to ignore because she kept right on going.

"I was on my way to school when this man came out of nowhere and grabbed my purse. My mother had given me a ten-dollar bill to do the shopping for the family after school so naturally, I was most upset."

"Naturally," I agreed, attempting to jolly her along.

"I met up with Mabel and told her what had happened. It was she who insisted I report it to the police, so we came along here, and on the way, it just so happened I saw the very man responsible. Wasn't that lucky? I do hope I'll get the ten dollars back. Mother will be so vexed with me."

I was listening with only half an ear to this sad tale, distracted by a weird pantomime Mabel was doing behind her friend's back. She was ducking and bobbing her head kind of in the way a robin does when it spies a worm wriggling on the ground and is trying to take good aim. Darting forward, she plucked an object from the back of Lorna's wide patent leather belt. But it wasn't any worm. It was a change purse out of which Mabel triumphantly fished a nice crisp ten-spot.

CHAPTER EIGHT

"Will you look at that," I said, giving Mabel an appreciative tip of the hat.

Lorna turned, flushing red as a strawberry when she saw what her friend had fished out. I had to give it to her. She tried her best to carry it off in high style.

"Why, how on earth did it end up there? Mabel Cummings, what a terrible joke to play on me. Letting me come all this way when you knew where it was the whole time."

"I didn't know it was there until I caught sight of it peeking out just now. Why would I think you still had it when you told everyone someone stole it from you?"

"Well… well…" Lorna huffed. "That man did bump into me. Maybe he changed his mind at the last minute and put it there."

"Without you noticing, I suppose," Mabel said with enough of an eye roll to win the Olympics of eye rolling if there was such a thing. "And this has nothing to do with that pair of shoes you've had your eye on in Bailey's store window."

"What are you trying to suggest?" Lorna spat out. I know all the signs of someone gearing up to make a dramatic exit, so I took the precaution of hooking one of my paws in the elbow nearest to me to put the brakes on any bright ideas she had about making a quick getaway from the scene.

"I believe," I said, "she may be hinting you had other ideas for how to spend the sawbuck your ma slipped you and don't mind throwing an innocent man under the bus, so how about we march back up these steps here and confess all. There's nothing so good as a clean conscience for a sound night's sleep, you know."

I could tell she wanted to argue, but the firmness of my grip on her arm must have convinced her she'd be wasting her breath. Flanagan took her confession in stride. Thought it was the biggest joke he'd heard all day and let her off with nothing more than a mild scold for wasting police time. I didn't agree it was funny at all but held my tongue and my temper so as not to make things any worse for Q.

After the girls left, I hung around on the front steps waiting to catch up with him when they turned him loose, but when he finally came out, he brushed past me without a word as if we'd never even passed the time of day before.

"Hey," I said, trying to keep up with him. "Slow down there, Q. You know I got a couple of bum legs. Give a guy a break."

He stopped so abruptly, I almost mowed him over, him being a bit of a lightweight and me built like a dump truck.

"Give a guy a break? Give a guy a break?" Q said very, very quietly. "No one gave me a break today, did they?"

"You don't need to be mad at me about it. I been trying to help you."

"You wouldn't understand, Mr. Malhaven," he said, drawing a ragged breath as though he was a drowning man. "The constant reminders I'm not one of you," he said with a frown at me that shook me up. "Being falsely accused of something I would never do simply for being who I am and in the wrong place at the wrong time. And my accuser walks free with barely a slap on the wrist, I bet."

He tucked in his shirt and straightened out his vest and tie, adding through gritted teeth, "I'm grateful for your help, but I'd prefer to be left alone."

Before I could stop him, he strode away at such a pace I knew it was no good me trying to catch him up. I felt bad about leaving it there, but then I figured maybe it would be better to let him cool off before I tried to talk to him again.

I decided to go grill Flanagan about the coin that Maudie let slip about and give him a piece of my mind about the screw up they'd made, but I shoulda known he wouldn't apologize.

"Whataya want from me, Jimmy? Nice-mannered young lady comes in and gives us a story. Who you think we're gonna believe? Besides, it all worked out, didn't it? What're you so hot and bothered for? Your pal is free as a bird, no worse for wear."

Remembering how worked up Q had been, I couldn't agree with Flanagan's breezy dismissal, but I also knew from old it was useless to argue with him about something we'd never see eye to eye on, so I let it go and moved on.

"What do you remember about that Janey Doe case? The little girl found in the park?"

"Huh?" Flanagan said, looking blank at the change of topic. "What's it to you?"

"You know Sister Honoria over at the Sisters of Mercy?"

"Sure," Flanagan nodded. "We get called over there now and again when some of the older boys get up to mischief. Honoria is a nice Irish lass. She was friends with my cousin Gracie when they was growing up. Honoria took the veil while Gracie went a very different way, I can tell ya," he said with a look that left me in no doubt what he meant. "Her ma ain't too happy about it, neither—"

Before Flanagan had a chance to take us on a trip around the moon to get two blocks down the street, I interrupted. "Yeah, well the good Sister called me in 'cause they've been having trouble. Practical jokes that have gone a little too far. And this girl, Janey Doe that was, seems to be at the center of it all, only they're calling her Lily White now."

Joey snorted. "Lily White! Don't that beat all."

"I know, I know. I got the idea not everyone thinks it's the best handle, but that's beside the point. Like I said, they been having trouble. Some of the nuns are blaming this girl. So much so, I had to break her out of there and farm her out to Victoria for safekeeping."

"I bet Victoria is taking real good care of her. That's one sweet lady you got there, Jimmy. You should go ahead and make an honest woman of her."

"Victoria is as honest as the day is long," I said, huffy to hear her good name thrown around. "She don't need me for that. We're taking things slow and easy after everything that happened."

"There's slow and easy, and then there's, I let a good thing slip through my fingers because I wasn't smart enough or quick enough to grab the brass ring, my boy. Don't come laying your head on my shoulder for a good cry if she finds another fella before you get around to asking for her hand."

"Let me worry about that, Flanagan. If I didn't know any better, I'd think you were trying to give me the runaround. All I wanna know is what you remember about the case. Did you guys ever get a lead on who this girl is or where she came from?"

"Nope. A couple of the boys are still working it. Following up leads that come in from time to time, but nothing ever pans out. It's as if she dropped down from the sky."

"Huh, like an angel, maybe?"

"She don't sound like much of an angel if she's causing all this trouble over at the orphanage."

"I didn't say she was causing trouble. Just that trouble started when she went to live there."

"Same difference, ain't it? I always tell you, you got a soft heart, Jimmy. First this fella at the paper, and now this girl. It'll get you in trouble one of these days, see if it don't. The world's a cruel place for orphans and outcasts. That's just the way of things."

"I know better than to get into a debate with a deep-thinker such as yourself, Joey. Just give me the facts, why don't you? For old times' sake."

"All right, all right. Not much to tell. We got a tip about a kid alone in the park. A couple of us went over and picked her up. She was shivering like a gelatin salad in an earthquake. All she had on was a blue dress and a pair of knit socks. Don't remember the color of the socks. No tags on the clothing. Looked homemade. The cloth wasn't bad quality, but it's a common pattern. Sold lots of places, so that didn't help neither. We advertised, sent out bulletins, checked missing persons reports. The usual. Couldn't track down anyone ready, willing, or able to own up to misplacing a tot. That's it."

"That's it? You sure?" I said, with a knowing look.

"What's wrong with your face, Jimmy? You know it ain't the prettiest at the best of times. I wouldn't scrunch it up like that if I was you."

"Very funny, wise guy, but I happen to have it from a good source you found something else on that girl. Something pretty distinctive from what I hear."

"You don't need to give me three guesses at who your source is. Must've been Maudie, and after she promised me to keep it under that rat's nest she calls a hairdo and all. Not that it matters much now. Turned out to be a dead end like the rest of it."

"Then there can't be no objection to describing this mystery object, wouldn't you say?"

"Tell you what, old friend, I'll do you one better by fetching it so you can see it with your very own two eyes."

I followed him in and cooled my heels in the lobby, smoking another cigarette and joking around with the boys in blue who came and went. It wasn't long before Joey was back. He pulled two big beefy fists out from behind his back, holding them out to me all balled up.

"Guess which one it's in?"

"What is this, Flanagan? Are we eight years old again?" I complained, refusing to rise to the bait.

"Ah, just a bit of fun. Don't be so sour. Here you go."

He opened his right fist and there it was. A coin, but not American, not by a long shot. How could I tell? I think the thing that gave it away was the great big swastika staring me in the face.

CHAPTER NINE

Icouldn't help but feel a chill down deep in my bones looking at that too-familiar devil's mark. I'd spent the war in the Pacific and hadn't run across too many Krauts personally, but nobody could escape the newsreel footage of those fanatics with their flags and banners and so-called fearless leader. The destruction, millions dead, the walking skeletons from the camps. I flushed hot and angry. Five years ain't long enough to forget. It all flooded back to me in a flash seeing that evil cross.

"Nazi?" I asked, stating the obvious.

"Not just Nazi. This particular one was only issued in the occupied territories in '40 and '41."

"That narrows it down, but what about it? Lots of guys I know brought home all kinda souvenirs from the war. Got a few myself."

"Yeah," agreed Joey. "We was hoping if we got a bead on someone, it might help clinch the deal if they were ex-service. We had so little to go on, we thought we should hold back on the only real clue. Don't guess it matters so much now, but I'm still kinda surprised Maudie told you. She made me a solemn promise, Jimmy."

"From what she said, you're holding something over her head. Maybe she's not so worried about it anymore."

Flanagan laughed. "No, believe me, it's not something she'd want to get out. But tell her not to worry. Not a word from me. Are you gonna write up a new story? Might not be such a bad idea to spread the word about this after all," he said, flipping the coin up in the air with his thumb and catching it. "Might scare up a new lead for us."

"I'll send one of the photog boys over from the paper to take a snapshot if it's okay with you. I gotta do some more research before I try to convince Morty to splash out on a new series. I'm mainly interested in helping out Sister Honoria and the girl. No family, and now the one place that should be taking her in and looking after her is trying to cast her out. She's awfully young to have gone through so much already."

"What'd I say? Soft-hearted, and soft-headed sometimes, too," Joey said, giving me the wink to let me know he considered me a pal all the same.

I wandered outside and hit the sidewalk, considering whether to head back to the paper and check in with Q. I'd never seen him so hot and bothered before, but he had good cause being hauled away on no more excuse than a scheming teenybopper mouthing off. It was no joke being a man of color accused of even the mildest crime by a white girl. In some ways, he'd been lucky, but I knew he wouldn't see it that way and I couldn't blame him. I gotta admit, I wasn't sure what I could tell him to make things better, so I decided to put it off. Maybe by the time he'd cooled down, I'd have thought of the right thing to say.

Instead, I drove back to the Sisters of Mercy figuring I could maybe pick up a bit more to chew on there. For one thing, I hadn't had a chance to investigate the scene of the crime in the kitchen. For another, I was curious about what the story was with Sam Leonard. I liked him, and Sister Honoria was always singing his praises as an A-one guy with the numbers. It was a big fall from glory to be turned outta his job. Being as incurably nosy as any other reporter worth his salt, I couldn't help but want to know all about it.

The scene had calmed down quite a bit by the time I got back to the orphanage, at least as far as I could tell. No sign of the kids or nuns. It was past lunchtime, so I guessed they'd all be in class. I headed back to the kitchen only to be stymied by as spotless a crime scene as you'd ever want to see. Every surface was shining. All the pots and dishes tidied away. And no, I'm not above digging through garbage in search of a good scoop, but all the trash cans had been emptied, too.

I shoulda realized the nuns would waste no time getting everything in shipshape order so they could make lunch for the kiddies. Kicking myself for not doing a proper looksee when I was there earlier, I went looking for Sister Honoria to see if she could add anything, hoping against hope the nuns had maybe found something useful to identifying the culprit while they were clearing up.

Honoria's office was empty, but I did run into Marlene Sutherland coming down the hallway.

"Back so soon, Mr. Malhaven? Is Lily with you?"

"No, I dropped her off with Victoria, and then…" It occurred to me Marlene might not know about her brother's run-in with the boys in blue unless he'd telephoned to tell her all about it. I had an awkward moment trying to decide if Q would want her to know or not. Feeling a bit of a heel, I decided I'd get more out of her if she wasn't upset by any bad news, so I finished up with, "… I decided to drop back by and check for any evidence, only everything's all tidied away."

"Yes, the sisters are terribly efficient," she agreed with a sympathetic grimace. "Though to be fair, the children were starving after the morning's excitement, and there was really no way to prepare anything for them with the kitchen in that state. If it makes you feel better, I was helping them out and didn't notice anything out of the ordinary way. I'm sorry you've wasted your journey back here."

"It's okay. Habitual disappointment is always on the menu for any dedicated reporter. You get used to it. Besides, I want to hear more about our Mr. Leonard. I have to say it don't sound like him to be cooking the books."

Marlene looked up and down the hall then beckoned me to follow. She led me back to the infirmary on the opposite wing from the kitchen. I woulda thought she didn't get much of a break from sick kiddies in a place that big, but all the beds were neatly made up and empty of inmates.

She shut the door and sat down at a small desk set up where she could keep an eye on her patients. I was more than glad to take a load off in a chair across from her.

"I'm glad you came back by, Mr. Malhaven. I wanted to ask for your help earlier but Sam—that is Mr. Leonard…"

I held up a hand. "Let's stick with Sam. It's less of a mouthful."

She smiled then, but not for long. "Sam's so proud. It hurt his dignity to be fired after all his hard work, but he doesn't believe in asking for favors from anyone. He's always made his own way in life."

I could tell she was proud of that. Anyone with half a brain could've told by the way she said it, she was not only proud of him, but something a whole lot more as well. Gave me a funny feeling. I'm a sentimental guy at heart and don't mind a bit seeing folks pairing off two-by-two like on Noah's ark, but I could only figure there was no future in it. No peaceful and happily ever after kinda future, anyways. Wasn't so safe in Carsworth City not to stick with your own kind. I tried to shake off the thought and concentrate on what Marlene was saying.

"But it's so unfair what happened. You said yourself Sam is a… a straight shooter, wasn't that what you said?"

"Certainly looked that way to me," I agreed. "Can't be easy keeping a big place like this going on handouts alone, but Sister Honoria always bragged to me about how he was able to stretch a dollar and keep the books in the black. What set off the fireworks?"

Marlene got a look on her face kinda like she had found something disgusting stuck to the heel of her shoe before spitting out, "It was all that man! Horace Ludgate," as though she'd also discovered the name for the wad of goo on her shoe and wasn't none too happy about it.

"What's his business when he's in town?" I asked.

"Being a wheedling busybody as far as I can tell. He appeared a few days before Christmas wanting to get hired on as an accountant. Sister Honoria told him we already had a very competent one, but he wouldn't take no for an answer and offered to check over the accounts for free in case he could come up with any additional ideas for stretching the budget. He spent a few days holed up with Sam's records before presenting what he said was proof Sam had been keeping a separate set of books, skimming money and pocketing it for himself."

"And Honoria took his word for it? A stranger over a guy she's known for years? Sister Honoria's no pushover. She's got plenty enough smarts to see through that kind of a boondoggle."

"That's what Sam thought, so he didn't take it seriously at first, but that man brought in a handwriting expert to attest the second set of books were all in Sam's handwriting. And I must admit," she said, biting her lip in frustration, "they are very good forgeries. But Sam and I know that's what they are."

"That's a serious charge this Ludgate character was bringing. Stealing bread outta the mouths of babes. Weren't the cops called in?"

"Sister Honoria didn't want Sam to get in any real trouble. She offered to forgive him if he paid back the money. But he doesn't have it because he hasn't stolen any! She felt she had no choice but to let him go. Then to top it all off, she hired that man to take his place."

"It's an awful lot of stock to put in a galoot who shows up on your doorstep out of nowhere. What do we know about this moocher?"

"I don't think Sister Honoria would have taken him so seriously except he had a glowing reference from a very important family. The Hasselwhites."

"I know the name. Big shots in the next county over, ain't they? Lots of money. I seem to recall there was some kind of tragedy. Somebody died."

"Too bad it couldn't have been him. Then we would never have even heard the name Horace Ludgate!"

We both jumped as the door to the infirmary sprung open and a yodeling voice sounded at us.

"Did I he-e-e-e-a-a-a-a-r-r-r-r-r my n-a-a-a-a-m-m-m-m-me?"

CHAPTER TEN

The yodel was owned by a singularly unattractive goop.
Slicked back raven hair so sparse up top his pink scalp was
shining through here and there. A doughy face with a nose as swollen
as a washed-up boxer who's gone one too many rounds, and one of
those pencil-type moustaches so thin it hardly seems worth the trouble
of having one. It certainly wasn't keeping those raw meaty lips warm.
If you're getting the idea I wasn't too impressed with my first sighting
of Mr. Horace Ludgate, you're not far wrong. His first speech didn't do
much to help.

"Hello, hello, hello! I was passing the portal to this sacred temple
of healing and couldn't help but overhear the melodious voice of our
pulchritudinous Nurse Marlene. Such an honor to hear my rather
plebian moniker springing from the lips of our very own reincarnation
of the goddess Aceso," Ludgate said with such a leer I'm surprised his
eyes didn't spring out of his head in the manner of those comic
lotharios featured in the cartoons at the movie house.

I'd met his kind before. Jokers who use ten-dollar words when a
nickel one would do. Throwing out references they think no one else in
the room is smart enough to get. In the newspaper racket, we learn to
put the stuff over with words the hoi-polloi can follow, but language is

my business, so I wasn't thrown off by this display of eruditeness. See? Two can play at that game.

I knew enough about Marlene to suspect she was well able to look after herself, but I couldn't stop myself from stepping in front of her. Instinct made me want to try and shield her from the gaze of such an obvious creep.

"Malhaven. Jim. Reporter with the Crier," I offered, sticking out a paw reluctantly because it was the right thing to do but with a sinking feeling I was about to get a fist full of sweat and rubbery skin for my effort. I wasn't disappointed, but I had to grin and bear it, maybe squeezing a little extra hard to try and prove a point the way boys will.

"So very, very pleased, Jim," he oozed. "Horace Ludgate, but my friends call me Horrie, and I do hope very much we will be friends. I pride myself on being a friend to all I encounter."

"Not such a friend to one Mr. Sam Leonard, I hear."

"Oh dear. Was that what you were conversing about with our dear Nurse Marlene? It was an immensely desolate situation, of course, and it pains me so, so much to know I was in any way instrumental in having to expose such transgressions. I'm an individual who wants nothing more than to spread joy and light, you know, joy and light wherever I go. Wouldn't you concur, Nurse?" he added, doing a surprisingly nimble end run around me so he could drape one flabby arm around Marlene's shoulders.

The look she gave him would have made most men turn to stone on the spot, but our Mr. Ludgate was immune to the hint. "Now, I do understand, dear one, that you felt very distressed for Mr. Leonard. Like me, you have a sensitive and sympathetic nature. But you must beware. There are certain kinds of men in the world who will try and take advantage of your innocence. You would do well to view this as a cautionary experience that will be of invaluable assistance in recognizing and avoiding such perilous pitfalls in future."

Not enjoying seeing Marlene shrinking away from this gent as though the piece of goo on her shoe had grown five foot six and a quarter inches tall and decided to give her a cuddle, I reached out a hand and hooked his other elbow. He made as if to resist, but there's not many his size can withstand the determined pull of a bruiser such as myself.

"You're exactly the fella I'd like to talk to," I said, dragging him toward the door. "Nothing so helpful as getting an intelligent man's perspective on everything that's been going on around here," I added, with a quick wink back at Marlene. "And I can tell you're one smart guy, Horrie."

"Ha ha ha. I must commend you, my good sir. Very few souls are perceptive enough to appreciate my worth upon such minimal acquaintance. Do excuse us, my dear Marlene," he called back over his shoulder. "Jim and I must confer man to man. I'm sure he will see through to the truth that has proven too painful for you to give the credence it demands."

I can't quite describe the sound Marlene made at this parting shot, but I hoped I was never dumb enough to earn the same directed at me.

Once pointed in the right direction, Ludgate was more than happy to lead me to the office that had been Sam Leonard's once upon a time. He took his place behind the desk there, leaning back in the chair with his stubby arms hugging his midriff and a satisfied look on his face as though he was king of the joint. I hadn't known Sam Leonard all that good, but there was no doubt in my mind I would trust him with my bank account a lot sooner than this smiling joker in front of me. Although, since I rarely had a balance of more than two figures, I guess that's not saying much.

"So, Jim. How can I be of assistance to you?"

"I'd love to hear your take on this whole situation. Between the bookkeeper turning out to be a crook, and all these pranks, it's kinda bad for business, ain't it? Although I guess you never run out of clients. There's not many places around to take in a poor orphan boy or girl."

"It is true that I am very proud of providing a safe harbor for those unfortunate children who find themselves abandoned and adrift in the maelstrom of life."

"I guess the nuns help out some, too," I noted, mostly to see if I could needle him but I must admit, it got my goat to hear him taking credit for the whole shebang, especially when he was nothing but a Johnny-come-lately to the operation.

"Ha ha ha. You have a delicious sense of humor, Jim. Of course, Sister Honoria and her staff do the yeoman's work of keeping everything running, but I am honored to play my own not insignificant role. At the end of the day, it is money that makes the world go around, isn't it?"

"I can't argue with that," I agreed, though I would have liked to just to try and wipe the smirk off his face. I'd been fooled before, but everything was telling me this guy was not on the level. "What do you think of these pranks then?"

"I think we'll find it a simple case of boys being boys. I was always a model student, myself, but we have all kinds here, you know. There are bound to be some rather bad eggs among them."

"So, you don't buy into this theory it's the girl Lily White that's somehow connected to it."

Ludgate suddenly lunged forward, resting his elbows on the desk as he leaned toward me, apparently wanting to convince me how sincere he really was.

"That poor, poor little innocent. It was so unfortunate I happened to be away on business this morning. My wife, Florrie, and I would have been thrilled to take Lily in while all of this foolery was being sorted out. I understand she's gone to stay with a widowed lady, but two parents, even temporary parental figures, are surely better than one. Wouldn't you agree, Jim?"

I guess no one had bothered to tell Ludgate of my connection with the widow in question, but I decided to let it slide for now.

"It depends," I said, stroking my chin like I was mulling it over. "I think the lady in question has quite a large house. Plenty of room for an army of kids if need be. You and the missus might find it a bit cramped at your place."

"Ho ho, Jim. That's where you're wrong. Mrs. Ludgate and I happen to be caretakers of a grand house ourselves. Perhaps you have heard of Hasselwhite Hall?"

I gave a whistle and a nod to assure him I was properly impressed.

"We are most fortunate to have been chosen to oversee the management of that famous estate while the family is on an extended European tour. We would of course send a telegram to Mrs. Hasselwhite to get her permission, but as she is quite tenderhearted, I have no doubt she would insist on us helping the poor child."

"And what would Mr. Hasselwhite have to say about it?"

"Sadly, Mr. Hasselwhite is no longer with us. A terrible accident. Mrs. Hasselwhite took her son to stay with relatives for several years after his death before embarking on their current tour. It is my belief she finds it too painful to stay in the house with all of its distressing memories but is too sentimental to part with the abode where she and her husband enjoyed happier days. But all of that is to say I told Sister Honoria we would be delighted to relieve Mrs.—I forget the exact name. Rather an unusual one. Foreign, perhaps?"

"Jankowski. Her husband was a Pole. Killed in the war."

"How tragic! So many good men lost. I was unfortunately disqualified from service because of a serious back injury that would have rendered me worse than useless on the front lines, but we also served who kept the home fires burning, don't you think? In our own small way that is."

I gave him something between a grimace and a smirk that I assumed he would interpret as agreement and was not disappointed. His type don't get sarcasm when it's directed at them.

"But as I was saying, I told Sister Honoria we'd be more than happy to relieve the widow of the burden of caring for Lily."

Deciding it was time to confess all, I said, "I happen to know Mrs. Jankowski. I delivered Lily to her in fact, and she was perfectly thrilled to help out, but I know she'll thank you for the kind thought."

His "hail, fellow, well met" act looked as though it was slipping into something more like pure annoyance at that.

"Really, Jim, I have to say I think it would be much more appropriate for someone who is affiliated with this great institution to be in charge of Lily's welfare while we get everything straightened out. Mrs. Jankowski is very kind, I'm sure, but doesn't have the aegis of being a part of this organization."

"I guess you could say so, although she was raised up here from an infant, and she and Sister Honoria are as thick as thieves. I think that gives her a certain standing. I wouldn't sweat it, Horrie. Every time someone takes one of these kids off your hands, it's all to the good, ain't it?"

His expression left me in no doubt. The friendly mask fell away, and I saw the real Ludgate under the blustery act. An angry man. Frustrated. And not least of all, afraid.

CHAPTER ELEVEN

I had to give it to Ludgate. The mask was quickly slapped back into place, and he didn't let my pigheadedness get him down. He gave it the good old college try about grabbing Lily back from Victoria for at least ten minutes before I could turn the conversation to Sam Leonard. I could tell he wasn't done yet with his campaign, but he was jovial as could be when he pulled down two sets of ledgers from a shelf behind his head and showed me the supposedly faked up set of numbers.

If it was a fake, someone had gone to a lot of trouble. I'm no mathematician, but comparing the two books side by side, even I could see how such a swindle might be done. And worse, the handwriting in both books looked identical, to the amateur eye at least. I had to admit to my friend Horrie that things didn't look so good for Sam.

"I knew at once you were a very astute man, Jim, and would immediately understand what I discovered. Sister Honoria took some convincing, of course. She was naturally loyal to someone who had been in a trusted position of employment at this institution for a span of many years. But she saw in the end this evidence is quite irrefutable. I am afraid our young friend Marlene has not been able to accept the truth. Between you and me, I believe she may harbor a tenderness toward this Leonard fellow. Completely inappropriate relationship, of course, but there is no accounting for women, is there? There is no doubt they are the weaker sex not only physically but emotionally as well."

"Inappropriate?" I asked, knowing better than to touch his opinion of women with a ten-foot pole.

"Yes, of course. We are both men of the world, Jim. Mixing of the races will only lead to dilution and weakening of the human species. Marlene would do well to look to her own kind. And even she can do better than a Jew. I tried, much as a father might to his daughter, to explain such to her, but I'm afraid she was not prepared to accept that truth either."

"That's interesting to hear you say, Horrie. Thought one of the reasons we fought the war was to make sure the Jews and everyone else got an equal chance."

He leaned way back in his chair again and put his hands behind his head. I recognized the signs of a man ready to share his own personal and far superior philosophy with me. At least I wasn't having to break a sweat to get this source to spill.

"I suppose you are referencing those unfortunate camps. It was regrettable, naturally, but in times of war, we must expect hardships on all sides. The Germans may have taken things a little far, but there is a kernel of truth in all political ideologies, don't you think? Like to like, you know. That is Nature's law in the animal kingdom. Why should it be any different for us? Of course, it was necessary to curb Hitler's territorial aspirations, and those terrible Japs. Imagine if we had lost and were being ruled over by Oriental savages such as that? I shudder to think. But even I can admire their discipline. That is something we are sorely lacking in this country. Look at the youth of today. Nothing more or less than a pack of wild animals when they gather together."

"Interesting point of view for someone such as yourself who's helping raise up kids. You must have teenagers here?"

"Unfortunately, yes. I have tried to convince the Bishop that setting a lower age than eighteen to discharge our young people would be all to the good. Sister Honoria did not appreciate my bringing up the matter with him, I'm afraid, but if only she could see how much more we could do for the younger children with the money we would save if we set the age limit to fifteen or sixteen. Why, when I was a boy, it was nothing for a lad of fourteen to already be working to help support his family."

"Kinda hard on kids today though, ain't it? With all the men back from the war, it's not so easy to land a job when you're young and inexperienced."

"I'm quite sure they would make their way. If nothing else, they could easily relocate to Chicago or another large city where there are more opportunities. This would reduce the strain on our local police and other governmental services and cut down on this hooliganism we hear so much about these days, Jim. Why, I do believe I've read several stories with your byline on that very subject in the fine newspaper you work for, so you know to what I am referring."

"Sells papers," I admitted, feeling guilty when he put it that way. Like I was contributing to the public panic about youth gone wild. Most of the stuff I reported on was smalltime pranks not much worse than my friends and I had gotten up to back in our day, but Morty always played it up big in the headlines. It's his job as editor to sell more papers, and he's good at it. But what is it about the older generation always wanting to blame the younger ones for society's downfall? As if we have all the answers the kids don't.

"Ha ha ha. Very good, Jim. Sells papers. And that is your business, after all, isn't it? Ha ha."

The jovial act was starting to wear out its welcome for me. I figured I'd gotten the measure of Ludgate—more than I bargained for even—and should move things along.

"That's right, Horrie, my friend, selling papers is my business. At least, that's what the boss tells me a dozen times a day. Guess I better get busy. Over half the day gone and no story to show for it yet. I don't want to get an earful when I get back to the bullpen. I do appreciate your time."

"Not at all, Jim. Not at all. Stop by anytime and you will find me here, crunching the numbers and burning the midnight oil."

I stood up to shake hands again, same rubbery experience as before, only there was more sweat this time. I couldn't tell if he was nervous or just a naturally moist guy. As I turned to go, a thought struck me.

"If you're here all the time, who's looking after this Hasselwhite joint? Sounds like a big job."

"You needn't concern yourself. My better half is more than capable of running the estate. In fact, my dear wife says I get under her feet and encouraged me to find a job to keep me out of trouble as she says. My training is in accountancy, and I do love to help my fellow man, so coming here was the perfect opportunity."

"Pretty lucky how an opening came up like that, too."

"You joke, of course, Jim. No one was more shocked than I when I offered my services gratis to go over the books to see if I couldn't give Mr. Leonard some sound financial advice only to stumble upon this dreadful scheme. It is really rather fortunate I came along when I did, isn't it? Who knows how much more money he would have siphoned away into his own pockets? As it is, we have had to make drastic cutbacks wherever we can to make up the deficit. Keeps me on my toes, I must say, Jim. And though I may not look light on my feet, I am more than up for the challenge. Ha ha ha."

Scrunching up my face seemed to give him the idea I was smiling along instead of grimacing at the second-rate comedy act. One of the rare advantages of having a scar rearranging your facial features is people tend to read your expression any way that suits them which is fine by me.

At least I thought he'd given up on the living arrangements for Lily, but he came around his desk and gave a last shot at it.

"Surely, now that we have gotten the measure of each other a little, Jim, you can agree Lily would do best to come home to my wife and me. I'd be delighted to run out to visit the good widow and pick Lily up if you'll give me the directions."

I debated the wisdom of setting this creep on Victoria, but figured he'd probably find out where she was one way or another, and I didn't have much doubt that Victoria's natural ability to put anybody kindly but firmly in their place would make short work of Horrie.

"Wynter's Hill. Few miles west out of town. Name in great big letters right over the front gate. Can't miss it. You'll be wasting your time. Mrs. Jankowski takes her responsibilities very seriously and won't give Lily up without an okay from Sister Honoria. But if it makes you feel better to see that Lily's in good hands, I can attest the hospitality of the house is always available to visitors."

"Very good, very good. I believe I've driven past this place. A cemetery, isn't it? You must agree with me, Jim, that is a very odd place to live?"

"Seeing as I lay my hat there myself, can't say I do."

And with that parting shot, I eased out the door before I had to spend any more time with the weasel. He was giving me an oily feeling all over, and I'd had about as much as I could take for one day. Or ever. But, boy, did I have a sinking feeling this wasn't the last I'd hear of these Ludgates.

CHAPTER TWELVE

Everything about Horace Ludgate was raising my reporter's hackles. I'd have bet the fifty-three dollars and nineteen cents I currently had stashed away in the bank that he was up to something, but I couldn't figure what. For all the talk about Sam stealing money from the orphanage, they weren't exactly rolling in dough to begin with. If Ludgate was trying to work a dodge himself, there were plenty of businesses in town, legit and under the table, where he could be raking in a lot more cash. Why would a man living the good life at a fancy mansion while the owner was AWOL indefinitely want to waste his time as a two-bit accountant for a charity outfit?

And what was with the digging in like a dog with a bone over taking charge of Lily? If he and his wife were so keen on the kid, wouldn't Sister Honoria have been happy to let them adopt her? Maybe she still held out hope Lily's real parents would be located. Or maybe she found Ludgate as repellant as I did. I might've been prejudiced against the guy for some of the awful guff he was spouting, but the idea of that big oily hand grabbing hold of Lily's small one and hauling her away anywhere gave me the shivers.

I stopped back by Sister Honoria's office to see if I could catch her and find out more about my new friend Horrie, but the room was still empty. I took advantage to use the blower on her desk and give Victoria a heads up about a possible greasy gentleman caller. I didn't have to wait through too many rings before she picked up the receiver at the other end of the line.

"Wynter Residence."

"Am I talking to the loveliest lady I know?"

"Depends on how many ladies you know, I suppose."

"Only one with amber hair and stormy eyes."

"I'm sorry. I thought I was talking to Jim Malhaven. Who are you, kind sir, and what can I do for you?"

"Very funny. That'll teach me to pay you a compliment."

"Sweetheart! You know you can pay me as many as you want. It's good practice for me. I'm still getting used to having a man in my life again who whispers pretty things in my ear. Are you coming home soon? If I know you, you've been on the run since you left us and didn't even stop to eat anything."

"I got a few more things to take care of, but don't worry, I'll grab a bite."

"Don't leave it too late. I don't want you to ruin your appetite. Lily and I have the cake layers out of the oven and are waiting for them to cool before icing, and Mr. Cressley is roasting a rack of lamb with all the fixings."

"You're making my stomach rumble. Sounds like awfully fancy doings. What's the big occasion?"

There was silence at the other end of the telephone. The kind of extra-hushed silence where I knew I'd put my foot in something. Given that this was the kind of thing I did from time to time, I'd learned to recognize the sound right off.

"Uh oh. Did I forget something? I forgot something, didn't I?" I asked, racking my brain.

"It doesn't matter. Nothing important," Victoria answered brightly. "Why were you calling, darling?" she added in a tone that told me I'd do better to let the issue lie for now.

"I wanted to see how things were going with Lily and warn you there might be an unwelcome visitor out your way. One Horace

Ludgate, or Horrie to his friends, and practically everyone who's anyone is his friend according to him."

"That doesn't sound promising."

"It ain't, and I'm sorry I couldn't convince him not to drop by, but you'll see he's not easily discouraged. He's the new bookkeeper at the Sisters of Mercy, and he's got a bee in his bonnet about how he and his good wife would be the best guardians for Lily. I tried to tell him Sister Honoria was jazzed to have her in your care, but he wasn't buying it. An unpleasant customer, but nothing you can't handle."

"Honoria has mentioned him to me a few times. He took Sam Leonard's place, didn't he? There was something rather strange about all that. She'd always spoken very highly of Sam."

"You're not wrong. Something stinks. I think I'll track down Leonard and get his side of the story. If he was stealing as much money as Horrie says, I'm surprised the cops weren't called in."

"I think Honoria hoped to protect him from that. I haven't met his replacement yet. I get the impression she has reservations about him, but it isn't so easy to find a competent person at the salary the Church can afford to pay. Why do you think he's interested in Lily?"

"I can't figure that either. I would say he's just a bighearted guy, but nothing else he said would back that up. Maybe you can pump him for more info if he stops by, but don't let him get ahold of Lily. Even on short acquaintance, I can tell you I'd trust him about as much as a three-card monte dealer. Speaking of Lily, how's our little ghost doing?"

"I suppose she is a bit like a ghost, isn't she? So pale and quiet. She's terribly bright for her age. She read the cake recipe herself and measured out all of the ingredients for me. I think she was enjoying herself in her own way. She's taking a nap out in the sunshine with Archie at the moment. He took to her straight away."

"That's good enough for me. That cat is a very discriminating judge of character."

There was a clattering in the background and a murmuring of voices before Victoria came back on the line.

"Livinia is here. She wants to speak to you before you go."

As there was no one around to see me, I didn't bother to hide the shock on my face at that news. Livinia was Victoria's aunt and a formidable lady. While our relationship was definitely not as frosty as it had been once upon a time, I can't brag we were the best of pals either. I believe I could safely say she more or less tolerated me but coming from Livinia that was about as good as you could hope for.

"Mr. Malhaven, I understand you are still in town. I'm sure you won't mind running an errand then."

See? That's the kind of a female she was. Confident it was in her rights to assign any task to anybody at any time. Victoria played along mostly, but she wasn't above standing up to her aunt when she needed to. Luckily, Livinia didn't rate my skill set very high, so I didn't get ordered around too much. I decided to play along to keep peace in the family.

"Always a pleasure. Any little thing I can do for you, Mrs. Cressley."

I couldn't help emphasizing the name a bit to annoy her. She'd been Livinia Wynter and proud of it for so long, she'd felt robbed that she had to drop the moniker when she got hitched. Victoria let slip her aunt had tried to convince Cressley to change his instead, but he dug in his heels on this occasion even though he worshiped the ground she walked on and usually wouldn't tell her no for any reason. Guess everyone draws a line somewhere.

Livinia gave me my marching orders. "There's a package that requires picking up at the haberdashery on Fleming Avenue."

"Old man Klein's place? Sure, I know it."

"Good. Then it will be no trouble at all for you to stop in and pick up the parcel. They'll be expecting you." And with that, there was a kinda final-sounding click as the line went dead.

I stared at the receiver for a half a second before dropping it back in its cradle with a shrug. I was tempted to ring her back and say driving all the way across to the east side of town and then back home was actually quite out of my way, but I thought it probable Sam Leonard lived over in that neighborhood, too, so maybe I could kill two birds with one stone. I flipped through the phone book in Sister

Honoria's office and sure enough, Leonard's address was listed on a cross street not too far from Fleming.

It wasn't hard to spot Klein's. A big, prosperous-looking joint with the name in fancy script in white on the dark green awning above a picture window filled with the latest in ladies' head gear. I'd never been in the store before, but I had a soft spot for it all the same. Klein had made the fedora I'd inherited from Victoria's husband as well as repairing it good as new when I was so unfortunate as to get a pistol shot through the crown. The bullet missed my melon, but I almost cried when I saw what I thought was a good hat ruined. Klein must have been a magician with hats because you'd never know to look at it now.

A bell above the door made me jump as I walked in, but the dark-haired young lady standing behind one of the glass display cases took it in stride, giving me a bright smile.

"Welcome to Klein's. How can we help you?"

Swiping my hat down from my head to be polite, I said, "I'm here to pick up a package for Mrs. Cressley."

"Oh, yes. Mr. Klein said to expect you. I'll let him know you're here."

I was surprised to think something so mundane rated the attention of the boss, but I didn't mind having a chance to shake the hand of the maestro behind my headpiece. He was a small man, wiry, with hair more gray than black, but his grip was strong in mine. Must be all those years molding felts, wool, and leather into place.

"You must be Mr. Malhaven. So happy to make your acquaintance, sir" he said, plucking my hat from my hand. "Ah, this was one of my best. Made it special for Lukasz Jankowski's wedding. A good hat for a good man. I hope you have been taking better care of it, Mr. Malhaven. I was quite shocked when Victoria brought it to me for repair, you know."

"Treating it as though it was made of glass, Mr. Klein. Don't you worry. I don't plan to be stepping in front of a bullet again any time soon."

"I should hope not. I would not have thought newspaper reporting was such a dangerous business." He reached under the counter and pulled out a fancy wrapped present.

"What's the occasion?" I asked without thinking for the second time that day only to see the gift card: *To Victoria, From Jim. Happy Birthday.*

Huh.

<h1 style="text-align:center">CHAPTER THIRTEEN</h1>

Klein laughed at me, and I can't say as I blame him. I must have looked like a bear caught in the headlights of an oncoming bus.

"Mr. Cressley let me know he had a feeling you might forget so he wanted to make sure you didn't end up in the doghouse with Mrs. Jankowski."

"Cressley? It was Livinia who got on the phone to tell me to swing by here."

"Well, of course. Mr. Cressley couldn't have, could he?" Klein said with a sympathetic look.

I'd forgotten in my mortification that Cressley couldn't talk. He must have passed Livinia a note to ask me to get the package. He was an organized guy and a thoughtful one, that Cressley, and he might have saved me from a world of hurt. Victoria wasn't the kind of dame to hold a grudge, but I would have felt seven kinds of heel if I'd shown up with nothing. In my eyes, she deserved the best and forgetting her special day made me feel I'd let her down.

"I guess you better tell me what it is, so I don't look too surprised."

"Mitzi, dear, fetch me my sketchbook," Klein said to the pretty dark-haired girl who'd been standing by looking amused at my expense.

She quickly fetched an oversized book from behind the counter. Klein flipped through a few pages then turned it toward me so I could see. "Here we go. Here's the hat I made for Mrs. Jankowski. I know the kind of thing she likes. Simple but stylish."

I was no fashion expert, but I could see what he meant. Victoria always looked a million bucks to me whether she was dressed up or down, but she wasn't a flashy dresser. I could see her with this cute little number perched on her smooth, sleek hair.

"Looks first rate, but how much is it?" I asked, knowing I only had a couple of bucks crammed in my pocket.

"Mr. Cressley took care of that, too. Now, now," he said, no doubt seeing I was about to argue the point. "As far as I'm concerned, the bill has been settled. You and Mr. Cressley can work out any other details at your leisure. I'm only sorry you had to drive so far out of your way to pick it up."

"That's no problem. I was gonna wander over to this neck of the woods anyway to look up a friend."

"Oh? Who are you visiting? I know most everyone who lives around here."

"Sam Leonard."

The dark-haired girl gave with a gasp. Mr. Klein looked over at her before asking me, "Sam? Why do you want to see him?"

"I only just found out about this trouble with his job at the orphanage. I want to hear his side of the story in case he got a raw deal. I'm a reporter, you know, and I like to get all the facts before making up my mind."

The girl spoke up then. "It was worse than a raw deal. They had no right to accuse Sam of such things after all the long hours he put in keeping that place running. He came home late every night and spent most every weekend there trying to make the books balance. They rely on handouts and couldn't always count on those, but Sam was always making contacts and helping the nuns find new donors. It's a crime the way they treated him."

"He's got you on his side, at least," I said, wondering if Marlene was aware Sam already had a girl before she set me straight.

"I'm his sister. Of course I'll always be on his side." She had tears in her eyes but looked determined enough to throw a right hook at anyone who said otherwise.

"Good for you, Miss Leonard. Sam's a lucky man."

She scoffed at me. "He's not feeling lucky right now. And the last thing he needs is a reporter raking it all up and printing in the paper that he's a criminal. Why, they didn't even call in the police. That should tell you something about the evidence they had. Sister Honoria and the other nuns should be ashamed of themselves. Marlene Sutherland is the only person who stood up for him."

"You know Marlene?"

"Yes. She's a nice girl. She tried to visit Sam a few times, but he doesn't want to see anyone right now. There's nothing anyone can do," she ended with a wail.

"Now, now." Klein patted her on the shoulder in a grandfatherly way. "Don't upset yourself, Mitzi. Why don't you take the rest of the afternoon off and show Mr. Malhaven here the way to your apartment? It might do Sam good to talk to another man, and Mrs. Jankowski thinks very highly of this one. I'm sure he'll help Sam out if he can, won't you, Mr. Malhaven?" he asked with a look at me that said I'd better, or he'd know the reason why. He might have been a small man in stature, but he had a look of iron about him.

"That's right," I assured them. "Nurse Sutherland is a pal of mine and what's more the sister of a pal of mine, and if she thinks Sam is on the level, I might be inclined to agree with her. But it'll take more than a couple of us believing in him to help him out of this jam. We need proof. Why don't you let me have a gab with him? Investigation is my business. I might be able to set the record straight."

She glared at me skeptically. I get that a lot. I look more like the villain of the piece than the hero with my rough looks.

"You must know Mrs. Jankowski, don't you?" I asked her. She nodded at me. "Well, look at this hat," I said, holding out the gray fedora. "You're in the hat business yourself. You can tell this is one of

Mr. Klein's very best, ain't it? It belonged to Mr. Jankowski who Victoria naturally thought a whole lot of before his passing, and she entrusted it to me for safekeeping. A lady such as her wouldn't do such a thing if she didn't think I was an OK guy, now would she?"

"I suppose not," Mitzi said. She heaved a mighty big sigh. "And I don't suppose we have a lot to lose anyway. Sam's taken all this… he's taken it hard. You'll see. Thank you, Mr. Klein. I think I will take the rest of the day off and see if Mr. Malhaven can't talk sense into Sam. Goodness knows I haven't been able to and staying holed up in the apartment all day by himself isn't doing him any good."

Klein ushered us out of the store after rushing back to get the package for Victoria that had gotten left on the counter in the excitement. I let Mitzi lead the way down the block, making polite conversation to pass the time.

"So, is it just you and Sam, then?"

"Yes, it is… now. Our parents…" She clutched her bag close to her chest like she wanted to protect it or herself. "They travelled back to where they were born in Poland. They wanted to try and bring back their parents, my aunts and uncles, our cousins. They took my younger brother with them. Daniel. He was eleven. That was in July of '39. We never heard from any of our family over there again."

That was a punch in the gut to hear. I could only imagine how it felt to her and Sam. They weren't the only ones to lose their family in the madness in Europe, but it was a tough blow.

"That's rough," I said. "I guess it's lucky in a way you and Sam stayed behind."

"We were both working already. Everyone agreed we should stay here to help save up money. It would have been to help everyone get settled. But they never came."

I glanced over at her. She looked grim but dry-eyed. Like it was a grief too deep and wide for tears.

"They meant to leave Daniel with us, but at the last minute, he begged and cried so to go that they gave in. We knew things were getting bad over there, but we thought we had more time. There's not a day I don't wonder what happened to them, but I can't decide if it would be better or worse to know."

Hard to know what to say when someone's whole family has been wiped clean from the face of the earth. I was glad when she stopped and pointed to a modest brownstone.

"This is it. First door inside and to the left is our apartment. I think I'll walk on to the market and pick up a few things. It might be better if you go in alone. Sam and I don't see eye to eye on things these days. You might have more luck by yourself."

"Anything else I should know before I surprise him?"

"You'll see. Walk right in. He never locks the door when I'm out. We could use some good luck, Sam and me. I hope you got some under that fancy hat of yours, Mr. Malhaven."

"I'll do what I can, Miss Leonard," I said, with a tip of said head-piece to her.

She nodded and walked slowly away down the street hunched over like an old woman. It made me sad to see her with head bent low as though her troubles were pressing her down into the earth. I marched up the steps and into the hallway of the brownstone, flinging open the first door on the left with a determination to help them out regardless of my reception.

What I got was a fist right in the kisser.

CHAPTER FOURTEEN

I spotted it in time to duck back and save myself the worst of the blow, but it was far from the greeting I'd been expecting. There was Sam Leonard, swaying on his feet like a fighter in the tenth round, and I gotta say, he'd seen better days. Dressed in nothing but boxers and a stained undershirt with a ragged growth of beard and hair standing on end, he was a far cry from the Dapper Dan I'd met at the orphanage.

The next thing I noticed was the strong smell of cheap whiskey. I'd drunk enough to know and to recognize its effects on the bum standing in front of me.

"What's the big idea?" I said, rubbing my sore chin.

"Jubarj… Jus' barge… Jus' barging in, argy bargy, argy bargy…"

As a song, it didn't have much rhythm and you couldn't dance to it, but he was giving it out with gusto, I'll say that for him.

"Argy, bargy, argy, bargy… Hey, who you?"

"Who me? Me Jim. You Sam. We've run into each other a time or two before now."

I could tell he was trying hard to place me by the way his eyes squint up like raisins and his head cocked to the side as though his brain was going into overdrive.

"Tired, go away."

I was tempted, but the way he was pitching about, my conscience stepped in and demanded I lend a hand.

"Here," I said, shoving him back and down onto an old, beat-up sofa with one hand. "Take a load off."

He had the look of someone who wanted to protest this ill-treatment, but then he listed over to one side and was out cold. I checked to make sure he was still breathing then rooted around in the kitchenette and found a half pot of coffee still sitting on the stove. Didn't take long to light the gas and heat it up. I took a cup back out and slapped him awake, choking it down him until he woke up enough to complain and take it out of my hand. He gulped the rest then bent over with his face in his hands, moaning like a tugboat horn in the fog.

I decided to wait it out. It wasn't long before he came to his senses enough to look up at me with a resentment I didn't feel I deserved for my kind attentions.

"What're you doing here? How did you get in?"

"I waltzed right in on your sister's invite."

"Mitzi," he said, craning his neck around in case she was hiding somewhere in the shadows of their tiny apartment.

"Don't worry. She walked on to pick up a few things. Gives you a chance to sober up before she gets back here and sees you in this condition."

He grunted. "It's nothing she hasn't seen before."

"Then maybe you should make sure she doesn't have to see it again. She seems a well-brought up young lady. Ain't you ashamed to be acting this way after all you've been through together?"

I wished I could take it back as soon as I said it 'cause it set off the waterworks like I hadn't seen in a long while. The messy kind.

"Mitzi's the best," he choked out between blubbers. "She deserves the best. She'd be better off without me. I'm no use to her. I'm no use to anyone anymore."

He started beating his hands against his head as if he wanted to beat the demons outta there. It was hard to recognize this sad sack as the snappy numbers guy I remembered from the orphanage.

Seeing as we weren't getting anywhere, I grabbed ahold of his wrists and pulled him up to his feet.

"Where's the shower? The shower?" I yelled, shaking him by the shoulders to try to get him to focus.

"D-d-down the hall."

"Let's take a trip then."

I hauled him out the apartment door and down to the shared bathroom at the back of the first floor, turned on the cold tap, and practically picked him up off the floor and flung him under the water, boxers and all. He sputtered and fought me, but I had at least sixty pounds and half a foot on him, so he didn't stand much of a chance. I soaped him down as best I could and rinsed him off before realizing we'd forgot to bring a towel.

"Stay put!"

I fetched a towel, bathrobe, and shaving kit from the apartment and stood over him while he stripped and toweled off, shrugged into the robe, and attempted to shave. His hands were so shaky I was afraid he was gonna cut his own throat, so I took over and did it for him.

I'm no barber, but by the time I was done, slapped some aftershave on his cheeks, and brushed his hair into place, he looked a lot more human than when we'd started. I pushed him back down the hall and helped sort out some clothes for him. He had finished dressing by the time the front door swung open and Mitzi walked in with a bag of groceries.

"Sam! Look at you! I'd never have believed it. Mr. Malhaven, I believe you are a miracle worker."

"I don't know about that, but I don't take no for an answer when I set out to help someone, I guess."

"It's wonderful to see my brother this way again. You both sit and I'll make us a fresh pot of coffee. I picked up babka, Sam. Chocolate, your favorite."

"I'm not a child you have to soothe with treats."

"Then stop acting like one," she said, eyes flashing as she slammed the groceries down on the small table in the kitchenette. She bustled around, flinging pots and pans and making more noise than was probably strictly necessary for brewing coffee, but I figured she had a right to be mad.

Sam sighed and looked at me. "Women. They don't understand, do they?"

"I dunno. Depends on what we're talking about. I'm not sure I understand because last time I checked, you were a fine upstanding citizen. Now I'm hearing tales you're some kind of criminal mastermind, yet I walk in here and find you looking like a bum who wandered in off the streets."

"Why are you here?" he asked, squinting at me all suspicious. "If it's for a story about me for the paper, do me a favor and take a hike. We have enough trouble as it is."

"I'm here because I'm curious. And because Marlene Sutherland is a nice young lady who happens to be worried about you. So here I am to get your side of things. That's what a good reporter does, you know. Gets all sides of the story before going to press. Why don't you fill me in on what I'm missing?"

"Is… is Marlene doing okay?"

"Why don't you ask her yourself?"

"I'm no use to her. No use to anyone now. I've been let go in disgrace. Accused of swindling orphans. Orphans! Sister Honoria was being fair in her way by not involving the police, but word gets around all the same. Who's gonna hire me now as an accountant with the reputation of being an embezzler and no recommendation?"

"Now, Sam," Mitzi protested. "You know Mr. Klein offered to take you on."

"As a delivery boy. Twenty-five bucks a week."

"It would be more than you're making now. Beggars can't be choosers, don't they say. And it would bring in money for us while you get back on your feet, or are you happy to mooch off me and spend up all our savings on the booze?"

I have to say Sam had the good sense not to try to answer what was a losing proposition. He hung his head while his sister returned to banging around pots and pans to show her displeasure.

"Listen, Sam. You don't have to convince me you got a raw deal, but we gotta convince a lot more people than just us. Why don't you tell me what happened in your own words? On the level. I promise not to print anything in the paper without your say so."

"Tell you what happened? I can tell you exactly what happened. A slime from the bottom of the ocean crept in the front door and oozed his way into my job, that's what happened."

"Let me guess, your pal and mine, Mr. Horace Ludgate?"

Sam looked at me with a look I only seen one other time on a man I watched go mad right in the middle of a battle in the South Pacific. He leapt to his feet and started laughing his head off.

"No, no, not just our pal. Horrie, a friend to all. A friend to all!"

CHAPTER FIFTEEN

J thought I might have to slap him around again, but Mitzi took a hand by slamming a tray with coffee and cake down in front of us hard enough to make me worry she was gonna break the dishes.

"Samuel Leonard! Stop that this instant. You've been wallowing like a quitter. What would Father and Mother and… and poor Daniel think if they saw you now?" She bust out the bawling, anxious to get rid of all those tears she'd been so stingy with earlier.

Sam looked as though she'd stabbed him right in the heart as he pulled her down on the sofa beside him.

"Ah, Mitzi, don't. You know I can't stand it when you cry."

"Then don't give me reason to."

"You know this has thrown me for a loop. I worked so hard and always did my best. I never expected to end up this way. Makes it tough to know how to go on."

"But we must go on, Sam. For them. We're alive and have our whole lives ahead of us. We owe it to them to make the most of it, don't we, Mr. Malhaven?" she asked, turning to me.

"Call me Jim. Both of you," I said, pulling out my handkerchief and handing it to her so she could dry her eyes. Luckily, I hadn't had cause to use it, so it was still nice and clean. My ma would've been proud of me, rest her soul. "All I know is in this life, there's only one direction to go. Can't go back, can't stay put. That means we gotta go full steam ahead. I get this was a blow, but if there's one thing I've learned, it's keep going even when you think all hope is lost. You'd be surprised sometimes what's waiting for you right around the corner."

I was thinking of a certain moment when the worst day of my life had turned into the best when I'd woken up and seen my Victoria looking down at me and come to find out we were both still alive and kicking against all the odds. It had taught me the truth of that old saw 'it ain't over 'til it's over.'

"I suppose you're right. I know Marlene puts a lot of stock in you. I'm sure you mean to help if you can, but I don't know what you can do about it."

"Investigate. That's what I do best. Looks like the evidence against you is all tied up in those cooked books Horrie has. What do you make of them?"

Sam shook his head. "I don't know what to think other than they are forgeries but done by an expert. If I didn't know better, I'd swear I'd written them. The handwriting certainly looks like mine. The notes and codes I add to the ledgers, all mine. Someone went to a lot of trouble to set me up."

"And by someone, we mean Horrie, I take it?"

"Has to be. He talked Sister Honoria into letting him hole up with the financial records for a couple of days with the excuse of being able to help me find places to cut costs. Hah! He emerged with that extra set of books and a lot of sorrowful looks at me as though he was awfully disappointed to discover such a thing. What a snake."

"We're in agreement there. Didn't take me long to finger him as a crook, but what I don't get is, what's in it for him? Can't be much to skim off the joint unless the high-society types around here are freer with the handouts than I've got them marked down for."

"That's the thing. Ludgate made it look in the forged books as though our donations were much larger than they are, but I know exactly to the penny how much was coming in. We barely had enough to keep the lights turned on and the children reasonably fed and clothed. I've been racking my brains to understand what his motive is in getting me kicked out. He obviously wanted the job badly enough to take a big risk, but why?"

"He seems kinda interested in one of the kids there. Some of the nuns staged a revolt and kicked her out over Sister Honoria's objections. They think she's doing the Devil's work. I took her to stay with Victoria Jankowski and Horrie was more than a bit peeved about it. Said he and his wife were the proper people to look after her."

"You must be talking about Lily White. I'm sorry to hear she's in trouble. She's such a sweet thing. She would come into my office sometimes and sit and draw her angel pictures while I worked. The other children teased her, so she was glad to be able to get away on her own. I know there have been some pranks since she arrived, but she always behaved like an angel herself, so quiet and well-mannered. I can't believe Sister Honoria sent her away."

"It's only temporary for her own safety until I get to the bottom of all this. Little girl found under mysterious circumstances. Can't or won't talk to tell anyone who she is. This Horrie goon shows up and shoves you out of the way and all these pranks start happening. Now he wants to get his hands on the girl since she's been let loose. I'm not someone who believes in that many coincidences. There's a connection here. We just gotta track it down. What do we know about this Ludgate anyway? Told me his wife and him are taking care of a fancy estate."

"Yes, Hasselwhite Hall. Marlene and I took a drive out there. She borrowed a car from her mother's employer. Mrs. Sutherland works for Carsworth, you know."

I tipped him the nod, aware Mrs. S was housekeeper for Louis Carsworth of the Carsworth City Carsworths and publisher of the rag where I made my living. Not a bad egg for being such a rich guy. He'd even paid Q's and Marlene's way through school. I could see him lending out one of his fleet of cars without a second thought.

"Marlene talked me into driving out there. I don't know what she thought we'd be able to find out, but it was tempting to see the place for ourselves. When I was first fired, I was so angry I wanted to do something, anything."

"And what happened?"

"Nothing. The place is a fortress. Ten-foot-high brick wall around the entire property and gates that were locked up tight. There was a buzzer set up with an intercom system. We rang it half a dozen times but got no answer. I was relieved to be honest. I'm no good at spying. Hadn't the slightest idea what kind of excuse we could offer for being there. In the end, we turned around and drove back home. Marlene and I argued on the way back. She wanted to try again. I wanted to forget the whole thing. After everything that's happened to our family, I feel we got no luck at all. There's not much point in fighting if the whole world is dead set against you."

"You're an awfully young guy to be feeling that way. Your sister here is going out every day and working. Might do you good, too. Why don't you take old man Klein up on his offer? Wouldn't it be better to be working a respectable job than sitting around the house looking at the bottom of an empty whiskey bottle?"

"I suppose. It would be a big comedown though. Guess I'm a prouder man than I realized."

"Nothing wrong with that, but there's different things to be proud of. Not giving up is one of them. I know what Marlene would want you to do if she was here, and I can guarantee it's not hanging around in your underpants hitting the sauce when you could be earning an honest dollar."

He got all red in the face again, and I almost expected him to take another poke at me, but instead he chuckled. "You won't tell Marlene how you found me, will you? I'd never hear the end of it."

"Cross my heart. We'll keep it to ourselves if you promise me I won't find you like that next time I come visiting."

"Promise."

Mitzi flashed a brilliant smile at me. It lit up her face the way a firework lights up the sky. "You've done him such good, Jim. Sam just needs a little hope right now."

"Well, fingers crossed I can deliver the goods then. I ain't failed yet and there's always a first time, but I seen plenty of guys like this Horrie. Always think they're smarter than all the rest of us put together, yet they always trip up somewhere along the way. Plus I got resources. Cop friends, informants, and a top-notch research genius in Marlene's very own brother Q. Which reminds me, I should go check in with him on a few tips I got."

We bid each other a fond farewell as they say in books. I drove back to the paper to see if I could get Q started on looking through the back issues for more about the search for Lily's family. I also wanted to make sure he was doing okay after the morning's trouble. He'd been so touchy, I'd thought it was a good idea to let him cool off, but I was worried about him. It had to sting to be swept up by the cops for nothing.

I hustled through the newsroom hoping to avoid my editor's eye, but Morty don't miss much. From behind the big glass window in his office where he kept an eagle eye on all the doings in the bullpen, he glared at me in a way that meant I better get in to see him double quick.

"Hey, Boss. I promise you I'm working on a hot one, but it may take a day or two before I have something to print."

He waved me off impatiently with one hand while shoving a paper in my face with the other. I may not have mentioned it, but Morty is a man who believes in being thrifty with his words.

Grabbing the paper from him, the first thing I noticed was the signature at the bottom. Marquis Sutherland. The next? The words "resignation, effective immediately."

CHAPTER SIXTEEN

"What? Where is he?"

Morty shrugged, pulled the half-chewed cigar down from its usual perch at the side of his mouth. "Gone."

As I said, Morty don't believe in spending words like they were going out of style, but I didn't need a whole song and dance to guess this had something to do with the events of the morning.

"Don't worry, Boss. He ain't serious. I'll get this straightened out," I said, folding up the letter and tucking it into my suit pocket.

Morty just shrugged again and stuck the stogie back in his mouth to mark the period on the end of the conversation as far as he was concerned.

I headed out to track Q down and talk sense into him but was flagged down by Maudie who was typing away at her desk as usual.

"If you're looking for that friend of yours, I'd give him a chance to cool down. He was all hot and bothered when he stormed through here a while back."

"Did he say anything to you?"

"Nah. But he was muttering under his breath something awful. Whatever it's about, he'll probably feel different in the morning. That's the way of it with men, ain't it? Do something in the heat of the moment then feel a fool when you've cooled off but too embarrassed to admit you made a mistake."

She had a point. I knew Q was worked up about being fingered as a crook, but I didn't expect him to go overboard by quitting his job. Sure, maybe some of the other guys at the paper had seen him being dragged out by the cops and would give him a razzing. It would be a nine-day wonder at best, but he was a proud guy. Maybe he didn't want to put up with it.

I walked back outside and got in the Champ, mulling over what to do. I was tempted to drive out to the Carsworth place and see if Q was there. I didn't want him to think I didn't give two cents about how he'd been treated, but it was awkward, too, what with Joey being my best friend and all. Maybe I wouldn't be so welcome.

In the end, I decided to let it ride until the next day. Maybe I was being a coward by putting it off, but it was getting late, and I needed to get home in time for Victoria's birthday party. Maybe Q would be calmer and starting to regret what he'd done by the morning, and it'd be easier to talk him around to admitting it then.

I drove back out to the boneyard we called home, stopping off at the caretaker's cottage where I lived to change into my best suit and tame down my rusty locks before heading over to the mansion, Victoria's gift in hand. I noticed a strange sedan parked out front of the mansion and wondered if an extra guest had been invited to our shindig. Anxious to make a good impression, I hopped up the stairs and flung open the door to an unexpected squabble.

There in the big marble lobby were the members of the household squaring off against one Horace Ludgate, who had a tight hold of Lily's hand. She was pulling with all her might against his grip with a look of pure hatred on her face that was something to see on such a young kid. For that one moment at least, she looked every inch the Devil's spawn the nuns had been complaining about. But it was easy for me to spot there was more than a little fear mixed up in that look of loathing, too.

Ludgate, Victoria, and Livinia were all talking a mile a minute, so it was hard to understand the subtleties of their arguments, but I got the gist of it. Horace was for hauling Lily away and the rest of them were against it.

Feeling quick action was called for, I strode up to our guest and gave him a bop on the nose. It was nothing more than a light tap, but he acted as though the heavyweight champ of the world had dealt him a knockout blow. Leaving hold of the girl, he fell heavily to his knees, clutching his schnoz with both hands and giving out with a high-pitched wailing.

Livinia sniffed. "Serves you right."

It ain't often she approves of something I did, so I had to grin.

Lily ran back to Victoria and hid behind her as I reached down a friendly hand to help old Horace to his feet. "Sorry, Ludgate. I'm one of those 'act first, ask questions later' kind of guys."

Eying me warily, like I was a grenade without a pin that might blow at any time, he ignored my outstretched paw and clambered to his feet, nearly keeling over again before steadying himself on his pins.

"Mr. Malhaven, this is quite outrageous. In point of fact, the reception I have received from everyone in this madhouse is nothing short of monstrous. I've come all this way, at no insignificant inconvenience to myself as I am a very busy man, and offered, as any good Christian soul would, to take charge of this poor orphan child, and have been met with nothing but suspicion, argument, and now violence! Never in my life have I experienced such undeserved and ill-mannered treatment. I pride myself on—"

"Being a friend to all, ain't it?"

"You perhaps think to mock my life's philosophy, sir, but I will still, despite all I have endured, extend the hand of friendship. Yes, even to you."

I gritted my teeth and took his oily palm in mine, the better to pull him close so I could keep an eye on the eel. I draped an arm casually over his shoulders to weight him down a bit. "I might have been a bit hasty. Apologies all round, but I thought maybe Lily wasn't so interested in going with you. What's your opinion, Lily? Would you rather go live with Mr. Ludgate and his missus?"

She answered plain enough without words by bursting into tears and grabbing Victoria's skirt in both her fists as though preparing to anchor herself in place against all comers.

"I think she'd rather stay with Mrs. Jankowski for now, but I'm sure we appreciate your interest," I said as I attempted to give him the bum rush out the door. But he was a slippery fish and managed to squirm out of my grasp. I had to hand it to him. He had a real never say die kind of attitude.

"Really, Mr. Malhaven, asking the girl what she wants is a pointless exercise. It is for we adults to decide what is in any child's best interests. They are too inexperienced and their minds too unformed to know what is most sensible for their own welfare. My wife and I have charge of a very comfortable house, and my position of responsibility at the institution ultimately responsible for Lily's well-being would logically support my position that we are the proper guardians for this poor girl."

Victoria gave him one of her cool looks that I knew from experience boded no good to anyone on the receiving end of it.

"Mr. Ludgate, as I have repeatedly, and remarkably patiently I might add, explained to you, I am an alumna of that same institution and have been charged by its head and my personal friend, Sister Honoria, with the care of Lily, a task I am most honored and glad to undertake. Until such time as I hear, from Honoria's own lips, mind you, that she would prefer you to take charge or that the orphanage is prepared to accept Lily back among its pupils, here she shall remain. I have also asked you repeatedly to please leave our house as you are upsetting everyone by your continued presence after I have already given you your answer. I was prepared to ring for the police and will still be happy to do so if Mr. Malhaven's arrival or your own common sense are not sufficient to persuade you to leave."

"Now, now, my good woman, there is no need to go to such extremes. I hope we may have a civilized discussion among ourselves without resort to any constabulary presence. I would urge you to reconsider your position. As a widowed woman with no children of your own, I had thought it would be obvious to you that it is far more proper for an older, more experienced married couple such as my wife and I to have charge of the child, particularly given your, ah, living arrangements, shall we say?"

"And what do you mean by that?"

"I was reluctant to mention it and hesitate even now as I am a man who abhors any unpleasantness, but it is—perhaps, unusual, is the best way of putting it—to have a single woman and a single man of comparable age living in such close proximity while unmarried. I have gained the impression there is some sort of... relationship between you and Mr. Malhaven. I'm not sure such an atmosphere, as it were, is the best for a young, impressionable mind. If I were forced to bring this situation to the attention of the Bishop, I'm sure he would agree with me."

Seeing as Victoria was about to blow her top and wanting to save her the trouble as it was her birthday and all, I was about to give the joker another bop on the nose when Livinia of all people stepped in, punctuating about every third word of her speech by waving a bony finger in front of Ludgate's face.

"If I am to understand that you are attempting to imply my niece would be involved in any activities not of the highest moral standards, and while under my roof and protection as well, you are an even bigger fool than I gave you credit for. And as for Mr. James Malhaven, while he can be an uncouth brute, he follows his own code of conduct that does no particular disgrace to his mother's memory. Furthermore, the day I allow anyone to stand in my house and throw insults in our faces has not yet arrived, you absolute cretin."

Victoria and I crossed glances and had to restrain ourselves from busting out laughing at this unexpected endorsement from a woman who had more than once intimated she regretted my very existence.

"Shall I demonstrate some of that uncouthness?" I asked Livinia.

"Please do, Mr. Malhaven."

With that permission, I pushed Ludgate, still protesting, blustering, and threatening, out the door Mr. Cressley had thoughtfully opened for me and gave him a hearty kick in the pants for good measure.

He stumbled and I was afraid I'd gotten carried away and he was gonna take a header down the front steps to the driveway, but he righted himself, shooting a look black as a thundercloud back at me.

"This isn't the last you've seen of me."

"That's what they all say," I said and slammed the door in his face.

CHAPTER SEVENTEEN

It wasn't long after that we heard a car start up outside and the sound of tires spitting up gravel down the driveway, indicating Ludgate had decided to beat a hasty retreat for the moment.

Victoria turned to her aunt and astonished her by giving her a swift peck on the cheek. "Thank you for being such a dear and standing up for us, Livinia."

That august person blushed pink. "Don't be ridiculous. The man is a complete buffoon. I am shocked the Sisters of Mercy would employ such a creature. I know quite a few people who sit on the orphanage's Board personally and will be expressing my displeasure both by telephone and in writing first thing in the morning."

Cressley rushed away to the kitchen to tend his pots and pans, reminding the rest of us we were overdue to attend a certain someone's birthday celebration. We made our way to the grand dining room with me stopping to retrieve Victoria's parcel from the floor where it had landed in the general mayhem. I handed over the slightly worse for wear box to Victoria with a flourish and got an enthusiastic kiss as a more than ample reward.

"Aren't you the sly one, sweetheart. And here I thought you'd forgotten all about it," she said with a smile, laying her soft hand against my scarred cheek in that way she had as though the ugly slash didn't mean a thing to her. One of the things about Victoria that gets me is the way she sees straight through to a person's insides and don't pay much attention to the outside packaging.

I sent Cressley a silent prayer of gratitude. I'd have to thank him in person later for being such a pal and arranging Victoria's present for me. He dotes on her almost as much as I do, and I like to think he don't resent having me around either. He's always been a valuable guy to have in your corner. This save of his was just another example of why.

To my surprise, Lily sat down to join us at the big table. I thought Livinia would have banished the kid to the kitchen to eat, but maybe she'd impressed that formidable figure with her good manners. Seeing the girl sit down and carefully spread her napkin in her lap then fold her hands, patiently waiting to be served, I could see why Liv would approve. Mrs. Cressley was quite the grande dame and approved of anyone who followed her own notion of behaving like a real lady.

Cressley did his usual round of serving. Livinia kept trying to convince him to hire a new butler and cook now that he'd been promoted to head of house. She thought it undignified for him to still do the housework, but he was stubborn about it, thinking no one could do as good a job as him and I can't say for sure he's wrong on that count. The food was always first-rate and his service top-notch.

He did sit down and join us at the table once our plates were loaded up and tucked in with as much gusto as the rest of us: roasted lamb, mint jelly, mashed potatoes, green beans, and the fluffy, buttery dinner rolls that were one of his specialties. There was a noticeable silence around the table as we were all busy stuffing our faces. Once we started to get our fill, conversation got off the ground with Cressley and Lily silent observers, though Cressley did write out a few notes in his elegant penmanship from time to time on the pad he always kept handy.

Livinia tried to quiz me about Lily's background in that high-handed way she had and obviously wanted to continue to air her griev-ances against our late unlamented guest, Ludgate, but Victoria and I kept turning the conversation to other channels. We were in agreement without saying a word that it wasn't a good idea to talk too much more about it in front of the girl, who still looked shook up from her attempted kidnapping.

At the end of the meal, Cressley brought out a seven-layer chocolate cake with a flourish and lit one big candle on top of it for Victoria to blow out. You might think it a shame she had to make her own cake, but she loved to bake so I knew she got a kick out of it and out of all the oohs and aahs as everyone took a taste. Then she opened up her presents: a beautiful gold pen from Cressley, a charm bracelet from Livinia, the hat from me, which I was pleased to see suited her every bit as much in real life as I'd imagined from the sketch Klein showed me, and from Lily, a drawing.

Victoria passed it around. I wasn't surprised to see it was one of the girl's angel pictures, similar to the ones I'd already been shown. Victoria made quite a fuss over it, then ushered Lily off to bed while Cressley and I cleared the table and started in on the dishes, Livinia naturally being above such mundane chores.

When Victoria came back downstairs, she and I ducked out the kitchen door for a walk. It was cooler now the sun had gone down, but that just made for good nuzzling weather. We parked ourselves on the bench in front of my cottage where we would sit and talk when the weather ain't too bad. We'd watched our fair number of sunsets together on that selfsame bench and it never got old, but tonight, we made do with a sky full of stars instead.

I filled her in on what little else I'd learned about the situation at the orphanage that I hadn't already told her. I thought about telling her about the predicament with Q, but something held me back. Victoria ain't the biggest fan of Flanagan's to begin with, and I couldn't help but think the morning's events didn't paint him in the best light. I reported on my visit with Sam, though, and my attempts to boost his spirits.

"It's such a shame. Honoria always thought the world of Sam and how hard he worked to keep the orphanage in funds. I hope you can help him," she said, settling in under my arm where she fit as though the space was made for her.

"I mean to try. This Ludgate character is up to something. I have to figure out what's in it for him to get ahold of the girl. What percentage could there be in adopting an orphan? There has to be one. No man is that persistent in the face of rejection without a motive. Good thing I came along when I did, huh?"

"Oh, I think I would have managed to put him in his place without your help if push came to shove."

"I have no doubt. The loveliest of women with a spine of pure steel. That's my Victoria."

"Your Victoria? Taking a lot for granted, aren't you, mister?"

"Well, you know I want to make you mine. I ain't kept those cards too close to my vest, have I?"

"I know, Jim. I'm still getting used to everything that's happened since last fall. I never thought I'd meet another man I felt the same way about as I did about Lukasz. And all those horrible things that happened, then finding out Livinia was my aunt after thinking I had no family all these years. It's been a lot to take on board. I'm not sure I'm ready for even more change yet."

"I know, I know. I ain't pushing. Just know I'll be right here in this very spot waiting to make an honest woman of you, and you'll have a hard time getting rid of me in the meantime."

"Honest woman, indeed!" she said, jabbing me in the ribs, but the smile in her eyes told me she wasn't really mad.

We sat there quite a while, enjoying each other's company, but I'll draw the veil over the rest of the scene. You can use your imagination. Or better yet, don't. It ain't polite.

When we finally called it a night, I went inside the cottage and stretched out on the bed, intending to rest a minute before changing into my PJs. Next thing I knew, I was waking up, feeling half drugged. Guess that heavy meal did a number on me. I picked up the alarm clock and seen it was two in the morning. Then I thought about what might have woke me up. Some kind of noise. I got sharp hearing, and it wasn't long before I heard it again. A metallic scraping sound, faint but enough to spark my curiosity.

There aren't many places quieter than a graveyard at night, so any noise other than the occasional hoot owl was plenty unusual. My investigative instincts on high alert, I jumped up and ran outside, hoping to get a better idea of where the noise was coming from. Didn't take me long to figure out something was happening up at the big house.

I'd learned to move as stealthy as a panther during the war. I know you're having a hard time imagining a big guy like me sneaking around, but when it's a matter of life or death in the jungles of the Pacific, you'd be surprised what you can learn to do.

Sneaking up toward the house, I kept an eye out for anything unusual. All the lights were out in the windows. Whatever was happening hadn't alarmed any of the inmates. Not yet, anyway. Luckily, there was a bit of a moon, and I was as familiar with the layout of the grounds by now as the back of my hand. Otherwise, I would have tripped a million times over all the tree roots and foot markers that littered the joint.

I hadn't seen any movement, but I heard the noise again. Now I was closer, I could tell it was coming from the back of the house. I was creeping in that direction when I heard a sound that never fails to set my heart to racing, even all these years after the war.

A gunshot.

CHAPTER EIGHTEEN

I burst around the corner just in time to get clobbered by a falling ladder. It knocked me to the ground in one fell swoop then kept me there as I got tangled up in the rungs trying to lift it off me. To add to my woes, another gunshot rang out much too close for comfort.

"Who's so trigger-happy up there?" I yelled. "Give a guy a break, would ya?"

Silence, then a haughty voice I knew all too well.

"James Malhaven, is that you? May I ask what you are doing trying to climb into my bedroom window at this odd hour of the night? Or at any time, for that matter."

"Mrs. Cressley, I can assure you, the impulse to do such a thing has never even once crossed my mind."

"Jim, darling?" a sweeter voice chimed in. "Is that you? Are you all right?"

"I been better. Could use a little help down here."

"Hang on, sweetheart. We'll be right there."

Ceasing my struggles, I lay back looking up at the stars. Even with the bit of moon that was peeking out, I could still see quite a few staring back at me. Pretty. Maybe I should take a moonlight stroll more often.

I was interrupted in my reverie by Cressley and Victoria riding to the rescue, him in a sensible gray flannel bathrobe and her in a less sensible but much more attractive matching rose-colored negligee and dressing gown. Between the two of them, they figured out how to disentangle my long limbs from the ladder and shift the thing off me which was a relief. I sat up gingerly, feeling around for any permanent damage and found none. I was gonna have a few impressive bruises, but at least nothing was broken.

Livinia arrived on the scene too late to help, naturally, and fully dressed. I had yet to ever catch her in anything resembling night attire even during the most dire of events. I think if the house was burning down around her ears, she'd still take the time to dress and fix her hair. Or maybe she slept that way to be prepared. I guess only Cressley knew for sure, and I wasn't gonna inquire.

"What is the meaning of this, Mr. Malhaven? Surely if you were trying to do maintenance on the house, it could have waited until morning. It is quite inconsiderate of you to wake everyone up in this manner."

"It wasn't too considerate to be firing bullets at me neither, but I'm willing to overlook it. That was you, wasn't it?"

"What if it was? A very natural reaction to someone trying to invade my bedroom in the dead of night, I should think."

"Suppose you got a point, but I didn't know you even had a pistol."

"It was Ernestine's."

"You don't mean the same one she used to—"

"Yes, of course. It is a practical-sized weapon for a woman, and one can't be too careful these days."

If that didn't beat all. If my sister and her loony twin had used a gun to go on a murderous rampage and then offed herself with that selfsame gat, I'm not sure I would have hung on to it even for sentimental reasons. But Livinia didn't have a sentimental bone in her body, so it made sense to her, I'm sure. Why spend money on a new gun when you got a perfectly good one right to hand?

I seen Victoria looking shocked. She was used to Livinia's thrifty ways but even for her, hearing her aunt had hung on to the pistol that put a period to her mother's life was a low blow. She'd had a hard time getting over all the crazy events of the previous fall, and I didn't want Livinia's miserliness raking it all up again. Getting stiffly to my feet with help from Cressley, I decided to reroute the conversation.

"Let me set you straight. I never climbed this ladder. I only got a face full of it when I came to see what the heck was going on. My guess is someone was about to use it when you scared them off. Did you see anyone?"

"No, I heard the ladder hit the side of the house. I always sleep with my window open. Fresh air, even on chilly nights, is imperative for good health. I haven't had a cold in over thirty years."

Resisting the urge to congratulate her, I nodded wisely to encourage her to keep talking, not that she needed it.

"I arose, pulling the pistol from my nightstand, and went to investigate. Seeing the ladder and knowing of no other interpretation than a thief attempting to infiltrate, I fired a warning shot. The Wynter family fortune makes us an unfortunate target for such criminal mischief. It wouldn't have been the first attempt. I have every right to protect my home, life, and personal property."

"And what did Mr. Cressley think about all these goings on?"

I thought for a minute I'd managed to disconcert her, but I'd found out on more than one occasion that Livinia was not easily put off her game.

"Mr. Cressley and I maintain separate bedrooms. Much more civilized."

I saw Victoria hide a smile at this pronouncement, and even Cressley looked amused. Livinia looked her usual poker-faced self.

"Well, whoever it was," I mused. "I'm afraid they're long gone by now. If I hadn't gotten involved in a waltz with the ladder, I might have been able to catch them, but there's not much use now. Why don't you all go back to bed, and I'll take a look around to be sure. And maybe sleep with your window closed just for tonight, Mrs. Cressley, huh?"

Livinia sniffed at that as she went back in the house, but we all heard the sound of the window slamming shut and the bolt being shot into place once she made it back upstairs. Cressley gave me a bit of a shrug, as if to say, what can you do with a woman like that, and went back in the house himself.

Victoria turned to me with that troubled look I'd seen too often on her lovely face and lay a gentle hand on my arm.

"Are you sure you're all right, Jim?"

"I'll be black and blue for a few days, but everything appears to be in working order. Could've been worse. That'll teach me to go rushing in where angels fear to tread."

She laughed. "If only I could believe that. I'm afraid I've had to learn to accept you'll always be the first to rush in."

"I ain't no angel, that's for sure, so maybe that's why."

"Speaking of angels," Victoria murmured, looking over my shoulder.

I turned around quick and immediately regretted it when my aching back protested. Standing there was a small ghostly figure, made more so by the white cotton nightgown she wore.

"Lily, dear," Victoria said. "You'll catch cold out here. Don't worry. It was a silly false alarm. Let's get you back to bed."

Lily trustingly took Victoria's hand as she was led away, Victoria shooting me one last look over her shoulder that caused me to waggle my fingers at her in an idiotic manner. She smiled and blew me a kiss. Totally worth looking the fool.

As they locked the kitchen door behind them, I started a circuit around the house looking for any signs of the intruder. I couldn't help but question whether this was a random burglary attempt. It had occurred to me looking at Lily that trouble followed her around wherever she went. Was this another in a long line of coincidences of which she was an innocent bystander? Or was there a pattern I couldn't see yet?

I enjoyed a good puzzle, but not when it brought unknown danger so close to home and the light of my life. I hoped I wouldn't live to regret bringing Lily to stay at the Wynter mansion. The place had witnessed enough evil and heartache. I didn't want to be in any way responsible for adding to the score.

It also occurred to me our Mr. Ludgate hadn't been too happy with his reception earlier. Was he determined enough to risk a breaking and entering charge to try and get his hands on the girl? If it was him, did he really think he could sneak into the house and spirit the girl away with no one the wiser? Even with all his bluster, there was a gleam of native intelligence in the man that made it hard for me to think he'd come up with such a cockeyed scheme, but desperate men are sometimes driven to desperate acts.

After fetching a flashlight from the cottage, I took a more thorough search around the grounds. It hadn't rained to speak of in a few weeks, so the ground was too dry to even find a good footprint. I gave it up and went back to bed only to dream a crazy mixed-up nightmare of Victoria sprouting angel wings, Livinia in a scarlet red negligee wrestling a giant eel, flying pots and pans, and Lily standing in the middle of it all, watching and smiling as Archie the cat wound around and around her legs.

I woke up with a start, heart pounding. Too early to get up, I passed the time turning over what little I knew so far in my brain. Dozed off again finally with only a single thought still buzzing around. Who was Lily? Find that out and everything else would fall into place.

CHAPTER NINETEEN

I'm usually an up and at 'em type, a habit left over from my
Army days, but I figured I deserved a couple of extra hours
of sleep after my nighttime misadventures. It was with more than a
groan or two that I finally crawled out of bed, my back giving me hell
from losing the fight with the ladder. And there's nothing like a weird
nightmare to make you feel muddleheaded, trying to sort out what was
real from what wasn't. I couldn't help but feel this mystery
surrounding Lily was going to bring even more trouble unless I figured
it out and fast.

Deciding I could use help, I downed a quick cup of java then
headed to town and the Carsworth place to see if I couldn't convince Q
to come back to the Crier with me. He still lived there with his ma. I'd
never been invited to the joint myself, being only a lowly working stiff
at the paper Carsworth owned, but everyone knew where his
house was.

I drove into town and turned toward the Northside where all the
best families hung out. No cramped brownstones here. Just big, gated
lots with fancier and fancier houses and gardens until you got to the
biggest one of them all. Guess when you got a whole city named after
your family, you got to keep up appearances. The place was all marble

columns and pink-colored brick with enough rooms to accommodate the entire staff of the paper and then some, if he ever lowered himself enough to have us over. Morty was the only one who rated an invite, and then only if Carsworth was of a mind to interfere in how his editor was running the Crier.

I explained myself to the bored guard sitting and working out a crossword in the gatehouse. He rang up to the house and confirmed with Q's ma I was legit and waved me through. I took his directions to follow the brick driveway to the back of the house in time to see Dorothea Sutherland emerge and beckon to me. She was as pretty as her daughter, but her face was creased with the kind of worry only a mother knows.

"Mr. Malhaven, I'm so glad you came by. I was going to try and ring you later at the paper to see if you couldn't help me make heads or tails of what is going on with Marquis. He came home from work early yesterday and hasn't been out of his room since. I couldn't even get him to take any food or talk to me. Do you know what's wrong?"

"I've a half a suspicion. Why don't you lead me to him, and I'll see if I can do anything about it."

And that's how I found myself for the second time in two days trying to perform a bit of amateur psychology. I'd been made Sergeant during the war and, being a few years older than the rest of the men in my platoon, I'd had practice lending a sympathetic ear and giving pep talks but not in a situation quite like this. I'd never seen Q as mad as he'd been the day before. Heck, I'd never seen him mad before.

I knocked on the door Mrs. Sutherland directed me to and got a whole lotta silence back. Tried the knob but the door was locked.

"Q?" I bellowed. "Jim Malhaven here."

Nothing.

"Your ma is awful worried about you. That's not a nice thing to do to her, is it, after all she's done for you?"

Silence.

I sighed and leaned against the door.

"Guess I'm gonna have to knock this door down. It's too bad. Might cause your ma trouble. She'd have to explain it to Carsworth.

Could raise all kinda questions. And you know I'm stubborn enough to—"

I didn't have time to react before the door was wrenched open and I halfway fell into the room. Wincing, I grabbed my sore back.

"Geez, give a guy a warning or something next time, why dontcha? I got into an argument with a ladder yesterday and the ladder won."

Q just stood and stared at me. He was neat and clean and all dressed up in his usual work duds which is to say a crisp white dress shirt, pressed gray flannel trousers, tie and sweater vest. The only thing missing was his black horn-rimmed glasses. I fished those out of my pocket and handed what was left of them to him.

"Thank you," he muttered, throwing them down on a dresser.

There being nowhere else to sit in the small room, I eased down onto the bed to give my back a rest, fiddling with my hat in my hands.

"It seems there's been a little misunderstanding at the paper. Morty's under the impression you up and quit."

He pressed his lips close at that, like I was gonna have to torture him to pry some kinda secret out of him, but that didn't bother me none. I'm more than used to carrying on one-sided conversations. I can talk all day if I have to.

"So, I decided to come by and straighten this out 'cause I need your help. Got a big story I'm working on. Well, it's not exactly a story. At least, not yet. More of a mystery. An investigation. Hey, maybe I should give up this whole reporting racket and go into the private eye business like in the movies, huh? Wonder if I could make more moolah as a dick than as a hack. Something to think about, ain't it? Anyways, I got this little girl, sweet as can be. Nobody knows her exact age or anything much about her, but she seems to be followed around by trouble and I know she's young enough she don't deserve that. Thought you might be able to help me out. See, she was found all alone in the park—"

"Janey Doe." He spat it out as if he couldn't help himself, but it broke the ice. "I remember the stories Miss Adams wrote about her. It was very sad. A child abandoned with no family."

"That's right. Ended up at the Sisters of Mercy. And that was when all the trouble there started. It's quite a tale to try and unravel. I sure could use an ace researcher on my side."

"I'm sorry, Mr. Malhaven. I appreciate the thought behind your coming out here to see me, but I really think it is best for me and best for the paper that we part ways."

"You know you can call me Jim. I've told you often enough. And is this about what happened yesterday? Because that was a simple misunderstanding, and we got it all worked out, didn't we?"

"I'm not sure I would call being arrested, roughed up by a couple of policemen, and thrown into the city jail for a crime I did not commit a simple misunderstanding."

"I get it. I'd be plenty sore about it, too."

"With all due respect, Mr. Malhaven, I don't think you do get it. You couldn't possibly know what it is to be under constant scrutiny and suspicion simply for the color of your skin and the type of treatment it opens you up for."

"No, I gotta give you that one. But this ugly mug of mine don't exactly inspire confidence in strangers. I've gotten my fair share of suspicious looks at least. Besides, I don't see how quitting the paper is gonna help."

"It's something I've been thinking about for a while. I'm grateful to Mr. Carsworth for the opportunity, but there is no chance of advancement for me at the paper. If I want to make my mark in journalism, I'll have to go to one of the big cities. I've written to the editors of the Defender in Chicago and the Amsterdam News in New York to see if they have any openings. I want to be doing stories on my people. See if I can't make a difference for them."

"Listen, I got nothing against you wanting to move on to bigger and better things. Sky's the limit for a smart guy like you, but no harm in staying on at the paper in the meantime, is there? Just while you wait to line something else up. I got a feeling this girl is in real trouble, and we ain't got time to fool around. Ain't helping out a pal better than sitting around here moping?"

"It's a moot point. I've already tendered my letter of resignation."

I took that self-same letter out of my pocket and tore it in two.

"What letter? C'mon, Morty ain't one to hold a grudge. I'll smooth things over for you. Besides, I got a feeling this is all tied up with other strange doings at the orphanage. That business with Sam Leonard is awful suspicious to me. And I know he and your sister are friends. Don't you think Marlene would want you to help me get to the bottom of it all?"

I could tell that got to him. Him and his sister were close as could be. I patted myself on the back for finding the right thing to say. It's hit or miss with me sometimes.

"I suppose I could come in and look up the back issues for you."

We were interrupted by his ma running in at the door looking flustered.

"Marlene called from the orphanage. That man she complains about—"

"Horace Ludgate?" I asked. "What's the goop gone and done now?"

"He's dead!"

CHAPTER TWENTY

That set me back on my heels and no mistake.

"Is that a fact? I'd better get over there and get the scoop. You wanted to do some reporting," I said to Q. "Now's your chance if you tag along with me."

"Wait a minute," he replied, digging around in a dresser drawer. He came up with a Brownie flash camera. "I might be able to get some good pictures for the paper."

"Always thinking. I like it. Let's hustle!"

We pulled up at the Sisters of Mercy in time to see a sheet-draped stretcher being loaded up into the morgue van. Q got a few shots off before they shut the doors.

My buddy Flanagan was standing on the front steps chatting with another of the boys in blue and gave me a look when he saw me coming.

"Been expecting you'd be on the scene before too long, Jimmy my boy, but even for you, this is Mr. Johnny on the Spot. How'd you come to hear about it?"

"Trade secret. A good reporter never reveals his sources."

"Hmph," he said, looking past me to where Q was hovering behind my shoulder. "I can guess. The nurse?"

"There ain't a law against it. Only natural she'd want her brother to come comfort her after such a distressing event. Why don't you go take a look for her, Q? I'm sure she could use a brotherly chat right about now," I added with a wink. Wouldn't hurt for Q to see what he could find out while I pumped Flanagan for info.

Q gave Joey a look that let me know he wasn't in a forgiving mood about the whole mix-up at the police station, but he took my meaning right enough and walked off. Flanagan's cynical gaze left me in no doubt he was wise to my tricks. We'd known each other too many years to have secrets.

"Gimme the story, Joey. Heart trouble? He looked the type."

"Won't know for sure until the coroner gets him under the knife. Coulda been, I suppose. All we know so far is he was found at the foot of one of the staircases. No obvious signs of trauma except for a nasty cut across his forehead, but since that had a bandage on it, don't seem likely it was caused by him falling down the stairs, does it? Unless someone took the trouble to fix him up not realizing he was already a goner, but no one has confessed to such."

"Who found the body?"

"The nurse did. Marlene Sutherland. Said she was on her way back to the infirmary when she stumbled across him. Felt for a pulse, then called it in, so she says."

"You got a reason to doubt it?"

"You know me. I'm not one to jump the gun, but one of the nuns was quick to fill me in on a little background. Told me Marlene has a boyfriend that got in hot water because of the deceased. Some kind of shady business. I'll have to talk to Sister Honoria about why we wasn't informed, but any road, makes me think Marlene or the boyfriend don't have much reason to feel very kindly toward the late Mr. Ludgate."

"You said yourself there's no sign of trauma. Sweaty guys his age drop dead all the time."

"We'll see. It's awful convenient when an unpopular fellow makes a lot of people mighty happy by turning up deceased at the bottom of a staircase. Guess I got a distrustful nature. Comes with the job. Besides, that ain't the only out of the ordinary occurrence around here. Come with me, Clark Kent. Got another puzzle for your investigatory skills."

Joey had never approved of my reporting gig as he expected me to follow him onto the force after we got out of the Army, so he liked to razz me whenever he could. I might not be Superman, but I was a pretty fair reporter, so it didn't bother me none. What are old friends for if you can't rib each other once in a while?

He led me through the building and out the back where the playing fields were. Over in a far corner, under a couple of massive oak trees was a graveyard I'd never noticed before. As we got closer, I realized it must be a cemetery for kids who'd died at the orphanage. One of the saddest sights I ever seen, those little gravestones, some with only a first name or an age and some not even that—the markings, if there had ever been any, worn away by Mother Nature and old Father Time.

I didn't have too long to muse though as Joey was quick to point out why we'd come. In a clear place to one side, where there was more dirt than grass or weeds, first thing I noticed was a white handkerchief tied to a long stick and raised like a flag as though to draw attention to the spot. On the ground was a pattern of neatly arranged stones, each about the size of a walnut, spelling out a command.

"*Bring her back*," I read. "Bring back who, do ya think?"

"You tell me. From what I hear, you know more about what's been going on around here than I do."

He had a point. Honoria had hoped to keep everything on the down low, but with a dead body, that plan was out the window. I decided to fill Joey in on what I knew. He was bound to find out anyway, so why not save everybody time and trouble?

When I got to the end of my tale, he asked, "You thinking what I'm thinking?"

"Depends on if you're thinking someone might be looking for a certain Lily White, aka Janey Doe. As far as I know, that's the only 'she' that could be said to be missing around here. And there's no doubt trouble seems to stick to her. When you have a string of unexplained events circling around the same person, makes me want to find a way to knot them all together. But we gotta keep an open mind."

"True, true. But I'm with you, Jimmy. If we don't find a connection between all of this, I will be mighty surprised, and I ain't often surprised by anything these days. For now, I better get a move on. Gotta go inform Mrs. Ludgate that she's a widow. Care to come along? You know how to charm the ladies. You may get more out of her than I can. I want to know a lot more about this Ludgate guy. Anyone who's that unpopular, usually there's a reason."

We made our way back through the orphanage, with me stopping to check in with Q and asking him to take a few pictures of the staircase and the graveyard out back in case there were any clues I'd missed. Marlene pulled me aside as I was turning to follow Flanagan to his patrol car.

"You will get to the bottom of this, won't you, Mr. Malhaven? I overheard one of the nuns talking to the police about Sam. It would be so easy for them to pin something on him. It's no secret Sam blamed Mr. Ludgate for losing his job, but he'd never hurt anyone. But you know what the police are like, especially toward people of Sam's religious persuasion. They'd rather charge him and close the case then spend time and trouble finding the real culprit."

"Whoa. Slow down a bit there. First thing, we don't know there's anything to charge anyone with. For all we know, Ludgate's ticker gave out. So, don't go borrowing trouble. And besides, you got me on the case. I ain't never failed to figure out a puzzle yet, and I don't plan to start now."

Waving off her thanks with my hat which I then firmly jammed on the old melon, I followed Joey out to his patrol car. We both lit up a cigarette and had a good time jawing and joking on the drive out of town. The Hasselwhite place was on a road leading south I rarely traveled, or I would surely have remembered seeing it.

As Sam had described, it was a big estate, surrounded on all four sides by a ten-foot brick wall with angry-looking spikes set in every few inches. Gave the distinct impression that casual visitors were not encouraged. We parked at the gate and Joey gave the intercom bell a few rings while I peered in through the iron bars. There were formal gardens and a well-tended lawn. Off to one side, I could see and hear construction equipment, and men yelling back and forth to each other.

Joey was having no joy with the buzzer. "Let's try whistling," he said.

Me and him were both champion whistlers. Used to have contests when we were kids to see who could whistle the loudest. We counted down from three and gave it our best shot. We were a little rusty, but it did the trick. Before too long, a beefy guy with a cheerful mug headed over in our direction.

"If you're selling something, you're wasting your time. They don't never let no one but my crew onto the place."

Flanagan flashed his badge. "Official business. You better let us in. We got news for the lady of the house."

"That don't sound so good. Hold on." He fiddled with an electrical box off to the side of the gate for a half a minute until they started rolling open.

We hopped back in the car and gave him a wave as we drove through and on up to the house. A stately mansion not quite as large as the Carsworth place but with the same air of wishing to impress upon the rest of us that only bigshots were welcome.

We went up the marble steps and rang the doorbell a few times with no noticeable effect until Joey got the bright idea to lean on the buzzer non-stop. It must have gotten on someone's nerves because the door finally swung open.

A wispy-looking bird stood there. She wouldn't have weighed 100 pounds soaking wet. Flanagan and I both towered over her as though she was a child. She had an unusual, crooked nose and sleek black hair and was dressed to the nines. Despite her small stature, she looked like she wasn't going to take guff from anyone, particularly a pair of goons who showed up unannounced and uninvited at her door.

"I don't know how you got through the front gates, but this is private property. I must ask you to leave immediately or I will be forced to call the police." She attempted the old shut the door in the face routine before Flanagan set her straight.

"I am the police, and we're here on official business. I need to speak to Mrs. Ludgate."

"I am Florence Ludgate."

"Wife to Horace Ludgate?"

"Yes."

"Then I regret to inform you that your husband has passed away. I'm very sorry for your loss."

She cocked her head to one side at us before saying, "How unfortunate. Thank you for letting me know," and slamming the door right in our faces.

CHAPTER TWENTY-ONE

lanagan and I exchanged a look.

"She took that better than most," he said.

I snorted. What an understatement. I'd never witnessed anyone take such news more in stride.

Flanagan did his leaning on the buzzer trick again. I guess it was annoying enough to fetch her back because the door opened once more.

"Yes," she said. "Was there something else?"

Joey threw me another look. A real cool customer if we'd ever seen one.

"Well, ma'am, I was hoping to come in and ask you a few questions if you feel up to it. That's kind of standard operating procedure in cases like this."

"Cases like what?"

"Unexplained death."

"Is it unexplained? Horace had a serious heart condition. It was only a matter of time before something happened. I don't know what else I could tell you. I presume this happened while he was at work. He always leaves before I get up in the morning, so I did not even speak to him today. Your time would be better spent talking to staff at the Sisters of Mercy if it is absolutely necessary to investigate what appears to be a quite straightforward occurrence." She cocked her head at us again as if we were strange birds that needed closer examination.

"All the same, ma'am. If we could just come in and talk to you for a few minutes."

She considered it a moment before nixing the whole deal. "I don't think so. If I'm not mistaken, unless you have a warrant, I am not obligated to let you in. I suppose I should say I appreciate the time you took to tell me in person, but really a phone call would have been sufficient. Good day, gentlemen."

And then she was gone. No amount of buzzer leaning fetched her back again.

"If that don't beat all," Flanagan said. "Can't help but make me wonder if she already knew about it. Nine times out of ten it's the spouse in murder cases, you know."

"First off, we don't know it's murder, and if it was, she'd have to be mighty stupid to call attention to herself like this. It'd be way smarter to invite us in for a cup of coffee and play the grieving widow to the hilt."

"Yeah, but I keep telling you, Jimmy, crooks ain't that smart. If they were, they wouldn't waste their time being crooks. They'd be fine upstanding citizens such as you and me."

We noticed the construction foreman standing and watching us with a grin on his face. Flanagan and I headed over to him.

"You don't look too surprised at our reception," Joey said.

"Nope. Ain't seen anyone get a foot in the door yet. Didn't figure you'd be the first."

"I'm Flanagan. This is Malhaven. I'm a cop. He's a reporter. Mind if we ask you a few questions?"

"Not at all. I'm Bill Logan. Logan Construction. Sounds grander than it is. Just me and the boys over there," he said, gesturing to a group of four guys taking a break under the shade of a tree. It was shaping up to be another unusually warm day for the time of year. Logan was stripped down to his undershirt already, showing off the rock-hard muscles of a man used to spending his days in manual labor. "A cop and a reporter? Must be big news of some kind."

"You could say. Horace Ludgate was found dead this morning at the Sisters of Mercy in town."

"You don't say. And she wouldn't even let you through the door for that?" He shook his head. "I can't say I'm exactly surprised, but you'd of thought she might make an exception this one time. So, Ludgate bit the dust, huh? Was it his heart? He used to tell me all the time about his delicate ticker, usually when I was trying to pressure him to pay my bill."

"What kind of work are you doing here?" I asked.

"What haven't we done? Been working on this place for years. Every time we finish one thing, they come up with another project. We've put in one room after another. A music room, conservatory for Florrie's plant collection, games room. That's where Horrie spends most of his time when he's at home. Brushing up on his billiards game. Redid the kitchen, all the washrooms. We're working on installing a pool at the moment. Real rocky ground out back. We've been having a hell of a time digging. Had to do some blasting."

"I don't get it," I said. "My understanding is the owner—wife and son, ain't it?—have been on an extended vacation since Mr. Hasselwhite's death. What's all the work for?"

"That's the million-dollar question, ain't it? The Ludgates claim it's all under orders from Mrs. Hasselwhite, but I never seen hide nor hair of her in all these years, and they're the ones reaping all the benefits from the improvements. I don't want to smear anyone, particularly the recently departed, but I can't help but wonder if the Ludgates ain't working some kind of a fiddle here. Fixing up the house for their own amusement with their boss footing the bill whether she's aware of it or not. But, hey, it's been steady employment for me and my boys, so I'll be the first to admit, I haven't asked too many questions. It's hard to come by these kind of big money jobs around here, and we all got mouths to feed at home."

"No one's judging," said Flanagan. "It's hardly your business. I'd of done the same and kept my head down, but you might want to start looking around for other work. We're not sure what's going on around here, but I wouldn't be too surprised if whatever we find might put a period to the home improvements."

"I was afraid of that," Logan said with a sigh. "But I appreciate the heads up. I guess we'll keep working for now, but I'll start asking around to see if I can line up something else. Even the golden goose has to die sometime, I guess."

He walked off to his men as Joey and I headed back to the car.

"What's next, boss?" I asked.

"Not worth doing much until the autopsy gets done. I'll see if I can hurry it along and run background checks on these Ludgates. I think you and I both know something stinks around here. The question is whether it's garden variety fraud or what. Why don't you see what you can find out and we'll meet up to compare notes?"

"It's a deal."

Joey dropped me back at the orphanage, and I headed inside to see if there was anything I could pick up that the cops hadn't. I was surprised to find Q was still there along with Marlene in Sister Honoria's office and filled them all in on the visit out to the Hasselwhite place.

"I'm worried I've done Sam a grave injustice," Honoria admitted. "From what you have found out already, Mr. Malhaven, I may have misjudged Mr. Ludgate's honesty. I felt I had no choice but to present the evidence of fraud he found to the orphanage Board, who ultimately made the decision to let Sam go. I was able to dissuade them from filing criminal charges in hopes Sam would pay back any stolen funds, but it now appears Mr. Ludgate was orchestrating a rather elaborate scheme of his own. I didn't suspect him because there didn't seem much to gain. We can't afford to pay anyone as much as I would want. Maybe he was hoping to steal money from the donations, but if what you say is true, he and his wife were living a very good life as it is. Why should he go to such lengths?"

"That's what we need to find out," I said. "Why did he go to so much trouble to get a job here unless it was to get close to the girl, Lily. He appeared obsessed with her. Came out to our place and tried to pressure Victoria to let loose of the girl. Volunteered him and his wife to take her in, but after meeting the Widow Ludgate, she ain't the maternal type. I can't help but think all these mysteries around that girl are connected."

"You're right, Mr. Malhaven," Q spoke up. "Marlene spotted a letter by Mr. Ludgate's hand when she found him."

"That right?"

Marlene chimed in. "Yes. It looked as though he had dropped it when he was… taken ill, I suppose. I'm afraid I took a look at it while I was waiting for the police. It was wrong, I know, but curiosity overcame me. It was an official-looking letter on the orphanage's stationary, indicating Mr. Ludgate and his wife were to be given custody of Lily."

"Say, that's something. Did you know anything about this?" I asked, turning to Sister Honoria.

"I most certainly did not and was quite shocked when Marlene told me. I can only think he intended to use the letter to trick Victoria into giving Lily over to him. Yet more proof of his plotting, I'm afraid."

"Sure is. Now we're getting somewhere. We just need to figure out why Lily is so important. Flanagan didn't mention the letter to me. Guess I can't blame him for playing things close to his vest, but I'll give him a ribbing next time I see him."

Marlene dropped a hand on my sleeve. "Oh, please don't, Mr. Malhaven. I wouldn't want to get into any trouble."

"Okay, okay. I can keep secrets too. It's a good thing you noticed it though. Confirms my theory we need to find out where Lily came from to figure out what's going on around here. That's good detective work right there."

"That's not all she found," Q added. He picked up an object from Honoria's desk that I hadn't noticed and handed it to me.

Soft and smooth. A single, long white feather.

CHAPTER TWENTY-TWO

I handed it over to Honoria. "This is more in your line than mine. Are we looking at an angel feather here?"

She snorted as she examined it. "More like goose, if I had to guess. My family raised them on our farm when I was a child, and I've seen plenty enough of them. I suppose a bird expert could tell you for sure."

"You shoulda turned this over to the cops. That's withholding evidence right there."

"I'm afraid I panicked," Marlene confessed. "I had it in my hand when I heard the police coming around the corner and hid it without thinking."

"Hid it where?"

Marlene laughed. "Tucked it down my blouse if you must know. Women hide all kinds of things there."

I might have blushed, but it didn't deter me from our clue. "Don't worry. I'll give it to Flanagan with some story or other. Might be important. Certainly is out of place unless you been plucking a goose getting ready for Easter dinner around here."

"Hardly," Honoria said. "We'll be lucky if we can afford some nice chickens for the children. I'm afraid we'll find our finances are in sad disarray with everything that has happened."

"Might be a good idea to call Sam Leonard back in. Let him work his magic."

"I'll talk to the Board. It's clear to me now Sam has been the victim here but convincing them may not be so simple."

"Mrs. Livinia Cressley may be able to help you. She got an eyeful and an earful of Ludgate yesterday and it put her right up on her high horse. A few of those Board members will be hearing from her today."

"That will certainly help. Mrs. Cressley is a force to be reckoned with when she takes up a cause. But even if we do prove Mr. Ludgate's treachery and clear Sam's name, I wouldn't blame him if he didn't want to come back to his old job. I feel it deeply I didn't do more to stand up for him."

"I'm sure he'd be happy to help," Marlene put in. "He knows you did what you could, and he believes in the mission here."

"Asking him might be worth a shot," I said. "Meanwhile, Q and I had better get to investigating. We don't know for sure Ludgate didn't pop off from natural causes, but I'm not gonna drag my feet waiting around to find out."

We left Marlene and Honoria strategizing about how best to approach the Board and Sam. I took Q out back to take some pictures of the message that had been left with stones near the graveyard. He clicked a few snaps before stooping down and rooting about in the dry leaves on the ground.

"Look," he said, holding up another feather in front of my face. "It looks like the one Marlene found inside."

"Good going, Q. Let's look around and see if there are others."

We scouted around and soon found more. They stretched in a line beyond the low chain-link fence marking the back boundary of the property. We vaulted over and found a few more in the vacant lot on the other side before they petered out.

"I don't buy that this is an angel shedding its wings, Q, but I can't figure it. Who walks around with a bunch of goose feathers?"

"A scribe in olden days, for one. Quills were commonly made from goose feathers. But nobody's bothered with quills since the invention of the fountain pen. Marlene was telling me Lily draws angel pictures.

Doesn't it make you think she's seen something that brought one to mind?"

"Something with wings, you mean?"

"Or somebody. Maybe a costume even. But to what purpose?"

"That's just it, Q. What kind of mug goes around dressed up in feathers? We figure that out, we'll crack this case wide open."

I dropped Q by the paper to start in on combing through the back files and developing his film roll in the paper's darkroom. Then I ran by the precinct to leave the feathers we'd found with the desk sergeant to pass on to Flanagan. Well, most of the feathers. I kept one for myself 'cause I had a kind of an idea about it.

The day was wearing on and I was hungry, so I decided to drive back out to the cemetery to see if I could fix myself a sandwich. That way I could check in with Victoria and let her know she'd be spared the dubious honor of having to entertain Horrie Ludgate for a second time now that he was kaput.

She was in the kitchen clearing the table from lunch when I walked in. The formal dining room was only used when Livinia was around, and Livinia never ate lunch. Something about keeping her girlish figure. Victoria was delighted to see me, which never gets old let me tell you. She sat down at the table to listen to the morning's developments while I put myself a cold roast beef and mustard sandwich together. I sat beside her and passed her the feather before tucking into my double-decker masterpiece.

She sat twirling it in one hand while she rested her chin in the other, deep in thought. "Whatever can it mean? First, Lily's drawings and now finding real feathers. There must be a connection. If only she could tell us."

"She still ain't said anything?"

"No, although I did catch her crooning a song to Archie while she was petting him. She stopped when she saw me, so I didn't have time to hear what it was. It sounded a bit like a nursery rhyme. But, Jim, she looked so scared. As though she thought she was going to be punished for making a noise. She's so solemn. I hate to think of what she might have been through."

"Yeah, I have a feeling it's not good, but it's interesting she was singing. Shows she could speak if she'd a mind to or wasn't frightened of whatever or whoever it is she's frightened of. Where is she now?"

"I told her to run outside and get some fresh air while I tidied up since the weather is so nice again."

"Do me a favor. Track her down and show her the feather. I want to see her reaction. I'll lurk behind a tombstone or something."

She laughed. "Wouldn't it be less trouble to give it to her yourself?"

"You're a lot less scary than a big lug like myself."

"And you don't give yourself enough credit, Jim. You have quite the way with the ladies, you know."

"As long as I do with one particular lady, that's plenty for me. Let's give it a whirl anyway. Things would be a lot easier if we could get her to talk."

We wandered outside and spotted her at a distance playing with the cat. Archie was jumping at a piece of string Lily was dangling just out of reach. The way they were both enjoying themselves, I kinda hated to break up the party, but Victoria marched on over. I edged behind a tall monument, wide enough to hide behind but still get a good view of the proceedings, and close enough to hear what was going on.

"Hello, Lily, dear. Are you and Archie having a good time?"

The girl nodded.

"I have something else for him to play with," Victoria said, pulling the feather out from behind her back. "What do you think?"

Her face lit up as she grabbed the white feather and held it to her cheek. It was the first time I seen her really smile. She looked all around as though she was expecting to see something else. Her face fell as she realized Victoria was all alone. It was clear the feather meant something to her. Something good. Whoever was behind the feathers, be it angel or human, wasn't what she was afraid of. At least we were getting somewhere by process of elimination.

So, if the angel wasn't a threat, who or what was? We knew now she could make sounds, so there was nothing stopping her from speaking except fear. Had she been scolded for talking or warned of punishment if she did? And if so, by who? After all, she'd been abandoned in the park and no one had come looking for her that we knew of, so it didn't seem as though anyone was interested in what she said or did.

But when I thought it over, I realized one person at least had been very interested in her. Horace Ludgate. And now he was dead. Victim of foul play or natural causes yet to be determined. Could it be the person Lily viewed as a friend, her angel, had gotten rid of Horace? The feathers were certainly evidence someone or something had been there at the time of his death. It was clear that finding out more about the Ludgates was a top priority.

I was so deep in thought, I got careless and didn't hear the steps marching up behind me until a voice detonated in my ear:

"Hey, Mister!"

CHAPTER TWENTY-THREE

shudder passed through me. That voice and those words could only mean one thing. I turned around to find Mikey Cummings gawking at me. He'd grown a bit since last time I run into him, but he was still dinky for his age which I estimated to be around ten now. Some people are economical with their words, but Mikey spent them like there was a run on the bank.

"Hey, Mister. Whatcha doing hiding? Are you playing a game? Is it Hide-and-Seek? I'm a whiz at Hide-and-Seek. I know all the best hiding places, and I'm small enough to fit just about anywhere. I hid in the trash can one time. And another time, I crawled under some loose boards in the floor. And then there was the time I hid by hanging upside down in Ma's closet in the middle of all her clothes. That was smart, wasn't it? I'm real clever at hiding. Nobody ever finds me. Not even one time. Ain't that something? You'd think someone would have found me at least once. I give up eventually when it's been long enough and usually everyone else is gone and I win, but ain't that something nobody ever finds me?"

Thinking of the rare peace and quiet that must bless the Cummings household whenever Mikey was in hiding, I'd have bet no great effort was expended in finding him. In fact, I'd bet a whole sawbuck the rest of the clan snuck off to the movies, gladly leaving him hanging.

Speaking of the rest of the gang, I noticed Mabel Cummings standing waiting for Mikey to wind down. She was holding a girl by the hand that looked to be about Lily's age, five or six or seven. I never been the best at estimating kids' ages. She looked almost the exact opposite of Lily though with tan skin, dark hair, and a beaming gap-toothed smile.

When Mikey paused to come up for air, Mabel broke in. "Hello, Mr. Malhaven. This is our sister Marnie. Mrs. Jankowski called and asked my mother if we would mind bringing her over after school to play with a little girl she has staying."

"That's right," Mikey piped up, having refilled his lungs. "Ma's waiting in the car. I asked if I couldn't come along 'cause we're great friends, me and you, ain't we, Mister? Remember when I saved your life, huh, huh, wasn't that something?"

Given that Mikey had very nearly been the cause of me getting a bullet through the skull, I might have been inclined to argue the point if I hadn't learned from previous experience that there wasn't a bigger waste of breath in the universe than trying to reason with this kid. Victoria arrived with Lily right then anyway, so I decided to let it ride.

"Hello, Mabel. Michael. And this must be Marnie," she said, holding out a hand that the girl shook energetically. "This is Lily. She's visiting with us, and I thought she might enjoy having someone closer to her own age to play with. Lily, do you want to introduce Marnie to Archie?"

I have to say Lily didn't look exactly thrilled at being gifted with a playmate. Thinking back to her experiences with the other kids at the orphanage, I couldn't blame her, but Marnie grabbed her hand and started swinging it fit to beat the band before yelling, "Kitty!" as she caught sight of Archie and ran, pulling Lily along after her. I kept a wary eye and was glad to see them settle into a game of catch the string with the cat.

Mabel's a smart cookie and must have sensed my doubts. "Don't worry, Mr. Malhaven. Marnie gets along with everybody, and everybody loves Marnie. She has a way about her."

"I can see that. Lily's had a rough time. We're trying to cheer her up a bit."

"I could stay, too, Mister. I know how to have a good time. Can't nobody say I don't know how to have a good—"

"That's enough, Mikey," Mabel intervened, seizing the gabbler by the hand. "Ma needs to get back to town, and I have homework to do."

"I'll run Marnie home straight after dinner, Mabel," Victoria volunteered. "Do thank your mother for me."

We waved them off, Mabel dragging a protesting Mikey every step of the way.

"That was a nice thought," I said. "Give Lily something to take her mind off her troubles."

"I hope so. I found a few puzzles and games up in the… the…"

I knew what she meant. The secret playroom her mother and her mother's twin sister used as an escape from their awful childhood. Her ma had used it as a hideout from the law during her last terrible days.

I pulled Victoria close and held her. She had a core of pure steel, but I knew she'd never forget that time, even though the sharpness of the pain had faded some. Victoria had lost her own twin sister—a sister she had just discovered—and found out the shocking truth of her parents, all within a space of nothing. Not many would have handled it even half as good as she did.

She wiped her eyes and pulled away.

"Thank you, kind sir, but I'd better go and let Cressley know we'll be one extra for dinner. That is, if we can expect you?"

"You can count on it. Be back as soon as I check in with Q and maybe Flanagan. See if there's been any developments. I gotta feeling it's better not to let the grass grow under our feet with all this. The Ludgate woman gave me a creepy feeling. Anyone coldblooded enough to take the news of her husband's death without blinking an eye might be capable of anything."

"Do you think Lily is in danger?"

"I hope not, but keep her close until we know for sure. Let's not forget someone tried to break into the house last night. It's not out of the question it was Ludgate, though maybe it was only your garden-variety sneak thief looking for easy pickings. But it's another coincidence in a string of them, and I don't like coincidences, particularly when they put certain people I have certain feelings for in the crosshairs."

"Don't worry, darling. I know how to take care of myself."

"I know you do. I pity anyone who tangles with Mrs. J."

She chucked me under the chin playfully with her fist with enough force to show me she could give an effective uppercut with the best bruiser in the ring if need be. Left a smile on my face as I headed back into town. I'd never known how lonely I was until I met Victoria. Hard to imagine life without her now. There'd be no life without her, if I was one-hundred percent honest with myself. I'd had a glimpse of it once before and prayed every day I'd never see it again.

Back at the paper, I headed down to the basement and found Q tidying up a stack of back issues. "Hello, Mr. Malhaven. Here are the papers with the stories Miss Adams wrote in them. You may already know most of it if you've talked to her."

"Yeah," I agreed, skimming through the articles. "Not too much more to go on here. Anonymous phone call. Found in the park. No ID to speak of. Nothing on her. No tags in the clothes. And no one coming forward to claim her even after all the publicity. The only thing not here is the coin they found on her."

"Coin?"

"Maudie mentioned the cops wanted her to hold back that detail. One of the photog boys went over to the precinct and got pictures of it for me," I said, pulling them out of my jacket pocket. "Handed them to me just now as I came through the bullpen. Came out pretty clear."

Q took the photos and examined them closely. They were good closeups of both sides of the coin, showing off the markings and letterings.

"Nazi issued," Q remarked. "Interesting. Could be a souvenir brought back from the war or from a private coin collection. Nazi memorabilia has become quite valuable since the war ended."

"Funny idea of collecting some people have. I'd as soon never see anything with a swastika again myself. Flanagan said this coin was only issued in German-occupied territories between '40 and '41."

"Might make it even more valuable then. There were probably a limited number minted. I can research it. See how readily available they are through coin dealers. Might tell us something about what kind of person could have been in possession of it before it was found on the girl. Also, I found another article in the back issues that might be relevant."

Q read out the pertinent info from a small paragraph at the bottom of an obit page.

"Mr. Francis Hasselwhite, found dead in the bathtub. A small radio set evidently fell into the bath while he was bathing, and he was electrocuted immediately. Death ruled accidental. The grieving widow and son are said to have left to visit with family before embarking on a tour of the Continent according to the new caretakers, Mr. and Mrs. Horace Ludgate."

"November of '45?" I said, noting the date on the paper. "The war was barely over, and Europe was a disaster zone. Strange time to go on a holiday there unless they had quite a long visit with the relatives first. And from what Horace was telling me, they ain't come back yet. Over five years now? That's a helluva tour. Kinda convenient they're out of the way while the Ludgates play at being lords of the manor."

"Rather opportune for the Ludgates as well that Mr. Hasselwhite had an accident?"

"Q, I'm afraid you got a suspicious mind. But then, so do I. Even if they offed the boss, though, how do they make sure Mrs. Hasselwhite stays away permanently? Why wouldn't she sell the joint if she can't stand to come back and live where her hubby met his maker? I sure would like to have a few minutes' chat with her, and we need to find out more about these Ludgates. I better see if I can track down Flanagan—"

"Speak of the Devil and he shall appear."

CHAPTER TWENTY-FOUR

I managed not to flinch as one of Flanagan's beefy hands crash-landed on my shoulder. Wouldn't be right to let him know he got the jump on me.

"Devil is about right, I'd say. Were your ears burning?"

"Now is that any way to welcome me when I come all this way to fill you in on the latest doings? Makes me feel you don't appreciate me, Jimmy, old pal of mine."

I saw Q looking on with a sour face that showed he wasn't exactly filled with the bon homie, as the French say, about Joey showing up, but Flanagan ain't got the most tact.

"If it isn't our resident pickpocket again," he said with a laugh, slapping Q on the back. "Hope you ain't still mad at our little run in. Only doing our job, you know."

"I'll be in the other room if you need me, Mr. Malhaven," Q said stiffly, retreating to the back room of the morgue.

"What's with him?"

"Joey, if I explained it to you for a million years, I don't think you'd ever get it. Why don't you tell me your news instead?"

"Doc finished the prelim autopsy. Pretty sure the geezer died of heart failure, but he's not so happy about that wound on the forehead.

Wanted to saw into his skull to check out the old gray matter. I didn't stick around for that. Hate the sound of the buzz saw slicing through bone," Flanagan said with a shudder. "He's got a theory from the look of the cut that it could have been caused by a bullet, but he couldn't tell for sure."

That shook me up some. Hadn't been too many hours previous to Horace being found at the foot of the stairs that Livinia had been taking potshots at a would-be burglar out at Wynter's Hill. Was it possible Ludgate was our mysterious intruder? And what would he have been after if not Lily? Was he seriously gonna kidnap her in the middle of the night?

The more I thought about it, the more it didn't sound so farfetched after all. He had definitely had an unhealthy obsession with getting his hands on the girl as evidenced by the letter found on him. Maybe after the failed snatching, he decided to go about things differently and came up with the custody letter scheme.

"Who do you think would be shooting at a guy like that, though?" Flanagan continued. "And why wouldn't he report it to us? The wound had been cleaned up and bandaged at least a few hours before his death according to the doc. The whole thing is so much hooey to me. More likely he fell and split his head open 'cause he wasn't feeling so good. Then he goes and has a heart attack a few hours later, don't you think?"

"It's not unlikely," I hedged, not wanting to encourage the bullet line of investigation. I wasn't Livinia's biggest fan, but Victoria had been through more than enough publicity and trouble with her family. Having her aunt questioned for reckless shooting wouldn't help none. "Either way, if it's only a bum ticker, you don't got much to investigate, do you? No murder after all."

"Guess not. Bit of luck for Sam Leonard. I was already measuring him up for a pair of handcuffs. But there's still something fishy about those Ludgates. I can't get over the way the wife just stared at us with dead eyes when we're delivering the news of her hubby's kicking off on the sudden. It ain't normal. But if the death is ruled natural causes, we won't have much excuse to investigate no more."

"That don't need to stop me. Reporters don't have to have a reason to investigate anything they've a mind to."

"Well, take it easy, eh? Don't want to have to be rescuing you again from one of your misadventures, my boy."

I brushed that off with a grin. We tried to get under each other's skin whenever we could. A habit from our carefree boyhood days. But he wasn't wrong. I had blundered in more than once during my career, sticking my nose in where it wasn't appreciated, and I had the scars and bum legs to prove it.

It seemed to me Ludgate was the linchpin of this particular scheme. It sure would be interesting to know what his widow was planning to do next. With the hubby gone, would she try to continue on at the manor house, business as usual? Or did this spell the end of whatever swindle they were trying to put over on the Widow Hasselwhite?

After Flanagan took off and Q emerged from hiding, we studied the stories in the paper some more looking for anything we might've missed. I read the full obituary on Hasselwhite. Last of a dwindling line of aristocrats. Inherited money. Married Margaret Elizabeth Hasselwhite, maiden name Smith. A son, Henry Horatio Hasselwhite. Guess they had a thing for the letter H. Eleven years old at the time of his father's death. So, he'd be about seventeen now. An unsettled life for a kid, traveling all the time. I wondered if he had a tutor. Probably, with that kind of money.

On a hunch, Q checked the back issues and found a society story on the Hasselwhite wedding. Wife came from modest beginnings, which was newspaper speak for she was poor as a hermit crab looking for a shell. No parents listed. No Mr. and Mrs. Smith who were tickled pink to be giving their daughter away to a walking pile of money.

I wondered what kind of relatives she had gone to visit, hers or his. Didn't sound like either of them had too many, but if we could track them down, might be able to get a bead on where Mrs. Hasselwhite and Henry Horatio were now. I had a feeling Florence Ludgate wouldn't be too cooperative in parting with that particular piece of information. The sooner her boss got back from her travels, the sooner Florrie might have some explaining to do about the expensive renovations. I still found it hard to believe the Widow Hasselwhite would spend so much money fixing up the place where her hubby died if she couldn't even stand to visit there.

This was all starting to add up to the lowest kind of fraud. Absent landlord, caretakers run wild. But the one thing that still wasn't making sense was Lily. There was no question Ludgate had an obsession about claiming her. Who was she to him that he would care enough to take the kind of risks he'd been running?

And let's not forget the unknown party in all of this. Our angel, or whatever you wanted to call him. Causing trouble at the orphanage, leaving messages, shedding feathers. He was also obsessed with the girl, and we had no idea in the world who he was or how to track him down.

"Q, my friend, as usual, we got more questions than answers on our hands. What do you suggest?"

"Lily appears to be the key to it all. So far, the only concrete clues we have are the coin she was carrying when she was found, the feathers, and the message."

"That message: *Bring her back.* Who wants her back so bad? If we get to the bottom of that, maybe everything else will fall into place."

"I'll start researching the coin. It might be able to tell us something. And I can take the feather home with me and ask Reggie Arnold about it. He raises all the animals out at Mr. Carsworth's farm. He usually comes by the house to report to Mr. Carsworth every evening. He may be able to at least confirm whether it is a goose feather or not."

"Carsworth has a farm? He's got more money than the rest of us put together. Why's he messing around with farming?"

Q looked amused. "Didn't you know Mr. Carsworth is convinced the atom bomb is coming? He's built a bomb shelter both at the house and out at the farm so he'll have a place to retreat to. He's been storing food and learning how to farm so he can be self-sufficient after the storm has passed. It's quite the obsession of his."

This was news to me. I'd seen the warning films same as anyone. What to do when the bombs start dropping. Duck and cover. More like duck and kiss the world goodbye if you asked me.

"Must be nice to have enough money to splash out on a thing like that. Guess all the Wall Street tycoons will survive while the rest of us are out of luck."

"I don't know. People of even rather modest means are building their own bunkers. But it has become quite the craze among the wealthy. No truly elegant home is complete without a custom-built fallout shelter."

"Makes me wonder if they have one out at the Hasselwhite joint. They've added about everything else to the place. I'll have to ask the construction crew next time I'm there."

"Are you going again?"

"Probably. We need to find out more about these Ludgates and what their big interest in the girl is. Best way to do that is go to the source. If I can't get in to see Mrs. Ludgate again, at least I can scout around some, see what I can find."

"Can I come with you?"

"I don't think that's a good idea, Q. You already had one brush with the law. A charge of trespassing wouldn't do you no good."

"You're not worried about it."

"Well, yeah, but that's because…" I hated to say the words but we both knew what I meant. Guys like me can get away with a heck of a lot of things that guys like Q can't.

The silence hung there a moment before I told him I'd think about it. First things first, though. I needed to make sure I got home in time for dinner. Cressley's cooking wasn't something you wanted to miss out on if you could help it, and I wanted to see how spending time with someone her own age had worn on Lily. If she would only open up and tell us what she remembered about her own short life, we might be able to get to the bottom of it all in no time.

But that would be the easy road, and me and the easy road ain't exactly bosom pals. But easy or hard, I wasn't gonna give up until I got answers.

CHAPTER TWENTY-FIVE

It was a surprise to find when I got back to the Wynter mansion that Victoria's car was nowhere to be seen. We don't usually eat until seven, which is the time Livinia had marked down as a civilized hour for dining, but Victoria often helped Cressley out in the kitchen ahead of time if she had nothing better to do.

I popped into the kitchen to find Cressley wearing the long white apron he wore wrapped around himself from his armpits down when he was cooking. He was stirring a pot with one hand while peeking worriedly under the lid of another.

"Good evening to the chef," I said. "Where's Victoria and the girls?"

Cressley smiled at me and turned the heat down on the stove before turning to find his pad and fancy pen that were never far from his side. He scribbled a note in his fast, elegant handwriting.

Fed the girls early and is running Miss Cummings back to town. Took Miss White with her. Thought she might enjoy the ride in the car.

"I bet she will. That's disappointing for me but gives me more to look forward to tonight. Seeing the light of my life when she returns and eating more of your first-rate chow."

Roast chicken. Peas. Escalloped potatoes. Must get back to the gravy.

He turned away to stir his pot.

"You're wasting your talents on us, Mr. Cressley. Your food is fit for royalty."

He gave me a shrug with a smile that told me he didn't mind the compliment. Cressley wasn't one of those false humble mooks. When he was good at something, he knew it and was proud of it. A great guy all around.

I went to sit outside on the steps and smoke a cigarette, enjoying the mild evening. That kind of weather don't last long in March, so better to drink it in while you can.

Wasn't long before Victoria's convertible came up the gravel drive. She had the top down and her hair wrapped up in a sky-blue scarf that brought out the honey highlights and made her eyes look bluer than normal. Of course, she always looked like a movie star no matter what she was wearing, so it's kind of a waste of time even mentioning it. She gave me a wave as she parked and hopped out. I seen she was alone.

"Hello, darling. Waiting for me? How sweet," she said, sitting down beside me and giving me a kiss to seal the deal. "I arranged for Lily to stay overnight with the Cummings. She and Marnie were having such a good time, it would have been a shame to break it up. Goodness knows, Lily seems to have had little enough fun in her life. I hope you don't mind. I think she'll be safe enough there."

"Sounds fine as long as she ain't overwhelmed by the horde."

"I think Mabel will see to it that she isn't. Mabel is quite capable, you know."

"She is," I heartily agreed, having seen before how she was able to control her brothers and sisters even though she wasn't the oldest of them all. Brains and determination can win more respect than mere age.

"Lily is such a sweet thing. I hope no matter what happens, she doesn't have to go back to the orphanage."

"I thought you said it wasn't so bad. You did alright there."

"I was always taken care of, but it's not the same as growing up in a loving home. I've been thinking—"

"You don't have to say it. I know all about you. You're thinking of taking her on permanent here."

"Is that so crazy? We have plenty of room and goodness knows there's more than enough money to take care of one more. This house has seen so much pain. It might help heal it, and me, to bring something good into it."

"It already has something good in it, and I'm holding her hand right this minute."

Victoria snuggled close. "You do think it's a silly idea then."

"Not one bit. She kinda creeps into your heart, don't she? Don't know why those nuns or other kids at Sisters of Mercy can't see it, but she's a sweet soul through and through. I'd bet my hat on it."

"Not the hat!" Victoria laughed that low, thrilling sound I loved to hear. My hat had been through a few adventures before I promised her to take better care of it. Though to be fair, trouble seemed to seek me out. I didn't go looking for it. Not exactly.

"You'll have to see what Sister Honoria thinks about it, though I can't imagine her objecting."

"It's not up to her, unfortunately. She makes recommendations to the Board, but ultimately, it's their decision who gets to adopt a child. It's rare they go against her advice, but it does happen."

"Why would they? Honoria's got the best interests of those little tykes at heart. Anyone could see that."

Victoria looked a little rosy which was unusual. Not much bothers her. "I believe the cases where they turned down the applicants, it was because the women didn't have a husband. Even though they had the financial means to support a child, the Board thinks it is only appropriate for homes with a mother and a father to receive children."

"Hmph, that is a stumper. I guess we could see if Mr. and Mrs. Cressley wanted to adopt her. They're a fine upstanding pair of newlyweds."

I shouldn't tease Victoria. Not like that. Her face fell and she looked away from me as if she was disappointed.

"Or," I added, "maybe you could find yourself a husband. I might know where there's someone with potential lurking around closer than you might think."

Her face lit up as bright as the sun in the sky. Every once in a while, I say the right thing.

"Why, Jim. Is that a proposal?"

"You mean, is that another proposal. It's not as though I ain't ever asked you before."

"I know. You're lovely to be so patient with me. It's not because I don't want to. It's just—"

"You don't have to explain yourself to me. You been through a lot. And you know I ain't going anywhere. I'll be right here waiting. But it's something to think about if it means you could adopt Lily. It wouldn't have to change our living arrangements or anything. It's only a piece of paper after all."

"Not to me. I took my vows very seriously when Lukasz and I were married, and I don't want to do any less with you. I'll… I'll think about it. Let me talk to Honoria first. It could be it isn't a problem after all. They may be so anxious to get Lily off their hands, they'll take any offer for her. I want us to get married when we feel the time is right, not for any other reason. I know it's been six months, but sometimes it feels like yesterday when we first met, it's all still so fresh in my mind."

I grabbed ahold of her hands and brought them up to my lips. "Victoria, you'll always be my one and only. You know that. Don't fret yourself, as my old ma used to say when I was hot and bothered about something."

A too familiar noise interrupted us, and Victoria laughed again. "I believe somebody might be hungry."

I grinned, grabbing my protesting belly. "That sandwich didn't last me long. I'm still a growing boy, you know."

We strolled inside arm in arm and enjoyed Cressley's delicious offerings, then took our evening turn around the grounds before parting ways for the night.

I was sitting in the dark in the cottage, smoking a last cigarette before going to bed when the shrill ring of the telephone jolted me up. Victoria had gotten tired of having to come find me whenever the paper rang me up at the big house, so she'd had an extension put in for me. Figuring it must be Morty wanting to roust me out on a late-breaking story, I thought about not answering, but the noise was annoying, so I picked up the receiver.

"Mr. Malhaven, please come quickly. We need—"

A click. Silence.

CHAPTER TWENTY-SIX

Only a few words, but enough for me to know it wasn't Morty, but Sister Honoria. I recognized the faint Irish brogue that softened her crisp tones. Could only mean one thing. More trouble at the orphanage. I thought about taking Victoria with me, but when I went outside, all the lights were off at the big house. Better to let her sleep for now and give her a call once I found out what was going on.

Thought about calling Flanagan, too. I didn't like the way the call had been cut short so abruptly. But I figured Honoria phoned me for a reason. If she'd wanted the police, she'd have already called them.

I cranked up the Champ and hightailed it back into town. Not much traffic that time of night so I pulled up to the Sisters of Mercy in record time. Unlike back home, every light was on in the place. The front doors were unlocked so I waltzed in and headed to Honoria's office. Found her there in deep conference with the two linebackers, Martha and Bertha. I couldn't have told you which of the three of them was more red in the face when I walked in after rapping a short rat-a-tat-tat on the open door.

"Mr. Malhaven, thank you for coming. That will be all for now, Sister Martha and Sister Bertha. We'll discuss this later."

"But Sister Honoria—"

"I said later!"

Honoria wasn't one to stand for a lot of nonsense, but even I was taken aback by the tone of her voice. It was certainly enough to make the two nuns back out of the office, but I could tell by the warlike look in their eyes they weren't done with whatever had brought them there to begin with.

Honoria sighed and sunk down at her desk with her head in her hands. I settled into a chair and perched my hat on my knee, lighting up a cigarette to calm my nerves.

"What gives? More pranks?"

"I suppose you could call it that, but if so, it isn't a very funny one." She handed me a piece of paper. I took it so I could read the words written in pencil: *Bring her back.*

"Same as the message out by the graveyard. Where did you find it?"

"You mean, where did we find them," she said, grabbing a disorganized pile of paper on her desk and shoving it over to me. Dozens and dozens of pieces of paper with the self-same message scrawled across them. *Bring her back.*

"Where did you find them all?"

"That's the thing. We found one under every pillow on every bed in the whole place. But the frightening part is they must have been placed there after the children went to bed. We strip and change the bedding once a week and today was the day. We had only finished making up all of the beds right before the children went to sleep. There was no time for anyone to slip them in before that. Do you see, Mr. Malhaven? We had someone walking freely through the building, visiting all of the children's beds when they were asleep, and no one heard or saw a thing."

"That's not so good," I agreed. "When did you get wind of it?"

"We discovered the first message when one of the children got up to go to the bathroom and noticed it under their pillow. We investigated and started finding them everywhere. I have a duty to keep the children safe, Mr. Malhaven. How do we know next time whoever is doing this won't cause them harm?"

"I see your point. But they already had the opportunity and went out of their way to not even wake the children, much less harm them. They're trying to get your attention. Let's see, it's one-twenty now, which must have made it about one when you called me. What time do the children usually go to bed?"

"Lights out by nine. Earlier for the younger children. Although, of course, we can't make them go to sleep. There is usually some talking until around ten most nights. Each ward has a nun monitoring it at night who tries to encourage the children to be quiet and rest."

"So, maybe by eleven or so at the latest, most of the kiddies would be asleep. What about the nuns?"

"One nun sleeps in each ward in case a child needs someone in the night, but we always have a very early start to our days. Most of them would have been tired and also asleep by then."

"Which means we're looking at a pretty small window of opportunity for someone to slip in and out, assuming it was someone from the outside."

"Who else would it be? None of the sisters or Nurse Marlene would have any motive for causing such a disturbance. I thought at first it was one of the children, but they're never unsupervised for long. Someone would certainly have noticed them writing out all these notes."

"Yeah, an outside job is most likely. We got the message. Someone wants her back, and I think we both know who the 'her' in question is."

"Someone's looking for Lily and is upset she isn't here."

"Exactly. It comes back to Lily again. She's been the key all along and until we find out who she is, I think you can expect more trouble. Looked like Martha and Bertha weren't too happy about it."

"No, they had the temerity to suggest we bring Lily back and leave her alone somewhere like a sacrificial lamb in hopes that whoever was doing this would show themselves. I try not to think uncharitable thoughts, Mr. Malhaven, but I can't help thinking it is the height of cowardliness to want to put a child into possible harm's way just to save ourselves worry."

"I can sorta see their point of view. Instead of calming the situation down, things have only escalated since Lily checked out of here. Ludgate's dead, and we've got an angry angel on the loose."

"You know as well as I do that there is a very human agent behind this. Lily is a flesh and blood girl, and there is someone out there who cares about her even if they aren't in a position to claim her publicly."

"The thing we don't know is whether they have her best interests in mind or not. Ludgate had an idea about claiming her, and I don't think it was because he had a heart of gold."

"I must agree. I was quite shocked to find out from the police that the letter he had giving him custody of Lily had my signature on it. It was a forgery, of course. Just as I see now the ledgers he supposedly found were also forgeries. But I wouldn't have been able to tell the signature wasn't mine if I didn't know I hadn't signed any such paper."

"A man of hidden talents, our Mr. Ludgate, it would seem. A forger and a liar. Wonder what else he was up to before he kicked off."

"I'm afraid we will find it was nothing to the good. I'm glad we were able to keep Lily out of his hands. He'd been pressuring me to allow him and his wife to adopt the girl ever since he started working here, but I kept putting him off. There was always something about him that made me hesitate to recommend it to the Board. How is Lily doing now?"

"I think she's happy enough. She's sleeping over with that Cummings brood in town tonight. They got so many, I doubt they even notice one more. She should be safe enough with such a crowd around her. Victoria thought it would do her good to be with some other kids for a change. Sort of lonely for a child out at the cemetery."

"Victoria is so thoughtful and kind. Such a shame she lost Karolina. She has a way with children. I'd hate to think she's missed out on having any of her own."

"It's early days yet," I couldn't help but chime in, "and I got a few ideas in that direction when she's ready. Speaking of which, I don't know if I should speak out of turn, but Victoria was talking to me today about applying to keep Lily on permanent. You know she couldn't have a better ma than Victoria."

"I agree, of course. Unfortunately, the Board has very strict guidelines about adoption. I have never known them to approve an unmarried woman's application."

"Even a respectable widow with plenty of room and cash like Victoria? That's nuts."

"Yes, again, I can only agree with you. But the majority of the Board is very conservative about these things. They don't realize times are changing. Now if Victoria were to marry…"

"You don't have to finish that thought. Don't think I ain't trying. I think she'll come around one of these days, but she's had a lot to deal with. She's still trying to get used to being one of the Wynters of Wynter's Hill not to mention everything else she's been put through."

"You are a wise man not to bully her into anything before she's ready, Mr. Malhaven. I'm sure it will work out. Anyone with eyes can see how you feel about each other."

"Why, Sister Honoria, you're making me blush," I said, and in truth, talking over my love life with a nun was making me feel hot under the collar. "I'm gonna take a look around outside if you can keep the lights on for a bit. We won't disturb the kiddies again tonight, but if you and the other sisters could take a look around in here and let me know if you see anything else unusual inside that would be a help."

We parted ways on our separate missions. I made a slow circuit of the perimeter of the building. First thing I found was the telephone wire to the building had been cut. That meant the miscreant was still hanging around when Honoria was on the telephone to me. They may have wanted Lily back, but they didn't want anyone phoning to the police either.

And it won't surprise you any more than it did me to know that the second thing I found was a long, white feather. Our angel had struck again.

CHAPTER TWENTY-SEVEN

Finding nothing else of interest, I drove back home and got some shuteye in what was left of the night so I'd be fresh for action. I needed my wits about me to untangle this web of clues.

I was knotting my tie in the morning when I heard a car go past. I shrugged into my suit jacket and went outside to investigate. It was Victoria bringing Lily back from town, but she wasn't the only passenger.

"Hey Mister! Whatcha up to? Are you gonna go do some reporting? Can I come? I could be a big help, you know. I'm a whiz at finding out things. And I'm quiet like a mouse. I can sneak up on people and listen to what they're saying and let you know and then you could write it up for the paper. That'd be a big help, wouldn't it? Whataya think?"

What I was thinking was I hadn't even had my morning cup of joe yet and was not prepared for a sudden Mikey onslaught, not by a long shot. Luckily, Victoria came to my rescue.

"Michael, dear, why don't you go with Lily into the house. I'm sure Mr. Cressley will be up and would be happy to prepare you whatever you want for breakfast."

"Oh, boy! Eats! I'm starving," he yelled, grabbing Lily's hand. "Which way do we go?"

Lily led the way to the kitchen door of the house with her usual calm solemnity, apparently indifferent to the constant stream of chatter in her ear.

"Give a guy some warning next time," I complained, as Victoria came over to greet me with a kiss.

"Sorry, darling. I wasn't expecting it either. Apparently, Michael has been suspended from classes for the rest of the week for being too disruptive."

"Imagine that."

She laughed. "I took pity on his mother. Between looking after the younger ones and the house, the idea of having Michael home all day was driving her to distraction, but it was Lily who suggested he come home with us."

"She did? How's that?"

"She took his hand and made some gestures that made it pretty clear she wanted to bring him with us. She's never asked for anything since she's been here, so I hated to disappoint her. How I'll make it through the day, I really don't know."

"You? You have the patience of a saint."

"Even saints have their limits, and Michael has a special talent for pushing people past them whether he means to or not."

She looked more than a little annoyed, which was rare for her. Before I knew it, I was volunteering to take him into town with me for the morning. I could have bit my tongue the minute I said it except the way her face lit up made me think it was worth it.

"Would you? I suppose Lily might be disappointed, but I have so much to do today and can't help but think he would find a way to get into trouble one way or another if I don't keep a close eye on him."

"Trouble is definitely tops on his list of talents. Maybe I can think of something to keep him occupied. We'll drop back by for lunch though. That may be the limit of what I can take."

"Perfect. I'll take care of what I need to this morning so I can spend the afternoon supervising the children. You are a dear," she added, giving me the kind of smooch that made the idea of a half day of potential torture more bearable.

We caught up with the kids in the kitchen. Mikey was still talking a mile a minute while Cressley flipped a batch of pancakes on the stove. As neither he nor Lily talked any, they made the perfect audience for Mikey's brand of non-stop chatter. His thrill at finding out he'd be my sidekick for the morning knew no bounds, and I was beginning to despair of my impulsive offer before I had what seemed like a bright idea even for me.

"I gotta mission for you, Mikey. A secret mission. Whataya think about that?"

"What do I think? I think you couldn't of picked a better guy, Mister. I'm your man. Ain't nobody better at being sneaky than me. I seen all the spy movies. Learned all the tricks. You know the best way to follow someone? You carry a newspaper so when they look back at you, you can pretend you're just standing there reading it. You see how that works? Every time they look back, they just see a guy standing reading a newspaper. Ain't that smart? Should we pick up a newspaper, so I'll be ready? A hat would be good, too. Maybe I should use your hat as part of my disguise," he added, reaching for my fedora where I'd laid it on the table.

I rescued it before he could grab it. "Where we're going, you got the perfect disguise already, just as you are. I wouldn't change a thing."

We drove into town, him pumping me all the way about his assignment. I could see a big future for him in the FBI. All they'd have to do was leave him in a room with a suspect and let Mikey talk 'em to death. I don't think there's too many that wouldn't crack open like a soft-boiled egg under that kind of pressure.

I was mighty relieved when we pulled up in front of the orphanage. "Here you go, kid."

His eyes got wide and filled with tears. "Gee, Mister. I'll be good, I promise. Please don't hand me over to them nuns. Did Ma tell you to bring me here? Tell her I'll be good from now on. I won't get kicked out of school again. Honest."

I had to hide a grin at his fright. I'd forgotten I'd once threatened to donate him to the orphanage if he didn't shape up. "Take it easy, kid. This is where your mission starts. I need someone on the inside. An inside man, see? Someone who can blend in with the other kids and find out if they know something. Real spy stuff. Just for a few hours."

He batted at his watery eyes with two grubby fists. "Honest? You ain't kidding with me, are you?"

"Honest. You got the gift of gab, young Mikey. I need you to mingle with the other kiddies. There's been a lot of funny business going on here. See if you can get anyone to talk to you about it. Maybe they know more than they're letting on to the nuns, right?"

"You betcha. I'll solve the whole thing for you, don't you worry. You hired the right guy for the job. Hey, will I get paid for this? I'm doing you a favor. That oughta be worth something."

Unsurprised at his quick shift from grief to greed, I dug a quarter outta my pocket. "Here's an advance. We can negotiate any further payment depending on what you find out. Can't expect to get paid in full until I see the quality of your intel."

"That's right. That's how they do it in the movies. A briefcase full of cash in exchange for the photos or info."

"Slow down now. I ain't got a briefcase full of moolah laying around. But maybe a buck if it's good stuff, how about that?"

He mulled it over. Guess he'd learned how to drive a hard bargain from the pictures as well, but he finally gave in.

I marched him up the front steps and presented him to Sister Honoria and had him kick his heels in the hallway while I explained my scheme to her. She didn't look happy about it, but desperate enough to try anything when I convinced her it couldn't do much harm. A little white lie, you might say. It was actually easy to imagine coming back and finding the place burned to the ground with Mikey standing out front explaining how it was all a big misunderstanding, but I crossed my fingers even he couldn't get into too much trouble in only a few hours.

I headed back to the paper and was surprised to find Q sitting at Maudie's desk chatting away with her as though they were old friends.

"Look what the cat drug in," Maudie called out to me with a cackle.

"Same back atcha. What are you two jawing about?"

"I asked your friend here to fill me in on the latest with this Janey Doe story you're working on. I took a shine to that little girl. I'd like to know her story's got a good ending. Most of the ones I write don't. Sob stories. That's my racket. Kinda gets you down sometimes."

I pulled up another chair and lit the cigarette Maudie offered me. "I'm with you, but if we can't find out any more about her, we may be at a dead end."

"Maybe it's better not to know," Q said. "Doesn't it make you think we'll find it isn't a happy tale when she was abandoned all alone with no one looking for her? Maybe it would be better for her not to know."

"I dunno," Maudie said. "If it was me, it would make me feel worse not knowing. Maybe someone had a good reason for dumping her off. Wanted her to have a chance at a better life. Don't forget the phone call. Someone wanted the police to know where to find her. They knew she'd be taken care of. Seems to me she did have someone who cared about her and maybe they're still out there somewhere. Maybe we could help reunite them if we figure out what the trouble is all about."

"There's definitely someone still interested in her," I said, filling them in on the latest news. "What we got to figure out is what drives someone who cares about her to abandon her, but still wanna keep tabs on her whereabouts?"

"Let's find out," said Maudie. "We're in the investigation business. Can't tell me between the three of us, we can't figure it out."

Q chimed in again. "There has to be a connection to the Ludgates. Weren't you planning on visiting the Hasselwhite estate again?"

"Yeah, but I don't know if it'll be so easy to get in without a police escort. They got the place locked up tight, and the Widow Ludgate was no pushover. I don't see waltzing in through the front gate again."

"Leave it to me," Maudie said. "I got a foolproof plan."

CHAPTER TWENTY-EIGHT

We piled in the Champ and took the drive out to the Hasselwhite joint. Maudie had me drop her off down the road from the gates so the construction crew wouldn't catch sight of us.

"Gimme about ten minutes or so after I get to the gate. I'll create a diversion and you two can get in and scout around, but keep on the down low. I don't have the cash to be bailing you out of jail, and I don't think Morty will spring for it neither."

"What are you planning to do, Miss Adams?" Q asked.

"Never you mind. I been on the beat longer than either of you been alive. I got tricks you never even heard of."

"All right, Maudie. Show us your stuff," I broke in to try and get the ball rolling. I didn't want to leave Mikey at the orphanage too long. Heaven, or the nuns, only knew what mischief he was getting up to.

Maudie waddled off down the road at a determined pace. No one can say she didn't still have plenty of spunk. We were parked too far away to see what she did, but we could see when the gates opened up to let her in. They closed up again double-quick, but I wasn't worried about that. We had scouted out an old oak tree growing close enough to the wall that we were able to shimmy our way up and over. It was a long drop and a hard fall for me on the other side that didn't do my dodgy legs or my pride any good. Q was nice enough to help me up without ribbing me about my lack of grace.

We were on the side of the house farthest from where the construction crew had their equipment set up, but we could hear the heavy machinery working in the back. I figured they must be digging out the swimming pool Bill Logan had talked about and hoped they were busy enough not to notice the two of us skulking around.

There was no sign of Maudie as we approached the house, which meant she had either talked her way in or been promptly ejected by the formidable Mrs. Ludgate. I was kinda sorry to miss that scene. When two headstrong individuals collide, it can be quite a sight to see.

Q was lighter on his feet and about a decade younger than me, so he darted around exploring and looking for ways into the house. I stood guard until he reported back.

"There's a concrete addition around the side over there. Looks like it could be one of those fallout shelters we were talking about. The interesting thing is the door to it has a security bar on the outside with heavy duty locks."

"Kinda as if they're trying to keep something in instead of out?"

"That's what it looks like. It would be interesting to know what's down there, wouldn't it, Mr. Malhaven?"

"Definitely. Things that are locked up nice and tight are always of interest to me. But doesn't sound as if there's much chance of getting in. Wonder if it connects up inside the house somehow?"

A big hand landed on my shoulder. "Could be, could be. Wouldn't you like to know?"

It was Bill Logan. I felt ten times a fool for letting him sneak up on us, but from his grin, I had a feeling we weren't in too big a trouble.

"Fancy meeting you here," I said. "Thought you'd be busy working right about now."

"I was until some lunatic old dame showed up at the gates claiming she was gonna pass out on the ground if she didn't get a glass of water from the house. I was curious to see if she could talk her way in, so I let her through the gates. Sure enough, she's been in there a good fifteen minutes or so. Has to be a new record for not getting kicked to the curb by our Florrie. Wouldn't be a friend of yours, I don't suppose?"

"She might be an acquaintance."

"Well, she's working some kind of magic. And who's this? Another sorcerer's apprentice? You got the whole paper down here trying to break in?"

"This here is Marquis Sutherland, another colleague of mine. Q, this is Bill Logan, head of the construction crew. We've got a feeling there's a big scoop here. Can't blame us for ganging up on it, can you?"

"It's no skin off my nose. I got the feeling things are gonna blow sky high here any minute, and we ain't seen a dime yet for the work we've put in on the pool. Just a lot of excuses. I wouldn't be surprised if Florrie did a bunk before too long without paying. With her husband popping off unexpected, she must be feeling the pressure."

Q piped up. "I was telling Mr. Malhaven about the bunker I found on the side of the house. Did you and your crew build it?"

"That was the very first thing we did. Ludgate told me Mrs. Hasselwhite wanted a first-class bomb shelter. Had me fit it out real nice. It's nicer than some of the dumps I've lived in. Bigger, too."

"Security's pretty tight. Have they got something valuable stashed away down there?" I asked.

"Your guess is as good as mine. I just follow orders. I learned pretty quick not to ask too many questions around here unless I wanted to get my nose bitten off. The money's good when we can get it out of them, so I stopped wondering about anything strange."

"Have you noticed other unusual things, Mr. Logan?" Q asked.

"Everything seems unusual to me. The house was already big when we started working on it. With everything we've added, it's probably doubled in square footage. Why would Mrs. Hasselwhite want to spend that kind of money on a place she's never set foot back in since I been working here?"

"You told me and Flanagan you thought the Ludgates were enjoying the add-ons themselves," I noted.

"That's certainly true of some of the rooms. But get this, they had us put in a full playroom with an oversized doll house and everything. Ordered all kinds of toys for it and stocked it up real nice. Now who's that for? I thought it meant Florrie might be expecting as unlikely as that was, but as far as I know, the room's never been used."

"When was this?" Q asked.

"That was the second thing we did. After the bomb shelter. At the time, the Hasselwhite kid would have been about eleven or twelve. Too old for the stuff they were filling up the nursery with. Besides, it was all done up in pink for a girl."

"Very interesting," Q agreed. "And you've never seen any children around the house?"

"Never seen no one but Horrie and Florrie. Of course, they keep themselves to themselves. And they close off parts of the house when we're working in there. Locks on a lot of the doors. My crew is always under orders not to go exploring. They made quite a fuss one day when one of the guys was poking around. Made me get rid of him on the spot or they threatened to fire me and the rest of the crew."

"Didn't it bother you how secretive they are?"

"Sure. Sometimes. The wife and I have talked about it many an evening. She don't want me mixed up in something that's not on the up and up. But I'm not breaking any laws I know of. Doing an honest day's work and getting paid for it. It's not my business where the money's coming from, is it?"

I was letting Logan know we weren't blaming him for making a buck wherever he could find the work, when Maudie suddenly materialized at my elbow, leaving me thinking maybe I needed to sharpen up my detection skills. Can't have people getting the drop on you left and right in my business.

"The jig is up, boys," she said. "Been tossed out on my ear, and she's called the cops, so we might want to hit the road. I'm sure your big Irish friend would get us out of any jam, but I don't want to be late for my lunch at the Automat. I think I've earned two slices of lemon cream pie today. That woman is made out of stone and spite. Enough to wear a person out."

Q and I didn't hesitate to escort Maudie off the property. Logan was kind enough to let us out the front gate, which is just as well as I couldn't see us hoisting Maudie up and over the ten-foot brick wall. We made it to the Champ and started back to town, passing a car along the way with a couple of our boys in blue that I recognized. They recognized me too 'cause they gave us a cheery wave with a rather satirical air to let me know we needn't worry about them giving chase. I figured they'd humor Florrie, then take a leisurely drive back into town.

Q filled in Maudie on what we'd learned, and Maudie cut right to the chase. "A nursery done up in pink? Sounds like they was expecting a little girl to come and stay with them. And there's only one little girl in this story, ain't there? Miss Janey Doe aka Lily White. It always comes back to that poor kid. What did they want with her? That's the question. That woman was hard as nails with me. Think if she got her hands on a helpless child."

It was something none of us wanted to imagine, and something I was gonna make damn sure didn't ever come to pass.

CHAPTER TWENTY-NINE

I dropped my two accomplices off at the paper and headed back to the orphanage. I figured Sister Honoria would never speak to me again if I left Mikey on her hands for too long. The nuns was used to dealing with all kinds but Mikey was in a class by himself.

Didn't shock me to find Mikey cooling his heels in Honoria's office when I arrived. She gave me a look when I popped in that told me plain as day that he'd worn out his welcome some time back.

"We're very glad to see you, Mr. Malhaven. Aren't we, Michael?"

"I guess so."

"Michael?"

"Yes, Sister Honoria."

"That's better. I hope you've learned a few things during your visit with us today that you can take with you when you return to your school."

"I'm sure he's been greatly improved by your example, Sister," I intervened, seeing the obstinate look on Mikey's face that foretold one of his unending spiels. I grabbed him by the arm and yanked him out the door before he annoyed her anymore. Sister Honoria was a good egg, but even she had a limit.

"I get the feeling you left quite an impression today," I said. "What did you get up to?"

"Nothing."

He was trying out the terse bit, but I'd never known him to be able to keep it up for long.

"That's too bad. I was hoping you could break this case wide open for me."

That did it. Mikey wanted to make sure I wasn't left with the impression he was anything but an expert at the whole spy gag.

"I would've, but those nuns don't fool around. All I was trying to do was pump the guy next to me in class for information, and next thing I know, I'm being marched down the hallway. How's a guy supposed to investigate when there's no one around to investigate, huh? I asked Sister Honoria a bunch of questions, but I wonder if she's hard of hearing because she never answered even one of them no matter how hard I tried. Do you think she's deaf, Mister? Maybe she should get her hearing checked out. She could get one of them ear horns like my grandpa used. He used to hold it up to his ear when we was talking to him except for me. He always said he could hear me as clear as a bell. I got one of those voices that carry, I guess. Like an actor on the stage. Hey, maybe I should go on the stage. Whataya think? Does that pay more than being a spy?"

"Well, you might be more successful at it. You gotta learn to be smarter if you want to get into the detecting business. You'll never find out anything if you keep getting kicked out of places."

"Yeah, the only thing I found out was this kid I was trying to talk to was crazy. You know what he was telling me before the teacher grabbed me? He was trying to convince me he'd seen an angel hanging around the cemetery they got out back in the dead of night. Ain't that the craziest thing you ever heard?"

"An angel? Did he describe it? How did he even see it?"

"Got up to use the bathroom, didn't he? Drank too much water probably. If you drink a lot of water, you always gotta go in the night. He was up around midnight and looked out the window. Said he saw the white wings glowing in the moonlight. That kid's off his rocker.

But I was the one got in trouble. That's always the way. Everyone gets away with everything except for me. Life ain't fair, is it, Mister?"

"That's a good lesson to learn, Mikey. But I'll tell you what. In this case, you got some first-class intelligence there. This isn't the first I heard tell of an angel hanging around that joint."

"Is that right? Gosh. Do you think it was a real angel? I thought that was just something they told us in Sunday school to scare us into being good. Do you think I have a guardian angel watching over me? Do you think he's here right now? Hey, Mr. Angel, if you're here, give us a sign or something. Make something appear or the car crash or something."

"Whoa, there. That's a little extreme, ain't it? Maybe the best idea is to try and behave as if there's an angel keeping an eye on you. Maybe there is and maybe there ain't, but I'd hate to make it all the way to the pearly gates before finding out someone had been keeping a ledger on me and them throwing me down to that other place, wouldn't you?"

There was a rare moment of silence. I thought maybe I'd found the key to reforming Mikey's wild ways through the threat of eternal damnation, but he's one of those hard cases.

"Naw. That place is for killers and robbers. I ain't that bad. I bet I could talk St. Peter into letting me in. I got a way with people you know."

As I could picture only too well Mikey talking the ear off anyone guarding the path to heaven, I had to admit he might have a point. St. Peter might wave him on in just to get rid of him.

"So, whatcha think about this angel? Is he haunting the joint like a ghost? Boy, I'd sure love to see that, wouldn't you? Do you think we could sneak back over there tonight and see if he's hanging around? Maybe you could bring a camera and we could even get a picture of it. I bet we could sell it for a hundred dollars. Wouldn't that be something? What would you buy with a hundred dollars? I want one of those machine guns you see in the movies. Rat-a-tat-tat, rat-a-tat-tat, rat-a-tat-tat."

The horror of picturing the ever-impulsive Mikey with such a weapon combined with the unending racket he was making was thank-fully cut short by our arrival back out at Wynter's Hill. Mikey leapt from the car before I came to a full stop and started chasing Archie around like a madman. I wasn't too worried for the cat. He's a cagey one and always knows instinctively whether people have his best inter-ests at heart. He bounded lightly up to the top of an obelisk and stared down, twitching his tail in amusement at his frustrated opponent.

Lily appeared and took Mikey's hand. She appeared to have a strange power over him. He meekly followed along as she led him back to the house for lunch. It was just the two kiddies and me and Victoria as Cressley was out running errands and Livinia was in her room resting as she usually did around midday. Mikey did most of the talking, but I managed to pull Victoria aside after we ate and fill her in on the latest.

"It's seeming more likely there is an angel, or someone running around dressed as one, doesn't it, Jim? But why would anyone do that?"

"We won't know until we can catch him and ask him. Guess it means a cold night staking out another cemetery for me. I'd hoped I was done with that."

She smiled. "At least you've had a lot of practice and you don't frighten easily. But do be careful. The last time you were investigating a graveyard in the middle of the night, you got shot."

"You don't have to remind me. Luckily, there was a lovely lady there to save me."

"Hm, does that mean I should come with you? I could keep you company while you wait."

"That would make the time pass quicker, but probably best for you to stick close to Lily. With Ludgate gone, I don't think we'll have any more unexpected visitors, but I don't want to take any chances until we get this all cleared up. I only have a passing acquaintance with her, but I wouldn't trust the Ludgate woman not to get up to something."

"I'll keep an eye out. I've loved having Lily here. She's such a sweetheart. What do you think will happen to her?"

"I dunno. I hope you won't be mad, but I asked Sister Honoria about what you said, about wanting to adopt her. She said you didn't have much chance with the Board without a husband."

"I was afraid of that. It's maddening. We have plenty of room and plenty of money to take care of her. Yet the Board would rather keep her in an institution than to trust her with an unmarried woman. Sometimes it feels as though we're living in 1851 instead of 1951."

"You know what I'm gonna say."

"I know, Jim. And it's not that I don't want to one day. But on our own schedule, not to please a bunch of fuddy-duddy old men with old-fashioned ideas."

She had a fierce look on her face that told me she wasn't gonna let this go without a fight. I couldn't help being mad at the Board myself. It felt like they were making Victoria dig her heels in against marrying me just for the principle of the thing. One of the perils of falling in love with a strong-minded woman is they got their own thoughts and way of doing things. It wasn't up to me to try and change her mind. I'd take her on her terms any day of the week over the risk of losing her.

But there were many times when I had saluted Mr. Lukasz Jankowski in my own mind. He'd succeeded in convincing Victoria to walk down the aisle dressed all in white when I hadn't. I wondered sometimes if I'd ever stand at an altar watching her float toward me like an angel herself. Made me wonder what he had that I didn't. I knew I was no prize to look at, but he couldn't have loved her any more than I did. I guess that's all I could do.

CHAPTER THIRTY

I headed back to the paper for the afternoon, feeling a bit low. I knew it was winning the lottery for a woman such as Victoria to put up with me, but there were times I thought maybe I wasn't what she was looking for after all. Her actions said otherwise, but even a tough guy like me ain't so full of confidence as you might think. It felt as though I was stuck in limbo without that ring on her finger. A pretty pleasant kind of limbo, but it left me with an unsettled feeling all the same.

I'd never even thought about getting hitched before I met her, and now I was letting it become an obsession. I tried to lock the thought away at the back of my brain and throw away the key. Pressuring her was a sure-fire way to get her back up, and I couldn't stand the thought of losing her. I was the luckiest man on earth to have any part of her. If it meant treading lightly around the idea of wedding bells, I could do that.

Checking in with Q seemed a good way to take my mind off my love life. I didn't think he'd of had time to find out much else since our morning adventure, but then again, he has plenty of drive and determination so I wasn't too surprised when he looked eager to see me.

"Mr. Malhaven! I was going to ring you out at the cemetery. I've been on the phone with a contact in New York. I had asked them to see if they had any information on the Ludgates or the Hasselwhites. In particular, whether they could find out anything from passenger liner records printed in the newspaper of Mrs. Hasselwhite and her son sailing to Europe."

"That's smart thinking. What did they find?"

"They couldn't find any record of the Hasselwhites sailing, but interestingly, they did come across a record of the Ludgates arriving in May of '45 on a Navy transport ship from Europe."

"You don't say? That's a strange thing. Ocean passage was pretty locked down to military personnel and other essentials toward the end of the war. How did they rate that kind of treatment?"

"It would be interesting to know, wouldn't it? They must have had friends in high places."

"Or bribed the right person," I added, being no stranger to the fact that corruption flourishes even during, or maybe especially during, times of national crisis. "Strange, too, that there's no record of the Hasselwhites' departure."

"Yes. Of course, it wasn't an exhaustive search. Just the major ship lines that had started taking passengers after the war. And it's possible they took an airliner. It sounds like they have enough money to do that, but transatlantic flying was still rare then."

"Ain't so common now, unless you got the moolah, but yeah, I guess that's not definitive. I sure would love to know where they are now. It's all to the Ludgates' good that they stay away as long as possible, but it's also mighty convenient."

"You're not suggesting Mr. and Mrs. Ludgate did away with Mrs. Hasselwhite and her son? There must be people who would notice if they were missing. Relatives or even lawyers or bankers. People with that kind of money don't disappear without somebody asking questions."

"You would think so, yet from what we can tell, these Ludgates are acting pretty free and easy with the cash, at least as far as the house renovations go. Wouldn't a lawyer have stepped in and asked questions by now if there was one?"

"I can do some more calling around. See if I can get any information on who handles their business or if there are any relatives."

"You do that, Q, because I think we have about as much chance of getting any information out of the person most likely to know, one Mrs. Horace Ludgate, as we do out of a statue posing in the park. And as she never leaves the house and won't let us in, no chance to even try."

Turns out I was wrong about that though cause when I pulled up back home, there was a shiny black Buick of the very latest model parked next to Victoria's Caddy. I roamed through the house until I heard voices coming from the sitting room where Livinia spent most of her free time, of which she had plenty. I walked in and interrupted quite the tea party.

Livinia was facing the door, sitting in one of the pink velvet-covered highbacked club chairs as though it was a throne, sipping on a cup of tea, while Victoria perched gracefully on the flowered sofa with her back to me. The other club chair was taken up by none other than the elusive Mrs. Ludgate of all people.

She looked like a miniature doll next to the formidable Livinia, but the weirdest thing about her was the rictus of a smile she had plastered on her face. It was the smile of someone who had never done it before, and didn't plan on doing it again, but had been told it was the kind of thing humans did when they were among other humans.

"Oh, Jim, it's you," Victoria said, looking around at the sound of the door opening. "Look, we have a visitor."

The way she said it conveyed as clear as clear to me without any more words that the visit was neither a welcome nor pleasant one, but I didn't mind getting another crack at Florrie. I settled myself down beside Victoria on the sofa and greeted our unexpected guest whose smile had disappeared rapidly at the sight of me.

"Ain't this a surprise. And a delightful one, naturally. Great to see you again. What brings you to our remote neck of the woods, Mrs. Ludgate?"

She gave me a look as though I was a bug on the floor that had started in to speaking and hardly deserved to be noticed.

"Have we met?"

"Sure, though you might not remember. I was with Flanagan. The cop that broke the sad news about Mr. Ludgate to you. Let me offer my condolences again. I'm kinda surprised to see you out and about so soon after such a blow. It speaks well of your resiliency, don't it? I'm sorry. I just got here. Did I miss anything?"

"Mrs. Ludgate was telling us she was here to take custody of Miss White," Livinia said with a sniff that was hard to interpret. Whether it was directed at me or our visitor, I couldn't say. Livinia could be enigmatic that way.

"That right? I was in town visiting at the orphanage this morning and Sister Honoria didn't mention a thing about it to me. Which reminds me, I hope little Mikey is staying out of trouble?" I said, half expecting him to jump out from behind the curtains or from underneath the sofa. I never felt one hundred percent safe with that kid around.

"I think so," Victoria answered with a smile. "He and Lily are helping Mr. Cressley with dinner."

"Poor Cressley," I muttered before turning back to our grim guest with a grin. "Well, sounds like Lily is doing all right here. We appreciate the offer, but I think Lily is best off with us for now. You may not know it, but there is a bit of a mystery surrounding her. I'm getting to the bottom of it, but in the meantime, best if Lily stays where she has a lot of people to keep an eye on her, and I'm sure you must be busy yourself. There are always a lot of details to sort out when there's an unexpected death in the family and all."

The look I got for that told me she'd a mind to squash me flat like the bug she thought I was. There followed an awkward silence that I was considering breaking when Florrie piped up.

"It was Mr. Ludgate's wish we adopt Lily. I have the papers here to prove it. I will speak to Sister Honoria, but there is no reason I cannot take Lily with me today. It would be very inefficient and inconvenient for me to have to make another trip out here."

Victoria and I both opened our mouths to protest but were beat to the punch by Livinia. If there's one thing that gets a high-handed person going, it's being told what for by another high-handed person, and Livinia was having none of it. For the second time, I had the pleasure of seeing her leap into action against a Ludgate.

She rose to her feet to make her stand. "Miss White is our guest and shall remain so until such time as Mr. Malhaven has discovered the true nature of her origins. He can be rather plodding, but he usually gets there in the end. We shall await the outcome of his investigation before any decisions are made about the child."

More faint praise for me that to most people would have felt like a slap in the face, but I was always appreciative of any kind words Livinia said about me, and anyways, I supported her overall position, so I stood up as Victoria also rose to her feet. The three of us towering over her might have daunted another diminutive person such as she was, but Florrie was unfazed. She just narrowed her eyes a bit as she looked up at us from the plush confines of the overstuffed chair. It was a look that promised nothing good.

After she got done giving us all the evil eye, she gathered her purse from the table beside her and rose to her feet as well.

"We shall see."

And with that cryptic statement, she walked out of the room without a backward glance.

CHAPTER THIRTY-ONE

"*A*n abhorrently arrogant woman. Good riddance," said Livinia.

I felt Victoria poke me in the ribs with her elbow, afraid I was gonna bust out laughing at the pot calling the kettle black, but I actually agreed with Livinia. She might have finally met someone who could give her a run for her money in the haughty dame department.

Livinia excused herself to change for dinner as she did every night, even though the rest of us showed up pretty much in whatever we had on. She believed in keeping up standards and wasn't about to give up the habits of a lifetime just because times were getting more casual.

Victoria and I sat back down on the sofa. I was glad to have her nestle in next to me to show me there was no hard feelings about the whole marriage argument.

"What an afternoon! First Mikey, then this. The Ludgates are, or were, quite a couple."

"Yeah, what a pair, but I guess it only goes to show there's someone for everyone. I sure wish we could find out more about them."

"I wonder if Mr. Cliburn knows anything about them?" Victoria asked, mentioning the lawyer that had taken over the Wynter family business after the unfortunate demise of their long-time family lawyer during the previous fall's brouhaha. "There aren't that many lawyers in town who handle the kind of complicated financial affairs of families like ours. I know because we had a hard time finding one when Mr. Monroe's firm folded. I could run into town tomorrow and ask him."

"Lawyers usually clam up about that kind of thing. Client confidentiality, you know."

"Yes, but I might be able to coax something out of him. I think he's a bit sweet on me."

"Hey, I don't appreciate the sound of that."

"Darling, he's seventy if he's a day. Besides, you know you don't have anything to worry about on that score. I'm strictly a one man at a time woman, and you're my one man."

You don't need a lot of words when the woman you love tells you something like that with a certain look in her eye. I'll just say I was sorry to hear the dinner gong go off that meant we had to jump and run. I was mighty comfortable right where I was, but we trudged off to the dining room as Livinia was always put into a fouler mood than usual if we kept her waiting.

It was one of the quietest dinners we'd had in quite a while. Cressley and Lily, of course, didn't say anything, but even Mikey was silent. He opened his mouth more than once or twice to spit something out, but a look from Livinia was enough to shut him up. I'd rarely seen him cowed before, but there's no doubt Livinia has her quelling looks down to a science.

After dinner, I volunteered to take Mikey back to town. I'd decided to go ahead and try staking out the graveyard at the Sisters of Mercy in case the angel decided to make another appearance, so it wasn't any trouble to drop the kid off along the way. Whoever the angel was, it was obvious he was mad about losing tabs on Lily, so it wasn't likely he was going to give up on his crusade before finding out what happened to her.

It had started to drizzle when we went out to the car. I almost changed my mind about the stakeout, but I'd stood out in worse before and I wanted to get to the bottom of this sooner rather than later. I wasn't happy about how we'd parted ways with the Widow Ludgate. Those last words of hers had sounded like a threat.

Mikey was not a bit happy that he wasn't to accompany me on the stakeout. He talked my ear off about it the whole way, but I kicked him out of the car at the Cummings' place, stopping to light a cigarette before roaring away, relieved to hear the last of the pest.

I checked in with Sister Honoria when I got to the orphanage so I could let her know what I was up to. She let me out a back door and I spied a good hiding place, a low bench under a spreading ash tree where I could sit in the shadow and wait. The branches of the tree protected me from the worst of the rain, and my topper did the rest. I pitied the men who'd given up wearing a hat. I've said it before, and I'll say it to the end of my days, there's no more useful piece of clothing than a good hat.

It was tedious waiting there, but at least the rain fizzled out. I was afraid to light up a cigarette to pass the time in case our so-called angel saw the glow of the butt. Instead, I amused myself by trying to remember the lyrics to as many different songs as I could. I'd done "The Tennessee Waltz," "Rag Mop," and a dozen more and had moved on to "Harbor Lights" when I spied something coming through the vacant lot that hugged the fence along the back of the property.

I stayed still in the shadows, not wanting to spook whatever it was, and thinking I'd as soon not have to get into a foot race. I used to be able to run like the wind during my Army days, but I'd had a whole lot more motivation then with bullets flying all around me. That was also before I'd damaged both my legs. It's a hell of a thing to make it through a war only to be half-crippled once you return to civilian life.

The thing, whatever it was, strolled along, taking its time. It finally got to the fence and hopped over nimbly. It hesitated there, then came and sat on one of the larger tombstones. It was dark under the trees, but I could make out what looked an awful lot like wings, gleaming white in the gloom.

"Hello."

I almost jumped out of my skin. Guess I'd been wrong about not being visible where I was, but if he wanted to talk, that suited me fine. Maybe I'd finally get some questions answered.

"Pleasure to meet you. Name's Malhaven. What's yours?" I said, getting up to move closer.

"Please don't come any farther. I'd have to leave, but I'd rather stay and talk to you. I don't often get the chance to talk to anyone these days. It would make for a nice change." His voice was reedy and uncertain as though he hadn't used it much. I figured better to keep him talking.

"Sure," I said, easing back down on the bench. "I want to talk to you, too. I think you might know a thing or two about what's been going on around here."

"I didn't mean to cause trouble. I liked to visit her and make sure she was happy. She always enjoyed my tricks, so I did a few, but I didn't think they would send her away because of it. Do you know where she is? I need to find her and make sure she's safe."

"Who are you? Her guardian angel? Those look like wings."

There was soft laughter. "They are, but the feathers are only for show. She said I looked like an angel with my wings, so I've been covering them with feathers. She thought them quite beautiful even before I finished. Now that I'm done, I wanted to show her, but she's gone. Do you know where she is?"

"She's safe. She's with a friend of mine. A nice lady. You don't have to worry about Lily."

"Lily? Is that what they call her here? It's pretty. Suits her. Lily," he said again, trying out the sound.

"Why? What do you call her?"

"By her real name, of course, but better I not say. Do you swear the lady she is with will keep her safe?"

"I think so, but safe from what? If we knew what the danger was, we could do a better job of protecting her."

There was a silence and then a hissing whisper. "Those people."

"That's not very specific. Can you give me something to go on?"

"The one working here and the other at the house. I don't like to say their names."

"Could it be you're talking about the Ludgates? Ludgate singular now. You know, Horace is deceased."

"Is he? I wondered. He got a very funny look on his face when he caught me inside the building. He clutched his chest and fell to his knees. I didn't wait around to see, but when he never came home—"

"Home? You mean the Hasselwhite place? How do you know? Are you staking out that joint, too?"

The figure in white got to his feet as though he'd said too much. I couldn't see him too well, but I knew he was poised for flight.

I hurried to say anything to get him to stay and talk some more. "Forget I said that. It don't matter. All I want to know is who Lily is. And what is she to you or the Ludgates? You gotta trust me when I say I'm only trying to help her."

There was a silence. I thought I'd lost him, but his voice came faint again. "I think I do believe you. You sound sincere. But most people I've known in my life weren't trying to help us. I don't know who to trust. I want her to be safe. She is everything I have left in this world. If she is safe, I can rest content. I wish I could speak to her."

"Does she speak? To you? She won't talk to us."

"Won't she? I didn't realize. She didn't tell me. She always followed my instructions, sometimes to a fault. I asked her not to talk to people about me and where she came from. I didn't think she would take it to such an extreme. She always takes her responsibilities very seriously. Is she having any fun where she is? I want more than anything that she should have some fun."

"I think she is, in her way. She misses you. She draws your picture all the time."

"Oh, the darling girl. How I do miss—"

There was a noise like a gunshot that startled us both, a rushing sound of feet running. Before I could make a move or stop him, the angel was off with a bound over the fence, disappearing into the night.

CHAPTER THIRTY-TWO

"*D*id I get him? Hey, Mister, did I get that angel? Did you see the rock I threw? I was too far away, but that was a good toss, wasn't it? It hit pretty close to where that guy was sitting. Where'd he go? What direction? I can run him down for you. You're too old to run as fast as I can and… hey!"

I'd sidled up close to my friend Mikey during this monologue and gotten a good grip on his arm before he could take off running like a lunatic hare. Counted to ten and back again before trying to speak. Did it a few more times while Mikey wriggled in my grip as if he was a worm caught on a hook.

"Ow! Lemme go! What's the big idea? I'm on your side. Ain't we partners? If I'd just aimed a little higher, I'd have got him right in the chest. Knocked the wind out of him and then he couldn't of taken off. Why'd he run away? I thought he was gonna fly, but he was running like an ordinary guy. I coulda caught him easy. Why didn't you let me go?"

I closed my eyes and tried to clear my mind before spitting out through clenched teeth, "What do you think you're doing here? Didn't I drop you off at your house?"

"Sure, but I thought you could use some back up, so I jumped on your bumper and rode over here on the back of the car. Don't that show I'm good at this spy stuff? You never even knew I was there, did ya? Ain't that something? And I been hiding out all this time and you never noticed. I'm beginning to think you ain't very good at this detective stuff. Maybe you should stick to reporting all that society guff like Ma reads and—yikes!"

I drug him to the fence and plopped him over it into the vacant lot, following more slowly myself, then escorted him around the block and to my car. I kept an eye out on the way, but I knew my angel friend was long gone. All we found of him was a lone white feather.

I drove Mikey back home, fuming all the way at my missed opportunity, barely able to think over Mikey's constant self-congratulations over his big contribution to my mission. Marched him up to the door and saw him inside this time under the firm hand of a harassed-looking Mr. Cummings before I felt safe to drive off again.

I tried to calm down on my drive home, thinking over what I'd learned. It wasn't much. Angel, as I called him for lack of a better name, obviously cared about Lily. He said he had instructed her not to tell people about him or where she'd been living. Did that mean he was the one who left her in the park and made the anonymous phone call? Had he been trying to save her from danger and place her with people who could help her? And if the danger was the Ludgates, what did that mean? Were there more answers at the Hasselwhite place? Everything seemed to revolve around them and that house, but who was Angel?

His voice had sounded young, unsure, hoarse. He'd said he didn't get a chance to speak to people often. Where was he living? How was he supporting himself if he didn't come out among people?

A young man, maybe a teenager? The only young man I'd run across in the story so far was Henry Hasselwhite, and he was off in Europe with his mother. Or was he? We had only the word of the Ludgates, and Q's contact had had no luck finding out how the Hasselwhites had left the country.

The more we investigated, the more sinister the prolonged absence of Mrs. Hasselwhite and her son was. I could see taking off for a grand tour to get away from bad memories, but then you either come back home or sell the house and get a fresh start somewhere. You certainly don't pay thousands of dollars to get the house done over if you've no intention of living there.

But if Angel was Henry, where was his mother? And if he was around, why wasn't he lording it over the manor instead of the Ludgates? Plus, none of it explained who Lily was, or Angel's or the Ludgate's interest in her. Henry was an only child. How did this girl fit into the picture?

It was late. My head was aching from Mikey's incessant chatter and my frustration with getting so little further ahead even after talking to one of our prime suspects. I tried to tell myself it was progress of a kind. Things always looked better in the morning.

And true enough, I woke with a renewed optimism. I'd made contact with our supposed angel. He appeared to be very much flesh and blood as far as I could tell, having not been able to get close enough to touch him. His voice had been thin and reedy, and his figure was slight from what I could tell from under those weird wings he had on, but other than that, I couldn't come up with much more of a description.

Still, it was something to have seen with my own eyes that there was somebody running around with a pair of wings. Now to put a name to him and unravel this mystery once and for all.

I got dressed and grabbed a cup of joe before heading outside. The weather had turned blustery and cold again, about what you'd expect from the week before Easter. I ducked back inside and grabbed my trench coat. When I popped back out, Victoria and Lily were sitting on the bench outside my cottage, with Archie curled up in Lily's lap. Victoria looked a million bucks as always, and Lily had a fancy kind of navy pea coat on and a matching knit hat and mittens.

"Say, this is a treat. Two lovely ladies at my door. And don't you both look like something out of a magazine. Did Mrs. Jankowski do some shopping for you, Miss Lily?"

She nodded with a slight smile lighting that solemn face, holding out her hands to me as if to say, see what I got?

"That's fine. Just in time, too. The weather's taken a turn, ain't it?"

I said, squatting down gently next to the bench so as not to spook Lily or the cat. "I figured when that rain came through last night we might be in for a change."

Victoria smiled at me. "We decided to try out Lily's new coat and come down and say good morning to you before you run off. Isn't that right, Lily?"

She nodded and ran her mittened hand along Archie's sleek black fur. He had his golden eyes closed and was purring fit to beat the band. He always knew a good thing when he had it.

"Archie's taken quite a shine to you," I said. "He don't put up with just anybody. Only those he can trust. It's good to know who you can trust, ain't it?"

She considered that question as seriously as she thought about everything. Not one to leap in with an answer, our Lily. She looked up at me finally and nodded.

"Like you can trust Mrs. Jankowski. She's a good friend to have, ain't she?"

Victoria put an arm around Lily's shoulders, and the girl settled in there as though she wanted to belong.

"And you know you can trust me, too."

She gave an emphatic nod, I'm not too modest to report.

"That's good, 'cause I want to talk to you about something. I ran into someone last night. Someone I think you know. He had a pair of wings."

Both Victoria and Lily looked startled. The girl made as if to get up, but Victoria took one of her hands in her own for reassurance.

"Now, take it easy," I said. "Don't worry. We had a nice chat. He's a real friendly fellow. I think he was lonely and glad to have someone to talk to. I think he's missing you an awful lot."

Tears welled up in her eyes.

"He told me how he wanted you not to tell us anything about him or where you come from, but he was sad to hear you hadn't been talking to us at all. Said to tell you that's not what he meant. He wants you to be happy and have fun and to be safe. He was worried about those Ludgates."

She got a look then I can only describe as mean. If a little girl no older than she was could learn to hate, she had learned to hate the sound of that name.

"I told him Mr. Ludgate had passed away. Did Mrs. Jankowski tell you that?"

A nod.

"And I want you to know we won't let Mrs. Ludgate anywhere near you. I don't know how you know them, or what they want with you, but I promise you I'm not going to let anything happen to you. I'd like to help your pal, too. I didn't get a good look at him, but he sounded awful down, as if he could use a friend."

Victoria brushed away a tear that ran down Lily's face.

"Don't cry, darling. We only want to help you and your friend. I know we haven't known each other very long, but Mr. Malhaven and I only want the best for you. Do you believe that?"

"Yes."

It was so quiet, we almost missed it, but Victoria and I exchanged a look of triumph at the soft sound.

My thighs were on fire from squatting so long, the old wounds letting me know it wasn't the smartest position to be in, but I didn't want to do anything to break the spell.

Victoria gave the girl a hug as a reward. "You have someone else who cares about you very much. Can you tell us anything about him? He might need our help, too. Mr. Malhaven is very clever. If he knows a little more, he might be able to help you both so you could see each other again. Would you like that?"

"Oh, yes," Lily breathed. "More than anything."

"Then who is he, dear?"

"He's… he's… my brother."

CHAPTER THIRTY-THREE

"Is that so?" I said. "What's his name?"

"Hank."

Hank. Common nickname for Henry. Now we were getting somewhere.

"Not Henry Hasselwhite by chance?"

"Yes."

Victoria and I exchanged another look, and I let her take over the questioning.

"And what's your name, sweetheart?" Victoria asked.

"Henrietta, but he always calls me Etta."

"And where does Hank live?"

"It's a big house. Hank told me it belonged to our father before he died. It should belong to him now, because our mother is gone, too, but those people," Lily added with a shudder, "had taken over, and we were just guests there. We needed to behave or…"

"Yes, dear? Or what?"

"He said they would kill us. They killed Father and Mother and would kill us, too."

She broke into sobs. Archie jumped down from her lap and skittered off as Victoria pulled Lily close to her.

"Poor darling. Don't worry. We won't let anything happen to you. How brave you've been all this time."

"I told Hank I would be brave. I promised him and that I would never tell anyone. He said he'd find a way to get me out of the house and he did, but I miss him so. I wish I was back there with him again."

I had to get up then to stretch my legs or I'd have been stuck in that position forever. Victoria pulled Lily onto her lap so there would be room for me to sit down beside them.

I settled in, hardly knowing where to start with the questions now Lily was talking. "If he figured out how to leave the house, why didn't he come with you? You could have gone to the police. Told them what was going on."

"He said they wouldn't believe him. He tried it once. Said they called him a crazy kid making up stories. They called that man to come and pick him up. He convinced everybody Hank was playing a joke. They didn't give him food for days after that. He didn't want to risk it again. He thought if he sent me away and stayed himself, they'd be satisfied and wouldn't go looking for me. He said they only needed one or the other of us, not both."

"Why did they need you?"

"He said if there was ever any question, they would claim they were our legally-appointed guardians. They had papers. So they could stay in the house."

"Did they treat you badly, dear?" Victoria asked.

"Not me so much. They mostly left me alone. I had a playroom and toys and as many books as I wanted from the library room. But they were hard on Hank. He played tricks on them. They didn't like that."

"Tricks like in the kitchen at the orphanage?" I said.

"Yes. I thought they were funny, but I was scared, too. They got so mad at him, and they wouldn't let him eat for days at a time to punish him. I wanted to save my food and give it to him, but they watched me too closely."

"Don't worry, darling. Mr. Malhaven will take care of everything now that we know, won't you, Jim?"

"Sure. Sounds open and shut. Particularly now with Ludgate gone.

I wouldn't think his missus was too keen to keep up the act. In fact, I'll be surprised if we don't find she's done a runner to get out ahead of the law. She must know the jig is up. I'll head into town and fill Flanagan and his boys in on the doings. Don't you worry, Lily, er, Etta, that is. That'll take some getting used to."

"You can call me Lily. I like it."

"All right, Lily. Don't you worry. You did the right thing by telling us. You stay close to Mrs. Jankowski today, and I'll take care of the rest."

She reached over and gave me a hug, strong for such a little thing.

I trotted to the car, confident now that we were getting close to the end of this particular mystery. I turned it all over in my head on the drive into town. The Ludgates had knocked off Pa Hasselwhite, gotten rid of his wife somehow, and were keeping the kiddies so they could produce them as an excuse to be running the joint in case anyone such as me got nosy. They'd lost control of Lily aka Etta and had been busy trying to get their hands on her again without attracting too much attention and risking the authorities shutting down their scam. I was still puzzling out why Hank didn't run away, too, but maybe he'd been brainwashed by the Ludgates to think no one would ever believe him if the cops hadn't.

I wondered if there was a record of the time he'd tried to get help. Probably not. Sounded like the kind of thing my buddy Flanagan and his pals would've laughed off as a joke, not even bothering to write up a report. I also wondered why there was no apparent record of Henrietta's birth. All the papers and records said Henry was an only child.

And we knew how Hasselwhite had died. Easy enough to bump someone off by dumping a radio in the bath with them, but what about his wife? Maybe that's where the European tour gag had come in. Two deaths would have been harder to explain. Easier to pass off Mrs. Hasselwhite's absence as an extended vacation to get over her grief at losing hubby, but what if they had really bumped her off, too?

The biggest question of all was who were these Ludgates to begin with, and how had they wormed their way into the household only to wreak havoc on this poor family. I guessed there'd be time to find all that out, though I didn't envy whoever had to interrogate Florence Ludgate. She would be a tough mug to deal with, but if she'd done what Lily said, she deserved the electric chair if anyone ever did.

Maybe Horace made a lucky escape by kicking off when he did. It must have been a shock to him running into Hank at the orphanage. Made it more probable he popped off from a heart attack after all. I figured the police would sort it all out after rescuing Hank and arresting Florrie. The one thing I didn't figure on was red tape tying us up in knots.

"Jimmy, old son," Flanagan said to me with a pitying air after I filled him in on the action, "we got a thing called due process these days. The higher ups are cracking down on us boys running around willy-nilly breaking in doors and arresting people. It gets in the newspapers and people get annoyed with us and write angry letters to the mayor. We'll need some kind of evidence and a warrant to even search the place."

"We got plenty of evidence. Lily's filled us in on what's going on, and I talked to her brother about it, too."

"You want me to go in front of a judge and tell him how an angel you couldn't even see clear and a girl who's caused nothing but trouble handed you a fairy story and expect him to pat me on the head and tell me I've been a good little cop? You obviously ain't familiar with the judges around here. But listen, as a favor to you, I'll take you with me back out to the Hasselwhite place and see if we can suss anything out. Some kind of hard evidence."

That's how we found ourselves back out at Hasselwhite Hall. Bill Logan let us through the gate again cheerfully. I think he enjoyed watching people getting thrown out of the house, like a hobby he had taken up to brighten his working day.

Flanagan leant on the doorbell, settling in for a long stay, but to my surprise and his, the door was wrenched open double quick. Florrie came out, closed and locked the door behind her, and stood staring at us. Joey ain't unnerved by much, but even he seemed nervous under this unexpected examination.

"Mrs. Ludgate, we've gotten information that you have someone living here we want to talk to. A Mr. Henry Hasselwhite. Is that true? And if so, can we see him?"

I was getting ready to start in to arguing with her when she denied it, but her next words shut me up quick.

"Of course it is true, and no, you may not see him. Good day, gentlemen."

CHAPTER THIRTY-FOUR

*Y*ou could have knocked me and Flanagan both over with one of those long white feathers Hank had been shedding as we watched Florrie march away in the direction of the detached garage that stood off to the side of the house. Luckily, her legs were short and ours were long, so once we recovered ourselves, we easily caught up with her.

Flanagan positioned himself in front of the widow, holding up his hands as if he was trying to placate a charging bull. "Now, hang on one minute. Are you admitting that you're keeping Henry Hasselwhite a prisoner?"

"Don't be absurd. Mr. Ludgate and I are his legal guardians. I have the paperwork right here." She pulled a wad of official looking documents out of her black leather purse. "I am on my way to our lawyer right now to see what I need to do to regain physical custody of Henry's sister, Henrietta. We had hoped to bring her home without all this fuss, but as obstacles are being placed in my way, I must take legal recourse."

"Why didn't you or Mr. Ludgate tell us this before if you have a legal right to them?" I said. "That don't make sense."

"The children are always playing naughty tricks. They are very willful. However, I promised their mother we would protect them from any trouble or bad publicity. It was her wish they be brought up quietly. There are many people who would desire to take advantage of children who are to come into such wealth. When Henrietta ran away, Mr. Ludgate took a job at the Sisters of Mercy in hopes of convincing Sister Honoria to give us the child without our having to reveal her origins or rake up past tragedy. It was our duty—my duty now—to keep them away from those who would exploit them."

She shot a glare at me, as though I was the one living the good life in a fancy house on someone else's dime instead of her.

"So, where's Mrs. Hasselwhite now then? I thought she was off on a trip with the boy?"

"A slight prevarication that was her idea. She cannot stand the thought of being in this house without her husband but wanted the children brought up in a stable environment. She is not a well woman. Flighty. One might even say unbalanced. We have brought up the children and made improvements to the house as she has instructed. I have all the relevant documents, but I think I have wasted quite enough time and energy explaining things that are none of your business. Now that you know I have legal guardianship of Henrietta, maybe you will send her home and save me and my lawyer the trouble."

"Well..." Flanagan started, giving me the eye. I could tell he wasn't necessarily buying this guff, but I'll give it to Florrie. She looked every inch a most respectable and reasonable woman, reciting off facts with an answer for every objection.

I jumped in for him. "I think we'll need to do some checking around first. No offense, but we've only your word for all of this. The children have told me a different story."

She looked at me narrowly. "There is ample documentation, including every telegram Mrs. Hasselwhite has sent us with instructions about the house or children. Lily is a very young child and has a limited understanding of the arrangement. And it is quite impossible that you have spoken with Henry, but if you had, you would have seen he was not only willful but unbalanced like his mother. I'm afraid these inferior genetic traits get passed down in families. If you doubt my word, you may speak to the family lawyer, Thomas Martinbock. The firm is based in Chicago."

"Chicago? I thought you were on your way to see him?"

"I am, so I'll ask you to excuse me. I intend to drive there and back today so I cannot delay any further."

She brushed past us and disappeared through a door into the garage. We both jumped back when the electric garage door slid up and she nearly ran us down backing out.

"What do you make of all that?" Joey asked me.

"Bunch of hooey with more holes in it than a slice of Swiss cheese. But it's the kind of convincing hooey that might sway a judge. Bet you dollars to donuts any documents she has are as fake as those ledgers at the orphanage, not to mention that letter with Sister Honoria's signature that Horace had on him."

"What about those telegrams she mentioned? Can't forge those."

"No," I considered the problem. "Might mean they have an accomplice overseas or more than one."

"Hang on. Now you're building up a whole complicated conspiracy. Out of what? The word of a couple of kids that sound like they might have a screw loose like the mother. What if the story is true? Mrs. Hasselwhite is a loon and the Ludgates were trying to keep it under wraps to avoid publicity. They've lost control of the kiddies and been unsuccessful in getting one of them back without it all being made public. Sure, they'd have been better off coming clean with us or Sister Honoria to start with and taking Lily or Henrietta back home, but lots of folks think they're too clever by half. Take matters into their own hands instead of asking for help."

"What about those ledgers? Those were forged."

"Says that guy Leonard. What's he gonna say? 'I been keeping a second set of books and stealing food from the mouths of babes?' I've said it before and I'll say it again. You're too trusting, Jimmy. You always want to adopt the outcasts and strays and give them more respect than they deserve. Most people like that got some kind of racket going on."

"People like what?"

"Oh, here we go. Don't start in on me. Just 'cause you went off and seen the world while I was stuck on desk duty in Washington don't make you smarter than me. I know you fought side by side with all kinds of guys, but they don't have no choice but to be on your side when they're being shot at. It's a different story when you get home. Then it's every man for himself. This ain't the war and these men ain't part of your platoon, Jimmy."

"The thing I learned in the war is not to take a man at face value. Look at his actions instead. I'll always stick up for anyone I see acting like a man."

We'd both gotten red in the face and were shouting pretty hard at each other, so we didn't hear Bill Logan until he was up on us.

"Thought I heard yelling. Was hoping you were giving Florrie what for. Didn't realize I was interrupting the buildup to a prize match."

Flanagan and I took a step back from each other. My fists were clenched. I'd come closer to belting my oldest friend than I ever had before, but I should of known better. It was one of the things we never saw eye to eye on, and it'd only been worse since I got back from the war.

"A minor disagreement," I said, trying to calm down. "Mrs. Ludgate has flown the coop."

"Hopefully not for good. We still ain't seen a penny on this pool dig. The crew and I are getting ready to go on strike until we get an installment."

Flanagan stepped in. "You know anything about a couple of kids living here? A boy, teenager, and a little girl, about six or seven? You must have seen them around the place."

"Kids? No way. It's always been just Horrie and Florrie enjoying the joint as far as I could tell. Though there is that nursery I was telling Mr. Malhaven about. Are you trying to tell me there's kids living in there?"

"That's what we're hoping to figure out. According to Mrs. Ludgate, she and her husband have been taking care of Henry and Henrietta Hasselwhite, brother and sister, and heirs to this palatial estate. You sure you never seen them?"

"Nope. Think I'd of noticed a couple of kids. But as I said, the Ludgates are real secretive. They keep rooms locked up when we're in the house. We're only allowed in the part we're working on at the moment. Seems weird all around, but then everything seems weird here. The Ludgates always gave me the heebie-jeebies and I've about had it. I put up with it while we were getting paid, but I think it's time to pull my crew out and find other work. I don't want to be mixed up in anything that's got the cops making regular visits."

"Before you go, you got any access to the house?" Flanagan asked. "Nothing official. We wouldn't mind a looksee while the woman of the house is off to Chicago for the day."

"I got tools. I could get you in, but you gotta promise she won't know about it. Horrie didn't bother me. He was all bluster. But something about that woman makes me not want to get on her bad side."

"We won't tell her you let us in if you don't mention we were in," I said.

"Come on then, we better hurry before I get smart and change my mind."

CHAPTER THIRTY-FIVE

*L*ogan led us around to a side door and used a screwdriver to jimmy the lock open.

"That's as much as I'll do," he said, turning to leave. "I'd rather not know anything else. I'm gonna go talk to my crew, see how they feel about packing up this job before anything hits the fan and splashes on us. Good luck to you."

We gave Logan the nod and entered the house. It was cool, dark, and quiet inside. We both made a point of not adding to the noise since we didn't know what or who we might happen across.

"In and out," Joey whispered to me. "And God help us if we find anything, and I have to explain what we were doing in here to begin with."

"Let's split up. You take the upstairs and I'll look around down here."

"Good idea. Make it quick and meet back here."

We continued down the hall until we came to a lobby where the front doors of the house were at. Joey made his way up a fancy-looking staircase, and I started a methodical look into all the rooms on the first floor. Not a lot to see in most of them. I would have been impressed once upon a time, but there wasn't much that was any fancier than what was in the Wynter mansion, except a lot of the furnishings looked newer, less old-fashioned. I guess the Ludgates had been splurging out not only on construction but on keeping the interior decorating up to date with the latest magazine spreads.

I was poking around in the kitchen, looking through a well-filled pantry when I found the only interesting item. A feather, same as the ones we'd found out at the orphanage. It was a good-sized pantry, the walls lined with shelving and stocked up with plenty of dry goods of every variety. Didn't look like the Ludgates stinted on food either. I wondered if our angel had dropped the feather there while rooting around for something to eat.

I decided to meet back up with Joey, hoping he had run into Hank upstairs. Florrie had made no bones about him living there, so he had to be somewhere. Wandered back to our rendezvous point to find Joey waiting for me, looking nervous.

"Find anything?" he asked.

"Only this," I said, showing him the feather.

"Another feather. All that tells us is maybe the boy has been here, but the Ludgate woman already confirmed that, so where does it get us?"

"For one thing, makes me wonder where he is now. I'm assuming since you're back down here that you didn't run across him upstairs?"

"No, all the doors were unlocked. I poked my head in everywhere. Even took a quick look up in the attic. Nothing much to be seen. Bedrooms, that playroom Logan mentioned. All neat and tidy."

"That's weird in itself. If there's a teenage boy living here, you'd expect to find a messy room somewhere if he's anything like we were at that age. And where is he now? He wasn't with Florrie."

"She said she wasn't keeping him a prisoner. Maybe he's out enjoying the fresh air somewhere? He's paid plenty of visits to the orphanage. Not as though he's being kept under lock and key exactly."

"Most of those have been at night or early morning. As if he wasn't supposed to be out. I'd sure feel better if we could've found him and talked to him. I have an uneasy feeling about the whole deal."

"An uneasy feeling don't amount to a whole lotta beans, Jimmy.

Let's get out of here. I'm breaking a dozen different laws by coming in here with you, and I'd just as soon keep my job until I hit retirement. This kind of thing is all well and good for you. You got a rich widow to fall back on if things go south."

I gave him a sour look. He knew I didn't appreciate him needling me about how much money Victoria had in the bank compared to my own pitiful account.

We stepped outside to find Logan and his crew had packed up and left. Guess they'd decided the work wasn't worth it the way things were going. I spied the concrete bomb shelter jutting out from the house. The steel bar guarding it was firmly in place secured by two wicked-looking padlocks. Even if we could have found the right kind of tools around to bust it all open, there was no way of doing it without leaving evidence we'd been there.

"Sure wish we knew what they were keeping down there," I said. "Don't you think it's suspicious the way it's all locked up nice and tight?"

Joey picked up a rock and pounded it on the steel door. We listened but heard nothing. He shrugged. "What can we do? Suspicions ain't evidence. Bring me something I can take to the judge, and for you, I'll see what kind of strings I can pull, but I'd be laughed out of his office with all we got to show for it now," he added, holding up the feather. "Feathers and angels ain't gonna cut it."

I followed him back to the car, frustrated, every instinct telling me we needed to get into that bunker and look around, but I didn't want to get Joey in trouble. He had a wife and a pension to worry about. Better to try and come back on my own after dark maybe. See if I could break in without making too much noise and waking up Florrie.

When Joey dropped me off at the newspaper, it wasn't yet lunchtime. For lack of a better idea, I popped down to the basement to see if Q had had any more luck. Make sure his feathers weren't too ruffled from meeting up with Flanagan again. He hadn't said for sure he was coming back to the paper for good, and I didn't want him disappearing on me again. Not only was he a top-notch researcher, he was a good guy and I'd miss him if he took off for greener pastures.

Not that I could blame him. He was right about there not being much opportunity at the paper for someone like him. I wondered if I could talk to Morty about giving him a try as a reporter. The other guys would probably give him a hard time, but if Carsworth put his weight behind the decision, they'd have to lump it.

Maybe that would be the smart way to go about it. Carsworth prided himself on his progressive views. I wondered if Q or his ma could put a word in his ear about it. Pleased with myself for having such a bright idea, I stepped off the elevator and headed to the morgue where I could hear raised voices. Stuck my head in to find quite the party assembled.

"What? Did I miss the invite?" I said.

Q, Marlene, Sam Leonard, and Sister Honoria all turned to gawk at me.

"There you are, Mr. Malhaven," Honoria said. "You're the guest of honor as it happens. Sam came by the orphanage to see if we'd heard anything else about the Ludgates or Lily. Marlene suggested we stop by the paper to check with you."

"I filled them in on what little we've found out so far," Q added.

"Little is right," I said. "And I'm not much better off yet, although there have been a few developments."

I filled them in on my meeting with Hank at the cemetery, Lily's story, and Flanagan's and my visit to the Hasselwhite place, including Florrie's claim to have documents proving her guardianship over the children.

Sam spoke right up at the mention of documents. "More forgeries, I bet! It must have been Horace's doing. He was obviously a master at it. Those ledgers he produced were works of art in their way."

"He should have put his talents to better use than framing an innocent man for theft," Marlene said, all indignant on Sam's behalf. He took her arm and gave it a squeeze, a gesture that was lost on none of us, but we all politely ignored it.

Sister Honoria turned to me. "I'm afraid we may find these guardianship documents are also very convincing. I certainly don't have a good feeling about turning Lily over to that woman. I've only met her once, but that was enough, may the Lord forgive me for harboring such an uncharitable thought."

"I got a feeling the good Lord might agree with you, Sister, but will a judge? That's the question. Unless we can prove Ludgate was some kind of criminal mastermind, they're not just gonna take our word for it." I pulled my fedora down off my head and wrestled with it a minute to help me think.

"I might have a lead," Q said.

"That'd be a big help right about now. I feel like we're hitting dead ends and running out of time. Mrs. Ludgate meant business with the lawyering. If she gets a judge to rule in her favor, we might not have a choice but to turn Lily over to her. If she is a Hasselwhite, she belongs out at the Hall with her brother."

Marlene objected. "But it was her brother who was trying to save her from whatever is happening out there. We can't turn her back over and go on about our business as if nothing ever happened. You wouldn't allow it, would you, Sister?"

"I might have very little say, I'm afraid. I answer to the Board. I'm already having enough trouble convincing them to hire Sam back on. If we can prove the Ludgates are involved in something criminal, we could solve both problems. That may be the only way to save Lily, help her brother, and clear Sam's name, but we still know hardly anything about them, so what can we do?"

"I think they might be Nazis. Would that help?"

CHAPTER THIRTY-SIX

This time it was Q's turn to be the center of attention as we all stared at him. In our excitement, we'd forgotten he said he had a lead, but this was hardly the one any of us were expecting.

"Pardon?" Sister Honoria asked Q, quite calmly, I thought.

"I was able to find a photo of the Ludgates taken at the time of Mr. Hasselwhite's death. It wasn't used for the story, but the print was still in the back files. I wired it to my contact in New York along with the photos of the Nazi coin found on Miss White."

"What coin? We were told when the police brought her to us that she was found with nothing but the clothes she had on. What would she have been doing with such a thing?"

"That's what the cops wondered," I said, "so they kept it out of the papers in case it led to someone, but they couldn't ever link it up to anything useful."

Q continued. "My contact in New York had a hunch and showed the pictures to a friend of his who is a member of a group hunting down Nazis who are on the run since the war. They think Mrs. Ludgate could be a female guard from one of the camps who they've been trying to track down. A Greta Hausner married to Volker Ludwig who also worked for the Reich. They had gotten word that the pair might have bribed their way onto a military transport to the States. That would match up with what we know of how the Ludgates arrived here."

"They recognized them from a photo?" Marlene asked.

"This group spends hours combing over photos and talking to survivors, making notes about facial features, height, weight, hair color. Anything that might help identify war criminals."

"I gotta admit the widow is distinctive-looking with that unusual schnoz of hers, but she's a tiny thing. I can't imagine her keeping guard over anything," I said.

"All the guards were armed," Sam chimed in. "It doesn't matter how big you are if you have a gun, the people you are guarding have none, and you have no conscience about using it on unarmed innocents. Prisoners were shot out of hand for the slightest infractions or for none at all. Just for sport. So we've heard."

Remembering Sam and his sister had lost their family to that madness, I was more than willing to take him at his word. I imagined he knew more about it than he wanted to. Even I had heard stories, though my corner of the war was far away from what was happening in Europe.

"But when they talk, they sound as American as me or you. Wouldn't they have accents if they were Germans?" I asked.

"Not necessarily," Q replied. "Many Germans are highly-educated and learn to speak excellent English. And they've had years to perfect it and try to blend in as much as possible. I checked and Mr. Hasselwhite wasn't in the army. He had an exemption for a previous back injury and was in America throughout the war. But if the Ludgates came from Nazi-occupied territory, it might explain how the coin ended up in the Hasselwhite house and from there, with the girl."

"You'd think they would be more careful than to be carrying something as incriminating as that with them when they came to the States," Sister Honoria said.

"I dunno," I said. "If they bribed someone to get over here, they probably weren't too worried about being searched or questioned. If you have enough money, you can get a blind eye turned to most anything. Maybe they wanted a memento of the good old days back in the Fatherland before everything went to hell."

"If they are Nazis, they deserve to be hunted down like dogs and shot dead in the streets as so many of my people were." Sam's voice was low and gruff with emotion.

Q said, "A team of these Nazi hunters are on their way here now to try and confirm whether Florence Ludgate is Greta Hausner. If they can prove it, they may be able to have her arrested."

"May? Of course she must be arrested!" Sam objected.

"I've learned it's not always that simple. Since the initial war trials, interest in holding those who participated on the German side responsible has died down quite a bit. The government has moved on to the Cold War and the threat that Russia poses for nuclear war. There are rumors that some Nazis are even being protected by our government. Recruited as possible spies against the Communists or for special skills they possess that are deemed valuable. These hunters have gotten close to capturing some suspects only to have all trace of them disappear."

"Huh," I said, scratching my head. "We're getting the idea Ludgate is quite the forger. That would be a valuable skill. He could forge documents, passports for American spies. With the government telling us there's a pinko hiding under every bed ready to start the socialist revolution here in the good old U.S. of A., I guess it ain't out of the question they'd pardon some bad guys if they thought they could get something useful out of them."

"That's a terrible thing," Marlene chimed in. "We must have our own experts. Why would they overlook these crimes?"

"This Cold War and nuclear threat has everyone running scared, even the government. Makes sense they might want to hang on to every possible asset they could."

Everyone turned to give me the evil eye.

"I'm not saying it's a good thing. Only from being in the military, I saw plenty of decisions made that had more to do with survival than morality. One war may be over, but don't forget, we ain't exactly at peace either."

Sister Honoria broke the not too friendly silence that greeted what I thought was quite an astute observation.

"It is a hard thing to think that our own government would lend support to known war criminals, but in some ways, that is neither here nor there. Whether this woman was a Nazi or not, I think those of us who have met her can only agree that turning Lily back over to her is the last thing we should do."

We all gave a rousing, hear, hear, and I summed up the current crisis.

"Widow Ludgate is on her way to her lawyer right now, so we're running out of time, and I'm running out of ideas. We need to track down Henry and keep ahold of him somehow. He's old enough that a judge would have to take him seriously if he has dirt to spill on the Ludgates. Serious enough to at least postpone any guardianship hearing until an investigation was done. But how to find him? Flanagan and I didn't see any sign of him at the house."

"But there was that fallout shelter with the extra security," Q said. "Isn't it possible he is being held against his will regardless of what Mrs. Ludgate told you?"

"Sure, but then how does he get out and about at night to flit around here and there? And don't forget, it was probably him that spirited Lily out of the house. He can't exactly be both a prisoner and on the loose at the same time, can he?"

"And what about those wings," Marlene said. "What could be the explanation for those? It's very eccentric to say the least. What possible use could they be?"

"Probably just a costume," suggested Sam. "Kid stuff like those superheroes in comic books. Something to amuse his sister maybe?"

"I don't know," I said. "When I was talking to him in the cemetery, he said the feathers were for show. Something for Lily. But he made it sound as if the wings themselves were not. But what do you do with a set of wings?"

"Fly, of course."

That was the unmistakable croak of Maudie Adams, coming in to join our shindig. I introduced her around to those she didn't know and asked her what she meant.

"Just what I say. What good is having a pair of wings except to fly with? Maybe he's figured out how to flap his arms hard enough to get off the ground."

Q stifled what sounded an awful lot like a snort before observing, "I'm afraid that isn't scientifically possible. No human would have the arm strength or speed to lift themselves into the air. Birds can only do it because their bodies are so lightweight. Heavier birds with underdeveloped wings such as penguins or the ostrich cannot fly. And there are many birds like the larger birds of prey that soar rather than truly fly. They launch themselves off a high place, using their wings like airplanes to glide."

"What if Henry launched himself off a high place with these wings?" asked Sister Honoria. "We did find Lily up on the roof of the orphanage looking over the edge. What if her brother had jumped and been able to glide down to the ground? It might have given her the idea to follow him."

"I suppose it's possible if the wings were sturdy enough and made of a lightweight material. But the added weight of the feathers themselves would be a factor. It would be more likely the wings would work without those."

"He told me he was adding the feathers for Lily's sake," I said, "because she said he reminded her of an angel. Maybe he's not taking that into account. If this is all true, wonder what'll happen next time he goes to jump?"

Q looked serious. "I'm very afraid, Mr. Malhaven, that he will not survive the attempt."

CHAPTER THIRTY-SEVEN

"We should find this kid and fast before anything else happens," Sam said. "We know Mrs. Ludgate is away in Chicago. There'll never be a better opportunity to find out what's in that locked room."

"I'm afraid you are talking about breaking and entering, Mr. Leonard. Marlene and I can have no part in such a thing, even for the sake of these children. We'd better head back to the orphanage before this conversation goes any further," Sister Honoria offered, with a wink to let us know she didn't exactly disapprove even if she couldn't join in.

Their departure left me, Sam, Q, and Maudie as co-conspirators. I tried to talk the others into letting me go it alone, having skirted the law more than once or twice in my checkered career, but they were having none of it. In the end, I loaded them all up in the Champ, and we headed south out of town again.

There was no sign of Logan or his crew when we got to the Hasselwhite estate, so I gave Q a hoist up and over the gate. He's a whiz with just about everything so it didn't take him long to figure out how to fiddle with the electrical box and trigger the gates to open.

I picked up a crowbar I kept in the trunk for such occasions to see about busting into the bunker, but Q held up a hand and pulled a small brown leather pouch from his pocket. He unrolled it to reveal the neatest little set of picklocks you ever want to see. Maudie snorted and gave him a walloping slap of approval on the back that nearly knocked him off his feet. He managed to maintain his poise and went over to the padlocks on the bunker, fiddling with them a few minutes before we were in.

"Good going, Q. Now we can get in and out without leaving any sign. You're a valuable asset," I said with a grin.

He grinned back before leading the way down a set of concrete steps into a dark hallway. Sam fiddled with some switches on the wall until a string of overhead lights lit up the way for us. I'll admit I started sweating. Last time I was in an enclosed place underground, I'd had a series of shocks and setbacks that had about done me in. I wasn't such a fan of confined spaces since then, but I figured I was the brawn of the operation in case such was needed, so I held my peace and followed along reluctantly behind the other three eagerly making their way forward.

Logan wasn't kidding about it being a swell joint. Everything was finished off nice and the hallway led to a series of large rooms with all the conveniences one could want in case of nuclear fallout. Pantry stocked with canned goods, washroom, bedrooms with real furniture, even a nicely appointed living room with comfy chairs and a fully stocked library, I guess to pass the time as you waited out the aftermath.

It was strangely inviting while still being eerie as all get out to imagine being trapped underground while hell broke loose above. I almost thought I'd as soon eat it in the big one as hang around waiting to die. Quicker and cleaner.

What there wasn't down there was any sign of life. No winged boy waiting to greet us. The bunker must have run under a good portion of the house above but when we reached the end of the hallway, there was another locked door. This one meant business. Smooth edged with no gaps to fit my crowbar in to get some leverage. The lock was so tricky that even though Q spent a good half hour fiddling with it while the rest of us cooled our heels, he couldn't make any headway.

We tried banging on the door and listening for a response, but it was the same as one of those bank vault doors, solid and thick. I doubted whether anyone on the other side, if there was anyone on the other side, could hear us or vice versa.

"Awful suspicious," said Maudie. "Nobody puts up a door like that without they got something valuable to hide."

The rest of us couldn't but agree, but there didn't seem much else we could do. Between the time it had taken to drive out there and the amount of time we'd spent hanging around, I was getting nervous Florrie might pop back in and catch us in the act. Reluctantly, we agreed a strategic withdrawal was necessary.

We were all disappointed and didn't talk much on the way back to town. No matter what we tried, we couldn't seem to get anywhere. I dropped Sam by the orphanage as he wanted to start taking a look at the books to see if Horrie had been up to any hanky panky. Then I took Q and Maudie by the paper. Q promised to do more research, but we both knew we were hitting dead ends every which way we turned.

I was sitting parked at the curb making up my mind what to do next, and not having a lot of bright ideas, when a familiar red convertible pulled up beside me.

"Hello, there, my good fellow. Need a lift?"

I smiled and jumped out of the Champ and into the seat beside Victoria. "Never turn down a ride from a lovely lady. What brings you into town? And where's Lily?"

"Mr. Cressley is keeping an eye on her. She didn't have much more to say after you left this morning, and I thought best not to pressure her further for now. I want to pick out an Easter dress for her as a surprise. Something special."

"That's the ticket. And maybe we can find one of those chocolate bunnies."

"Yes! And an Easter basket. Who knows if she's ever had one before. I want to make this holiday memorable for her, no matter what happens next."

An impatient toot from behind reminded us there were other cars on the road. Victoria drove off smoothly, finding a first-class parking spot right in front of the Mimzy's department store downtown. We headed to the tearoom first as it was lunchtime and filled up on a Reuben sandwich and coffee for me and a Waldorf salad for Victoria. In between bites, I filled her in on the progress, or lack thereof, since I'd last seen her.

"It's maddening the police can't do more to help, isn't it, Jim? It's obvious something is very wrong at the Hasselwhite place. I'm disappointed Detective Flanagan wasn't of more help."

"Joey's just playing it by the book. The bigshots are cracking down on the freewheeling ways of the past. They gotta answer to the public, and the public don't always appreciate cops being such go getters now that crime isn't as big a deal as it used to be during Prohibition days and such. The cops spend most of their time keeping an eye on these juvenile delinquents everyone's so worried about. Without a judge's approval, I don't think we'll see Flanagan and his boys out at the Hall again anytime soon."

"Then it's our responsibility to come up with hard evidence against the Ludgates. Something the police, or a judge, can't ignore. I know I may not be able to keep Lily forever, but the thought of her in the power of that woman makes me shudder. She'd be much better off back at the orphanage."

"We're on the same page there. Florrie is a strange one. Cold as ice and nerves of steel. Even if the police did bring her in for questioning, I doubt she'd let go of any secrets. Not even under torture."

"Do you think it's really possible she and her husband were Nazis? I hate to think our own government has any hand in protecting them if it's true."

"As I was saying to the rest of the gang, this situation with Russia has got everyone spooked. If the Ludgates have any information or skills to offer, I can see that outweighing any crimes they might've committed. Our war with Germany is in the rearview mirror. It's all about the Commies now."

"You make it sound very pragmatic, Jim, but think of the atrocities those people committed."

"I ain't defending it. Only saying it's possible. We'll have to figure out a way to find out more about them on our own."

"I forgot to tell you I checked in with our lawyer. By chance, his firm handled the Hasselwhite estate until shortly before Mr. Hasselwhite's death. When the Ludgates came to stay, his firm was discharged. He was told they were switching their account to a larger law firm in Chicago. He knew nothing about what had happened since then other than reading about Mr. Hasselwhite's death in the papers. I got the impression he was still rather miffed to have lost such a big account."

"I bet. There's obviously money to burn the way they've been adding on to the place. Not bad pickings for a lawyer."

"Yes. He did say the Ludgates were old friends of the Hasselwhites and had been offered the job of caretakers as a favor to them. He only met them once but did not have a high opinion of them. When I told him we were suspicious of irregularities, he said he couldn't possibly speculate but wouldn't be surprised."

"He ain't the only one," I said, throwing my napkin on the table and grabbing the bill before Victoria could pay it. I might not be able to afford to take her to the finest place in town, but I could cover lunch at the local department store.

We split up after to make better time, me heading for the candy department to pick out an Easter basket. Victoria headed upstairs to the children's section where she made short work of picking out a cute little sky-blue dress covered all over with frills for Lily.

She dropped me by my car, and I followed her home, not having any better idea than to maybe quiz Lily some more about anything she could tell us about her brother or the Ludgates, but we were in for another surprise when we got there.

We pulled up to the house to find Livinia sitting on the front steps with Cressley laid out like a corpse, head in her lap.

Victoria jumped out of her car double-quick, and I wasn't far behind.

"What happened?" I asked.

"And where's Lily?" was Victoria's question.

Livinia said nothing, looking grim even by her usual standards. She handed us a sheet of paper with a scrawl that looked nothing like Cressley's normally elegant penmanship. Given his condition, I guess we could overlook that. You could make out the words fine all the same:

She's gone.

CHAPTER THIRTY-EIGHT

Victoria gave a cry and knelt down by Cressley. I could see he had a bump the size of a ping pong ball rising from the side of his head under the sparse gray hairs there, but his eyes were open and looked clear enough. He struggled to get up, but Livinia had him in a death grip. She didn't often show it, but I think she actually loved that guy.

"Don't be absurd, Cornelius. You must lie still until we can get you medical assistance," Livinia said before turning to us. "I was in the rose garden and heard some sort of commotion. I came around and found Mr. Cressley in this condition. He wrote me this note from which I assume he means to tell us that Lily has run off."

Cressley started shaking his head "no," then thought better of it as he groaned and closed his eyes. Guess it didn't do his noggin any good to be jostling it around.

"Not run off," Victoria said. "Taken?"

Cressley held up a thumb to indicate she was right on the money with that guess.

"Who was it?" I asked. "The Ludgate woman?"

He shrugged and pointed to his head.

"You didn't see? They knocked you out?"

Another thumbs up, then agitated pointing at the driveway.

"He's been doing that since I found him," Livinia sniffed. "I'm not sure what he's trying to tell me. If someone did take the girl, then obviously they drove off down the drive, but they'll be long gone by now."

Cressley looked discouraged and then cupped a hand around one ear.

"What on earth does that mean?" Livinia said crossly.

"Shhh," Victoria said. "Listen."

We all shut our traps and obeyed. I didn't hear anything at first, but then it came, soft and unearthly.

"*Me-oooooowwwww.*"

Victoria and I looked at each other and both said what was on our minds, "Archie!"

I jumped up and followed the sound only to find the poor fellow stretched out in the ditch that ran along the gravel drive. One of his front legs was at such an awkward angle I was afraid to touch him. Victoria came up and gave a gasp, then ran back to the house. In a few minutes, she was back with a soft towel which she used to gently wrap our fallen friend and started barking out orders I was glad to follow.

"Jim, help Mr. Cressley to my car. I'll carry Archie. We'll drop Livinia and Mr. Cressley at the hospital, and Archie off at the veterinarian's then drive on to the police station. Surely, Detective Flanagan will have to take us seriously now."

With Victoria taking charge, we were sorted out quick and on our way. Livinia sat in the backseat supporting Mr. Cressley while Victoria held Archie on her lap, softly crooning to the frightened animal. Victoria's Caddy was a fast ride, so it didn't take long with me breaking most of the traffic laws on the way to get into town and drop off our patients.

Then it was on to the precinct house where a harassed-looking Flanagan appeared after being paged by the desk sergeant.

"What can I help you with this time, Jimmy boy? Trouble with unicorns? Or maybe you seen a stray leprechaun?"

"How about a missing child," Victoria said, with enough tartness in her tone to take even Flanagan aback. "Is that something you can help us with? Or do I need to go directly to your superior officer?"

"Now, now, let's calm down, Mrs. J. Didn't see you there at first. Thought it was just more of Jimmy's tricks. Of course we can help you. This is Lily we're talking about I'm guessing. Where's she gone to?"

"Are you serious? If we knew that, we wouldn't be here, would we?" Victoria asked, still fuming. It takes a lot to rile her up but when she is, everyone needs to stand back.

I thought about stepping in to help my buddy out, but on second thought, figured it might light a fire under him to let Victoria handle it. It was easier to brush off an old pal than a member of the Wynter family. It made the Police Commissioner and Mayor nervous when taxpayers with money and influence got worked up.

"Er, no, that's a good point, Mrs. J. Why don't we have a seat, and you can tell me all about it?"

"We don't have time for that. Who knows what danger that child is in? You need to get a warrant and go with us out to Hasselwhite Hall. There's only one person with an interest in taking Lily, and we also suspect she is keeping another child prisoner. If that isn't reason to act, what is?"

"You're talking about the Ludgate widow. Any witnesses?"

I put my two cents in. "Cressley, but to be fair he got bopped on the head good and didn't see exactly who done it, but who else would it be?"

"You know, Jimmy, kids get snatched up from time to time. Especially girls that age. There's all kind of perverts running around out there. How do we know it isn't something like that? We could be wasting time barking up the wrong tree while he gets away with her."

Victoria looked taken aback, probably remembering a similar situation that had happened over in the neighboring town of Farrelton a year or two back. They never found the girl in that case.

But I wasn't having it. "Joey, you trying to tell me with all the trouble that's been following this girl around. All the mystery around the Ludgates and the Hasselwhite place, a random bad guy happens by the cemetery and targets her as well? That's pushing bad luck to an extreme, ain't it? It's a thousand times more likely that this is exactly what it seems. Florrie got tired of waiting around for us to give Lily up or for the lawyers to start fighting it out and took matters into her own hands. I hadn't been able to fill you in yet, but we got reason to believe she was a Nazi prison guard. You seen for yourself she's hard as nails. I wouldn't put anything past her."

"Nazi, huh? Same as the coin? That would be something, for sure, but she's still taking an awful risk. So far, we got nothing concrete on her or the hubby, but kidnapping is a whole other ball of wax. They still get the chair in this state for it. Why would she bother if she was so confident she'd got the law on her side?"

"Maybe with Ludgate's death and us poking our nose in, she feels time is running down on her. Lily is a witness. I hate to say it, but maybe Florrie is tying up loose ends before she disappears."

"Oh, Jim. If that's so, we must find her now. Every minute we delay could be disastrous."

"I know, honey. Don't worry. I'm going out there with or without backup, and I ain't quitting until we find out where those kids are."

Joey snorted. "What are you? A one-man army? Don't be a fool. If this woman is desperate and an ex-Nazi, she won't think twice about offing you if you go running out there like a chicken with its head cut off. Best thing you two can do is go home in case this is all a misunderstanding and Lily shows back up. I'll call the D.A. and we'll make a case to a judge. It won't take more than a few hours, and then we can take the whole squad out there and do a proper search."

"But—" Victoria started to protest, but I squeezed her hand softly with my own. We're often on the same page, so it didn't take more than that for her to get my message. "Of course, you're right. I apologize. I'm just upset, naturally. But we'll leave it all in your capable hands, won't we, Jim?"

"Absolutely. My boy Flanagan here has never let me down yet," I agreed with a heavy punch to Joey's shoulder that made him wince. "Let's go check on poor Mr. Cressley and don't forget Archie, too. He's a cat," I added for Flanagan's benefit. "Got caught up in the action somehow. He's a good cat, too. We mustn't forget Archie."

Flanagan gave us both the fisheye as if he suspected this sudden change of heart, but what was he gonna do? He couldn't detain us on suspicion of taking the law into our own hands, could he? Victoria hooked her arm through mine, gave Joey a cheery wave, and dragged me out the door. On the steps she turned to me with a raised eyebrow, not even needing to ask the question.

"Oh, yeah, we're gonna raise a little army of our own and go see what's what. If we're fast enough, old Florrie won't even know what hit her."

CHAPTER THIRTY-NINE

We swung by the paper first and picked up Q. At his suggestion, we invited Maudie along, too, figuring she might come in handy, being a tough old bird. She looked thrilled to bits to be part of a real live rescue attempt. Next, we stopped by the orphanage and made short work of explaining our mission to Sister Honoria.

Appreciating the seriousness of the situation right off, she wasn't so reluctant to get involved this time around. She promised to gather up Sam, Marlene, and those linebackers, Martha and Bertha, for extra assistance. The orphanage had a bus they used to take the kids around for treats. It wasn't fast, but it would get them out there hopefully in time to be of help.

We decided not to wait around but go on ahead as a scouting party, with the orphanage squad to follow as second team coverage. Victoria's a mean driver herself and her Caddy made short work of the miles. We were back out at the Hasselwhite place in no time. We'd discussed a few different strategies on the drive and had hit upon me hoisting Q over the wall and letting him check out the garage to see if the Buick was parked inside. That would at least tell us whether Florrie was back on the premises or not.

While Q was on reconnaissance duty, we waited in the car down the road from the gates so as not to call too much attention to ourselves, not that the red Caddy was exactly inconspicuous. Victoria was impatient to do a frontal assault, but I was worried about spooking Florrie into some kind of action we'd all regret. Maudie passed the time by filing her nails, the sound of the emery board scritch-scratching driving me batty enough that it was more than a relief to see the gates rolling open. Q poked his head out to wave us in, letting us know the Buick was nowhere to be seen.

Victoria parked in an out of the way spot behind the garage so as to give us the element of surprise if Florrie returned. Then we decided to split up. First, Q picked the lock on the side door, letting me and Victoria in to search the main house proper. He and Maudie continued around to the bunker to see if they could find anything more there than we had during our last visit.

Me and Victoria made quick work of the ground floor then headed up the grand staircase to the rabbit warren of rooms on the second. The doors were mostly standing open and none were locked. Every room we looked into was neat and tidy except for the last, a large bedroom with a view overlooking the back gardens and the hole in the ground where Bill Logan and his crew had started the swimming pool.

This room was a mess. Clothes thrown every which way, suitcases standing open half-packed, toiletries knocked over and spilled making a mess of the fancy antique vanity standing along one wall. There was also an old-fashioned rolltop desk with papers cascading across the top and onto the floor.

"Someone was in a hurry," remarked Victoria.

"I think Florrie's got the wind up and decided to make a quick getaway. Maybe it was taking too long to pack up, and she took what she could carry fast. We may not see her out here again after all."

"Oh, Jim, don't say that. If she doesn't come back here, how will we ever find her and Lily? She could be anywhere by now if she drove away from the cemetery and headed out of town."

"She knows the police will be able to look up the make and model of her car and the registration number. If she's smart, she's headed for the train station or even an airport to switch to faster transportation. There's a regional airport between here and Chicago. No commercial flights, but lots of small planes going in and out all the time. If she had enough money, hiring a pilot to take her across the country or even down to Mexico would be a snap."

"Maybe we should split up when the others get here. Half of us go to the train station and half to the airport?"

"Maybe, but let's take another quick look around to make sure we aren't missing anything. I don't think she's coming back. Why don't you stay up here and have a look through these papers and see if there's any clues there. I'll take another pass downstairs."

We agreed to meet up in the kitchen after our investigations. I poked in and out of the rooms on the first floor again, but everything was neat and tidy until I got to the pantry off the kitchen. Another mess, canned goods knocked off the shelves, dried goods smashed and spread across the floor. I was trying to figure out whether Florrie had been gathering supplies for a journey when I heard a commotion outside. Sounded like shouting.

I ran to the front door and undid the deadbolt, flinging it open to find two groups of angry visitors having it out on the front lawn. The first was our backup team, Honoria, Bertha and Martha, Marlene and Sam. They had piled out of the rusted old bus that was the best the orphanage could afford. They were confronting Bill Logan who had pulled up in his Chevy pickup truck. I hastened down the steps to keep the peace.

"The gang's all here," I said, holding out a conciliatory hand for Logan to shake. "How do, Bill? Thought you guys were all washed up out this way?"

"We are. I came by to gather the last of our supplies. We left lumber and blasting supplies out back that we can use on another job. Since we ain't been paid diddly squat for the pool, I figure I'm owed at least that much. But I got more right to be here than this crew. What's going on anyhow?"

"Spur of the moment search party. We got a missing girl and maybe a boy, too, and plenty of reason to suspect they might have been held here against their will. The cops are busy filling out paperwork and rounding up a judge, so we decided to do a little private investigation of our own. Make a citizen's arrest if need be."

"You don't say. Guess I'm not surprised. Those Ludgates were some creepy customers. It's none of my business what you do. I don't want no trouble. I'll take my stuff and leave you to it," he added, disappearing around the back of the house.

I was filling the rest of the folks in on our lack of progress so far when Victoria came down the steps with a legal pad in her hand.

"Look, Jim, these are notes about pilots for hire at the airport you were talking about. She might be planning a flight after all, don't you think?"

I took the pad and looked over the list, headed with the name of the airport and phone number. Sure looked like she was investigating a plane ride as the best alternative for making herself scarce in a hurry.

"This might be our best lead unless Q and Maudie found anything down below."

"Not a chance, Jimmy," Maudie croaked from behind me. She and Q had appeared while we were studying the list. They looked discouraged. "We searched the place thorough. There ain't nothing down there that's any help unless we could get behind that locked door. Stands to reason something back there must be valuable or why all the trouble to keep it in a bank vault?"

"I believe Miss Adams is right," said Q. "I tried again with every trick I know, but I can't get the lock to budge. There appears to be no way for us to find out what they are hiding back there."

"Did you try the secret door?" This tidbit was from Bill Logan, trudging back to his truck with a load of supplies.

We pretty much all bust out with a "Secret door?" at the same time then stood there with our mouths hung open.

He laughed at the sight. I think he was tickled with the reaction he got.

"Sure. Follow me."

We trooped along after him into the house and through the kitchen to the pantry. He shoved aside the mess on the floor and pulled on a couple of pieces of shelving, kind of like a puzzle, then stood back with a grin on his face as he tapped the back wall of the pantry.

We watched in amazement as the whole wall swiveled in, revealing a secret passage

Bill grinned at us. "Just like the movies, ain't it? Abracadabra, boys and girls!"

CHAPTER FORTY

*L*ogan was pretty pleased with his parlor trick. I was at the front of the crowd and peered in to see a set of steps leading down to the basement. Now that feather I'd found in the pantry when Flanagan and I were searching the house made more sense. Maybe Hank had been using the secret door to get in and out of the bunker. But then if Florrie was keeping him prisoner, that didn't add up either.

"Florrie knew about this, didn't she?" I asked.

"Of course. It was her idea. She wanted a way to go and come from the house as well as outside. I guess she figured if the bombs started dropping, they should have more than one way to get in and out."

"So, this side ain't locked up like the outside?"

"No, you should be able to get into the safe room from here."

"Safe room?"

"That's what the Ludgates called it when they showed me the sketch they'd drawn up. It was meant to be a secure room against any invaders. They were pretty sure we were in for a full-scale Commie invasion. Kind of an obsession with them. I personally don't see it. We showed old Hitler and Tojo what was what, didn't we? Don't guess we can't show mean Joe Stalin a thing or two if he gets too big for his britches."

Not wanting to get sidetracked into a discussion of world affairs when we had a little girl to rescue, I just gave him a nod and ventured down the stairs followed by the rest of the crew. The rooms here were more utilitarian than the living quarters on the other side. The first one we looked into was stacked full of boxes.

I dragged the nearest one down and ripped open the top to find another swastika staring me in the face. Pulled out the full uniform that went with it and showed it to the others crowded into the narrow hallway behind me.

"Nazis!" cried Sam. "Those scum. Living here in luxury after what happened to my family."

"Looks like it," I agreed. "Guess they held on to some mementos. Maybe they expected a Fourth Reich to come along soon and they wanted to be ready to suit up."

"This is shocking, but it doesn't help us to find Lily. We should stay focused on that," Sister Honoria reminded us. "This woman may be ruthless. Lily could be running out of time."

"If it isn't already too late," Victoria added softly. Honoria reached over to give her a hug, both women's eyes filling with tears.

"Right you are, Sister," I said. "Let's take a quick look around in case there's anything else here that can help us."

The first thing we found of interest was a room with a printing press and sophisticated-looking stamps and other gear.

"This is a good setup for forgeries," said Sam, rifling through the papers on one of the tables. "With this equipment, you could forge passports, documents. Anything you need."

Marlene gasped and picked up some small photographs. "Look, photos of Lily."

Sam grabbed them. "Right size for a passport photo. Maybe she's planning on taking Lily with her after all. Use her as a bargaining chip if we get too close?"

"That would be good news," I said. "As long as Lily has some value to her, she won't harm her."

Martha and Bertha had wandered off down the hall and came back to report another locked door at the end of it. Bill Logan and I went to investigate.

"That's funny. This wasn't here before, and we didn't install it. Looks the same as the heavy-duty door we put on the other side. They must have gotten someone else to put it in though. I didn't know anything about it."

"Makes sense they'd want both ends secure. Maybe they didn't want you to know all their plans. Didn't want to put all their eggs in one basket. Don't suppose you happen to know where they kept the keys to these things?"

"As far as I know, they always kept the keys on them. Horrie and Florrie each had a set. I guess the police might have his now unless they turned his effects back over to his widow."

"Can't you work some magic and help us get in there? We still don't know what's happened to the boy. I hate to think he's trapped in there while we're out looking for his sister."

Logan leaned over and took a good look at the lock. "If it's the same as the door we put in on the other side, you'd need a master locksmith to get this open. They're designed to be unpickable. You'd be better off trying to blast it," he said with a chuckle.

"Say, how about that? Didn't you say you got blasting materials you're picking up?"

"Wait a minute, buddy. That dynamite we got is heavy duty. It's for blasting rocks. One stick would bring this whole house down on our heads."

"Maybe we could modify it." This was Q who had walked up on us and overheard our conversation. "Could you take it apart so we could use a small amount of explosive to blast out the locks?"

"That's tricky business, son. And dangerous. One wrong move and you could find yourself singing in that heavenly choir."

"I've studied the properties and science of dynamite. I think I could do it, Mr. Malhaven."

"I dunno, Q. Sounds risky. We can't afford to lose you. We better wait until Flanagan and his gang arrive. Maybe they still got the key Horrie had."

"You said yourself the boy may be in there. Maybe he's in trouble or hurt. I do know what I'm doing."

Logan butted in. "How did you come to know so much about it? You planning on blowing up city hall or something?"

"No, I took a lot of science courses in college."

"College? Are you kidding me?"

Q started to bristle before Logan added, "Gee, I always wanted to go to college, but we didn't have the money for it. I had to quit school and go to work. I can't complain. I done alright, but there's lots of things I'd love to know more about. I guess if you're confident about it, I can help you out with this explosion gag. I've got lots of experience with it. With your book learning, if we put our heads together, we can probably figure something out."

"I still don't like the sound of it," I said.

"I don't guess you're the boss of us, are you?" Logan said with a grin. "Just tell my wife I love her if I go up in a puff of smoke."

Victoria came up. "Jim, I really think some of us should go to the airport in case Mrs. Ludgate is trying to get away. Aren't we wasting time here?"

I looked at Logan and Q. They looked determined, and they were right, I wasn't their boss.

"Guess I can't stop you trying but for the love of God be careful, won't you? You won't do the boy any good if you blow him and you two up both."

"Don't worry, Mr. Malhaven. Trust me."

"I trust you, Q. I just don't trust explosives."

We all trooped back upstairs. Q and Logan went off to start their experiments far away from the house. I crossed my fingers they knew what they were doing.

Victoria jumped in the driver's seat of her Caddy, and I took shotgun. Sam and Maudie filled out the back seat. We decided to leave the nuns behind to keep an eye out in case Florrie decided to show back up after all, and also in case our scientists accidentally blew themselves up. At least they could pray over the remains. Marlene stayed behind in case she could patch them back together.

The mood in the car was tense on the way to the airport. It was about forty-five minutes out of town. Victoria broke the speed limits but luckily, we didn't attract any attention of the police persuasion.

The airport wasn't big enough for a flight tower. Just a couple of hangers and one long runway for takeoff and landing. There didn't look to be a lot of activity, but one of the hanger doors was standing open, so we headed that way. First thing we saw was a shiny black Buick parked outside the hanger. The next was a very blonde set of pigtails. Lily, and she wasn't alone. Florrie was standing next to her with one claw grasping the girl's shoulder. The other claw was doing something even more sinister. Holding a gun pointed at Lily's head.

CHAPTER FORTY-ONE

The Widow Ludgate wasn't much taller than Lily herself, but with that gun, she didn't need to be to have the upper hand of us. We jumped out of the car, but Florrie was no fool. Instead of waving the gun around at us, she kept it pointed at Lily. That brought us all up to a halt.

"Don't come any closer. Get back in the car and drive away now if you value her life."

Victoria called out, "Please let her go. We won't interfere, but why take her with you? She'll only be a burden to you."

"It never hurts to have an insurance policy, and I don't plan on giving this one up. I'll ask you one more time to turn around, get back in the car, and leave."

I piped up then. "You know we can't do that. Not while the girl's in danger. You can't take all of us on, you know."

"I don't have to. One bullet in this child's brain. That's all it takes. I've done the same many times before, so don't underestimate me."

That got Sam riled up good. "How many innocent lives have you taken? Do you think we will just let you fly away, Nazi? You must stay and face the consequences for your crimes."

"You don't know what you're talking about. My husband and I are under the protection of your own government. We've performed many valuable services for them."

"If that's true," Victoria said. "Why are you rushing off?"

"Things have come to a head here, and I have no wish to be relocated again. I prefer to live life under my own terms from now on. My husband always advised caution, chose not to continue our great cause, content to wallow in luxury, while so many of our compatriots suffered and died, but I have never stopped believing. There are more of us around than you might think. Some of our greatest leaders still live and have need of allies to resume the fight. Our Führer would expect no less from us."

"In case you ain't noticed," I said. "The war is long over, and your guys lost it, big time."

"The war will never be over until all impurities," she spit out, with a mean look over to where Marlene and Sam were standing close together, "are cleansed, and the great Aryan race is acknowledged as the natural rulers of all others. This child here is of pure blood and will be one of many who will join the fight."

"What about her brother? I don't see him around."

"He was weak and imperfect. Like his mother. The new world order demands strength and discipline."

"So, where are they at then?"

"Do you expect me to stand here and tell you all my secrets? I'm not a tinpot villain in a bad dime novel. I'll leave the rest to your no doubt adequate investigatory skills. I have neither the time nor inclination to tell you my entire life story."

"What are you hanging around for then? You got things to do, places to be. What's the hold up?"

She pointed over to a wizened old man with a scraggly white beard and coveralls who had appeared from behind the Cessna parked in the hanger. "The pilot is making a few last-minute repairs. He has promised me it won't take long, and then we'll be on our way. There is really no point to you staying here any longer. I will not give up the girl, and you will not risk her life by attempting to stop me."

"The old stalemate, huh? Hey, bub," I called over to the pilot. "You might want to think twice about helping this lady out."

He wiped his hands on a greasy rag and walked over to our get-together.

"What's the hullabaloo? When I said I'd run you down across the border, you told me you were going on holiday with your daughter. Who's the rest of this crowd?"

"People with nothing better to do than harass a poor widow, I suppose," she sniffed.

"Poor widow?" Victoria snorted. "This woman is kidnapping a child. Do you want to be an accessory to kidnapping? There are heavy penalties for being involved in such a crime."

The old guy held his hands up and started backing away. "Now wait a dang minute. I don't know nothing 'bout that. This lady said she'd pay me to fly her and her daughter down to Mexico."

"Why do you think she is holding a gun to the child's head, man?" asked Maudie. "That ain't the act of a loving mother, is it?"

"Well," he said, rubbing his beard with one hand as if he was having the first deep thought he'd ever had in his life. "That does seem a might peculiar now you mention it."

Florrie was having none of that. "It is immaterial to you whether it is peculiar or not. I am paying you triple the going rate and you know it. It's more money than you'll ever see again in your lifetime. If I were you, I wouldn't trouble about anything else."

"That's true. It is a lot of money, and I sure could use it. But what about that little girl? Is she your daughter or ain't she?"

"Again, I would advise you not to worry about anything other than the rather large sum of money you've been promised."

"Promised is the word, ain't it? Ain't seen any yet. How do I know you even got that much cash on you?"

"It's in my suitcase. I'll be happy to show it to you when we get on the plane to take off."

"About that. These repairs were kind of tricky, but I think I got it more or less put to rights."

"More or less? That does not inspire confidence."

"Maybe the big fellow there can help me push the plane outside. I'll need to start up the engines, and make sure I didn't miss nothing."

"Fine, but only after we are on board."

"I can't say as I'd recommend it. If I did miss something, the engine could catch on fire. Could be hairy getting everybody off in time. But it's up to you."

Florrie stared hard at the pilot. I have to say he looked pretty innocent and concerned.

"Very well, but no funny business."

"Lady, I ain't got a funny bone in my body." He gestured to me, and I went over and helped him push the small plane out toward the runway.

I suspected something was up when he gave me the wink with one squinty eye. He jumped in the cockpit and revved the engine. It roared to life causing the propeller to start up. I ducked away to get out of the danger zone and the plane was off, making short work of the taxi down the runway and liftoff. I walked back over to the group to find the widow as red in the face as a pickled beet.

"You know," I offered. "I get the idea he ain't coming back. Probably would've been a good idea to have him take your suitcase off the plane before he tried it out. That's the kind of smart thinking might have occurred to someone of the master race. You must be off your game today, Florrie. Or maybe you ain't quite the genius you think you are."

Her mouth flopped open one or two times like a fish gasping for air, but I got to hand it to her, she recovered quick. She marched Lily out of the hanger and over to the Buick parked nearby without another word. I made a move toward her, and she fired off a shot in my direction without a second thought. I ducked just in time. My hat flew off my head, but I didn't have time to worry about it because right about then, I became aware of another thing flying.

It was hard to see against the bright sun that was starting to sink low in the sky, but I caught a glimpse of something. It looked an awful lot like an angel in flight.

CHAPTER FORTY-TWO

*A*bunch of things happened all at once. Florrie screeched and let out another shot, into the sky this time, aimed at the feathered apparition. Lily pulled loose from her and ran to Victoria who caught the girl and held her close. Sam and I rushed Florrie and managed to knock the gun from her hand.

She was a tiny thing when all was said and done, so it was lucky we didn't break her in two piling on, but it seemed like she survived okay. I found that out because as we were trying to get her up off the ground, she broke loose again, lunging for the gun. Maudie appeared out of nowhere and swung something at her, causing poor Florrie to go down like a sack of Idaho's best potatoes.

"What was that?" I asked.

"Lead sap," Maudie said, holding it up proudly. "Never leave home without one. It's come in handy more than once."

We all chuckled a bit in relief. Found a piece of rope to tie Florrie up and discourage her from any more escape attempts, then we all started looking around the airport and at each other.

Maudie asked the question we was all thinking. "Where did that guy go?"

"Did everyone see it?" I asked. Nods all around.

"Of course," said Sam. "It was as large as life, but where did he go?"

Victoria was making soothing noises to Lily, but the rest of us scouted around with no luck, except finding a few white feathers on the ground near the car.

"Maybe he slipped away in the confusion," Sam suggested.

"But to where?" I asked. "And why didn't he stick around once he saw we had the woman under wraps? You'd think he'd want to check on his sister now that the danger is over."

A quiet voice spoke up. "No one is supposed to see him." It was Lily, clinging to Victoria who had picked her up and brought her over to the group.

"Why, sweetheart?" Victoria asked.

"He's a secret. A secret just between me and him."

"But we want to help him, like we're helping you. Don't you want that? You could be together again."

Lily just closed her eyes and buried her face in Victoria's shoulder, refusing to say anything else. We decided the best we could do was load everyone up and head back to the mansion. Check if any progress had been made on the doors or if the cops had finally shown up. Victoria took Lily and Maudie in her car while Sam and I loaded up the unconscious Florrie in her Buick.

It was a long drive back. Florrie came around about halfway through and started kicking at the doors. I screeched to a halt, and we flung her into the trunk for safekeeping for the rest of the trip. She still made plenty of noise, but at least we knew she couldn't break out of there.

We drove up to the Hasselwhite place in time to hear a small explosion. We jumped out expecting the worse, only to find a grinning Q and Logan coming around the corner of the house. They both were a little the worse for wear with a noticeably burned patch in Q's sweater vest, but they looked like the proverbial cat that swallowed the canary.

"We figured it out, by gum. This one here's got a bright future in munitions work," Logan said, slapping Q on the back.

Q looked modestly pleased. "We were double-checking that the charge would be strong enough but not too strong before trying it on the door. We should be all set to give it a go now, Mr. Malhaven.”

The nuns and Marlene had come around to see what the commotion was. Sister Honoria crossed herself and said a prayer when she seen Lily was safe and sound. Martha and Bertha still looked sour about Lily, so I set them to work opening the trunk of the Buick and keeping our belligerent prisoner under control.

I filled everyone in on what had happened out at the airport.

“Not much point in opening those doors now, is there?” asked Logan, looking disappointed. “If the boy is out running around, may not be much to see down there.”

“I’m still curious,” I said. “Call it reporter’s intuition, but I find it hard to believe they have that much security and nothing to hide. Besides, we can’t let all your hard work go to waste.”

We decided the fewer the better underground as Q tried to open the door, so he and Logan and I went down. I couldn’t do much besides provide moral support as they fussed with the explosives around the door and ran a long fuse down the hallway so we didn’t have to be too close to the danger zone.

“Here we go,” Q said excitedly as he lit the end of the fuse. We put our fingers in our ears and ducked into one of the rooms farthest away. It seemed like forever before we finally heard the blast. It wasn’t as loud as I’d expected, and I was thinking we’d find the door hadn’t budged, but I should’ve had more faith in Q. The lock and latch were blown clear, so it was a simple matter to push the door open and step inside.

There was some dust settling from the explosion so it took a minute before we could see that we were in a continuation of the hallway with rooms on either side. We heard a coughing noise from behind one of the doors.

“The boy,” Logan said excitedly, reaching for the handle. It was locked but Q was able to pick it in half a minute flat.

What the opened door revealed was far from what we expected. A woman stood there, thin and pale. It was hard to tell her age. She looked worn and troubled, her hair a stringy mess of gray and blonde.

She wore an old dress, a style that hadn't been popular for years. She cowered back at the sight of us until Q stepped forward and took her arm.

"Don't be afraid. We're here to help you if you need it."

She cleared her throat a few times and croaked out lowly, "I do. I do. Is this a dream? Are you real?"

"Yeah," I said. "I know I may look like a nightmare, but we're the good guys. But who are you?"

"Mrs. Margaret Hasselwhite."

I whistled. "Mrs. Hasselwhite. You don't know how pleased we are to make your acquaintance. We thought maybe you were six feet under somewhere. Have the Ludgates been keeping you down here all this time?"

She went even paler than pale at the sound of that name. "Where is she? Is she coming back? Can you get me out of here before she does?"

"Don't worry, ma'am," Q hastened to reassure her. "We have Mrs. Ludgate secured. We're only waiting for the police to arrive. She can't do anything to you."

"I… I can't believe it. It's been so long… so long. I'd given up any hope. What about my children. Henry and Henrietta? Are they safe? How I've longed to see them, to hold them again."

"Henrietta's upstairs right this minute," I said, deciding to focus on the positive as we didn't know where Hank had gotten to since we last seen him at the airport.

She half-fainted at this news. I encouraged Q and Logan to help her up the stairs into the fresh air and reunite her with her daughter while I completed the search. We still hadn't found where they'd been keeping the boy, and I was curious about what was behind the other door.

There was debris in the hallway half-blocking the room. It didn't look as though it had been entered in a long time. I cleared away the trash and tried the doorknob. It didn't want to give. I gave the door a quick once over. It was an ordinary looking wooden one, nothing special. I decided rather than wait for help, I'd open it the Neanderthal way.

I backed up as far as I could and rammed my shoulder into the door. It gave a little but not enough. It took two more tries before I busted through. When I did, I kind of wish I hadn't. It was hard to take in what I was seeing.

The room held a narrow bed like my old Army cot. Laid out on it was a body, dried out and mummified the same as you see in those pictures of the Egyptian bigwigs. It was too far gone to make out the features good. The only recognizable thing was what it was all wrapped up in.

A pair of wings, covered in feathers.

CHAPTER FORTY-THREE

$\mathcal{I}$ reached out and touched the wings. A cloud of dust rose up to greet me. I'm not sure how long I stood there. I couldn't take in what I was seeing or make any sense of it. I was broken out of my stupor by the sound of heels tapping down the hallway.

Before I could pull myself together and stop her, Victoria walked into the room and let out a gasp.

"Jim! What on earth?"

"I don't know if it's on earth or heaven or hell. You tell me."

"That can't be—can it?"

"The boy? Henry Hasselwhite? Are there two sets of wings like that in the world?"

"Maybe he came back before we got here somehow and left the wings?"

"Look at the dust. These wings've been here a long time. As long as this poor soul I imagine."

"What are you saying? You saw the boy in the cemetery. Talked to him. We all saw him today at the airport. And Lily has been seeing him all along."

I was shook to the core. "Don't ask me what I'm saying. You know I don't believe in that kind of stuff. This is more in your line, ain't it?

You're the one convinced Lukasz's ghost saved our lives. All this time we been thinking our angel was someone playing dress up. Maybe… maybe…"

"It was a real angel after all? Oh, Jim. The poor boy. Do you really think it's Henry?"

"As far as we know, everyone else is accounted for. Maybe Mrs. Hasselwhite or Florrie can shed some light on this for us. I hope I'm wrong."

I pulled off my trench coat and lay it gently over the face of the thing on the bed. Whoever it was, they deserved some respect and privacy in death.

Victoria and I went back topside to find everyone but the Ludgate woman and the linebackers gathered in a small parlor on the first floor of the house. Marlene was tending to Mrs. Hasselwhite. Victoria went off to the kitchen to see if there were the fixings for a cup of tea.

Lily was sitting near her mother on the sofa looking bewildered. Her mother kept reaching over and trying to take her hand, but Lily pulled back every time, finally hiding her hands in the pocket of her coat.

Worried Mrs. Hasselwhite was gonna start quizzing me about her son, I decided to take the initiative. "What can you tell us about what's been going on here?" I asked, not sure if she'd feel up to talking. Not only did she feel like it though, she acted like she was gonna make up for years of being shut away all in a moment.

"It's been a nightmare ever since those people came to stay with us. My husband had friends in Germany and, I'm ashamed to admit, was sympathetic to their cause, so he agreed to let them come and stay with us, ostensibly as caretakers. I argued with him about it. Told him it was too dangerous with Henry in the house and another one on the way."

"You were pregnant?"

"Yes. No one knew about it yet but Francis."

"What happened after they got here?"

"It was all right at first. They weren't the most pleasant people, but they did take over a lot of the responsibility for running the estate and were doing a good job at it. It was only when Francis… when he died, that I realized something was terribly wrong."

"Died? Or murdered?"

"I thought it was an accident at first, but I heard them talking about it, about how easy it had been. How it would make it simpler to run the estate the way they wanted to and divert money to their cause. They caught me listening. Threatened me. Threatened Henry and my unborn child. I promised them I wouldn't tell, but they didn't trust me. That's when they locked me away. I thought they meant to kill me, too, but they decided to keep me around. I signed documents for them. Approval for expenditures, that kind of thing. Mrs. Ludgate said she believed in keeping as many insurance policies, as she put it, as possible. You never knew when they might come in handy, she would say."

"And you had the baby?"

"Yes, no doctor or midwife. She attended me. Did what was necessary. They even let me keep the baby with me for the first year or so. Until she was weaned. And then one day, they came and took her. I've never seen her again until today."

The poor woman reached out again to her daughter but dropped her hand when she saw Lily shrink away.

"What about your boy? Henry?"

"I used to see him at first. They would let us visit together. But gradually that stopped, too. She used to complain to me about him. Said he was an evil child. Always causing trouble and getting up to pranks. I begged them not to hurt the children. Said I would sign any papers they needed. Horace laughed at that. Said he could forge my signature as well as I could write it. I heard them arguing once. He wanted to get rid of me and the children. Said it was too big a risk. She put her foot down. Said if anything happened to him, she might need me to sign the papers. Horace had heart trouble. She was always worried something would happen to him and she would need a backup plan. I guess I was the backup plan."

"She's the type to want to hedge her bets, for sure."

"Such a horrible woman," Mrs. Hasselwhite shuddered. "I can't believe this. I thought I would live out the rest of my life in that prison. Never see my children again. Where's Henry? Have you found him?"

Victoria was coming in with a cup of tea and a plate of cookies just then. She and I exchanged looks as she handed the cup to Mrs. Hasselwhite and answered her.

"We're not sure yet. The police will be on their way soon, I'm sure, and we'll be able to figure everything out then. Why don't you try to drink and eat a little? You need to work on regaining your strength."

The woman accepted the offerings and sipped and nibbled a bit as I said, "I think it's about time I called up the precinct and see what's what. Light a fire under Flanagan if he isn't already on the way out here. I'd say we got more than enough evidence now."

I found a telephone in an office across the hall and talked to the desk sergeant. He said Flanagan and the D.A. were down at the courthouse talking to the judge. I passed on that there had been some interesting developments, and he promised to send someone over to let Flanagan know.

Marlene and Sister Honoria stayed to keep Lily and her mother company while the rest of us regrouped outside. I filled everyone in on what Mrs. Hasselwhite had said. I wasn't sure whether we should mention our other find or not, but Victoria jumped in with the information before I could stop her. I can't say I blamed her. It was by far the most startling discovery of the day, and that's saying something.

Bertha and Martha crossed themselves and started muttering the rosary under their breath as if they were warding off evil spirits.

Sam swore and said quietly to the Ludgate dame, "Is this true? Is that Henry Hasselwhite down there?"

"He was troublesome. It was all his own doing. I told him he would get his next meal when he apologized for his poor behavior. It's not my fault that he was so stubborn."

Sam swore again. "He was only a child."

"He should have learned better manners. I told Horace he indulged him too much. Even going so far as buying him supplies for those silly science experiments of his to try and keep him busy. Wings and feathers, indeed. Foolishness and unnecessary expense. Horace always was too soft."

I could tell Sam wanted to take a swing at her. I wasn't far behind in seconding the sentiment, but we were interrupted by a dark sedan pulling up the driveway. I thought at first it was the cops, but the dark-suited gentlemen who stepped out of the car weren't the police. One was a young man, the other a distinguished older man with a weary face.

The older man marched over to us, photo in hand, the other following behind more slowly.

"Greta Hausner. You are wanted for crimes against humanity."

CHAPTER FORTY-FOUR

She looked at him with contempt and then spit, a nasty glob that landed on the lapel of his dark coat. The man took out his handkerchief and carefully cleaned away the spot with no more emotion than the robot in that science fiction film that had just made such a splash at the local cinema.

Sam stepped forward as though to attack Florrie, but the older man lifted his hand and Sam respectfully stood aside.

Q spoke up. "You must be Mr. Solomon? I'm Marquis Sutherland. I was told you would be coming to investigate."

The older man removed his hat and laid it over his heart as he bowed slightly. "Eli Solomon. My son, Asher," he added, gesturing to the younger man. "We appreciate you, Mr. Sutherland, for bringing this matter to our attention. We will take it from here."

"What does that mean?" asked Bill Logan. "Ain't the cops on their way? What kind of cops are you two?"

"We answer to a higher power than civilian authority. We are agents of God's will."

"Dirty vermin, that's what you are. Lower than the worm on the ground," shouted Florrie, aka Greta. "You have no authority over me."

"Hate to agree with the Nazi witch," Maudie chimed in, "but

Flanagan and the boys ain't gonna appreciate it if their prime suspect disappears before those slow sad-sacks get themselves out here."

"Maybe they shouldn't have been so slow then. Early bird gets the worm, finders keepers, and all that," I said.

Victoria gave me a look. "Jim, you're not considering turning her over to these gentlemen, are you? I appreciate your mission, Mr. Solomon, but this woman has committed serious crimes here. Fraud, kidnapping, murder. She needs to pay for them."

"Those are but a drop in the buckets of blood and misery that can be laid at her door. Greta Hausner was a notorious camp guard. She has been high on our list of fugitives. She will be dealt with and will pay for all her crimes. God's retribution may take time, but it is always sure." Solomon reached toward the woman.

"Jew! Don't you dare touch me with your filthy hands!" Florrie struggled in the linebackers' hold, taking them by surprise and managing to break free. She got a good head start running, but then Maudie of all people tripped her up and sat on her, putting a swift end to her prison break.

"Get off of me, you cow!"

"When you stop wiggling like one of those worms you was talking about, we'll see."

Florrie gave it the good old college try before she finally gave up. Martha and Bertha took her in charge, looking chagrined at their previous failure and determined not to let it happen again.

"Let's all calm down a minute," I said, looking around at how hot and bothered everyone was. "Maybe we should wait until the cops come and sort out who has what rights to our friend over there by the book."

Mr. Solomon shook his head. "I'm very sorry to have to tell you, if that happens, not only will this woman not pay for her transgressions during the war, it is doubtful she will pay for any of these other crimes you speak of. She and her husband are on lists of ex-Nazis that are known to be under government protection. This is a program very few know about. It is not to the government's advantage that she should be brought to trial here where such facts may become public. I think you will find in very short order that federal agents arrive in town and spirit her away. They will even provide her with a new identity so that she may start over in another place."

"That can't be true," Victoria cried. "Our own government would never be complicit in allowing a murderer to roam free."

"These are unsettled times, my dear young woman. People forget the Nazis. They think this is a thing that belongs to the past. That we can forget about this madness. Now it is the Communists we fight and Russia. History marches on. There are comparatively few of us weakly fighting for justice for our people when compared to the inestimable power of world governments."

"What do you think, Florrie, or should I call you Greta?" I said. "Would you rather take your chances here or go with these gentlemen?"

"Don't be stupid. I will wait here. Nothing would induce me to go with these Jews. They have no morals. Who knows what they would do to me."

"No morals." Maudie cackled. "Look who's talking. You call what you did to that family moral?"

"We all do what we need to survive. Francis Hasselwhite believed in our cause, but he was weak. He was having second thoughts about providing us shelter. He has only himself to blame for his fate, and the fate of his wife and children. The woman and girl are still alive, aren't they? And the boy would have been, too, if not for his stubborn nature. Two little words. I'm sorry. That was all I asked for and he could have had all the food he wanted. But he was too proud to bend his knee to me. The same as some of those vermin in the camps. I took pleasure in exterminating those who would not acknowledge our superiority. I would do it again gladly."

You can imagine how that speech went down with our crowd.

Bill Logan threw his hands up in defeat. "This is all above my pay grade. I'm taking my supplies and heading home. World politics, murder, secrets. No, thank you. I'm a simple man, and I'd just as soon I knew nothing about any of this."

He made good on his word, jumping in his truck and roaring off.

I looked around at the rest of the crowd who were staring at Florrie as if she was the vermin she liked to talk about so much. I met everyone's eye, one by one, and without anyone saying a word, got the message.

"Mr. Solomon," I said. "I wonder if you could do us a favor. I think we might adjourn to the house to have a good sit down and talk this all over. There's a lot to consider here. Weighty questions. Not something to be decided in a minute or two. In fact, it might take us a while. Would you and your son mind keeping an eye on our prisoner here while we deliberate? I suppose it's a lot to ask."

"Not at all, Mr.—"

"Malhaven is the name, Jim Malhaven. Pleased to meet you. I won't bother with introductions all around right now. There'll be plenty of time for the formalities later. We'll leave you in charge while we're gone. What do you say?"

"A very wise decision, Mr. Malhaven. Such serious discussion should not be hurried."

"Not a bit. We'll take our time. You and your son make yourselves at home."

The rest of us turned as one to go. I thought the linebackers might object to this scheme on religious grounds, but they were the practical sort and followed along.

I heard Florrie yelling after us. "You can't leave me here with these… these… men. You cannot trust them."

I turned and tipped my hat to her. "Oh, I think we can trust them to do the right thing. They appear to be fine upstanding citizens to me."

She was still yelling as we walked away into the house. Everyone else headed back to the parlor, Victoria and I lagging behind.

She suddenly grabbed my hat from where I was still playing with it in my hand.

"Jim! Look!"

There in the crown was a neat hole through the front and the back. It wasn't the first I'd seen like that. I suddenly realized what had knocked my hat off for me back at the airport. I'd been so busy since then, I hadn't noticed. What are the chances I'd missed being shot through the cranium twice in one lifetime and both times it was the hat that got it instead?

"Gee, Victoria. I sure am sorry. I promised you I'd take better care of it and here we're gonna have to ask Mr. Klein to fix it up again."

"I'm not bothered about the hat. Mr. Klein can work magic. But no one can fix your head if you get a bullet through it next time."

"Hopefully there won't be a next time. Besides you never know. Maybe it would scramble up my brains and improve my thinking."

She lay her head against my shoulder as my arms automatically went around her.

"Even you can't make me laugh at such a thought. Promise me you won't get shot at anymore."

"The quiet life for me," I agreed. Good thing she couldn't see my fingers crossed behind her back.

CHAPTER FORTY-FIVE

It was another hour before Flanagan and the rest showed up with sirens wailing. To say he was peeved to find he had missed all the excitement is the understatement of the year. He was even more upset when he couldn't lay hands on the prime suspect. He took me out on the steps of the house to grill me about it.

"Whataya know?" I said. "Those gentlemen looked the trustworthy type. How was I to know they'd make off with her?"

Flanagan gave me the eye. "I suppose the possibility never even crossed your mind when you left them alone with her. Gimme a break, Jimmy. You knew they weren't gonna wait around for us."

"That hurts, Joey. Just 'cause I ain't always the smartest guy in the room, you don't gotta rub it in."

"Alright, alright. No point crying over spilt milk. I've put out an APB but given you can't give me a description of their automobile, nor of the gents in it, and the fact that they got a good head start, I don't have a lot of hope. You've left me with a hell of a mess to clean up. I'm gonna have a lot of explaining to do."

"We tried and tried to tell you, Flanagan, so don't give me a sob story. If you'd gotten here sooner, things might have turned out different."

"We gotta follow rules unlike some goons who get to go off half-cocked at the slightest whim. You're lucky I don't have you all up on breaking and entering charges."

"I can see the headlines now: 'Good Samaritans Arrested for Saving Imprisoned Woman from Nazi War Criminal.' That should go over swell with the fine citizens of our fair city. And I'm sure Mrs. Hasselwhite won't mind at all you having a go at her rescuers. It's not as if she has the kind of money that makes important people sit up and take notice."

Joey snorted and stalked off. I knew he'd cool down. In a way, we'd saved him a lot of trouble. I didn't doubt for a minute that Solomon had been right about the Feds sending in someone to take over the case. Easier to leave justice to someone else and clean up the mess left behind.

They'd already taken poor Henry out on a stretcher, loading him up for the morgue. The coroner had a quick look and said he'd probably been dead for months. Something about the atmosphere down in the basement had made the perfect conditions for mummification instead of the more usual decomposition. I guess I was glad for Mrs. Hasselwhite's sake. She'd insisted on seeing him before they carted him off, and while it wasn't a walk in the park for her, it was easier to take than the other.

I wandered back into the house, and out of a kind of morbid curiosity, down to the basement again. There I found Henry's mother and sister huddled together, the wings across their laps. I was gonna withdraw and leave them in peace, but Mrs. Hasselwhite beckoned me in.

"Is it true, Mr. Malhaven? Mrs. Jankowski was telling me you saw him, spoke to him, long after he must have… must have been…"

"I spoke to somebody, but it was dark. Just a voice in the night, a pale figure, wings. I don't know what to tell you. I don't believe in that kind of thing myself, but I don't know that I can give you a good explanation for it either. Only thing I can think was someone else borrowed these wings and was running around in them, but who it could've been, I can't say."

"It was Hank." This was Lily, so quiet I almost missed it.

"Was it, Henrietta?" her mother asked.

"Etta. That's what he always called me. He used to visit me in my room upstairs. Play tricks to entertain me. He got in trouble. It was my fault. He was only trying to make me happy." Tears slid down her face at the memory.

"Don't cry, Etta."

"Lily. It's Lily now. Etta was just for him."

"All right, Lily. It is a very pretty name. And don't blame yourself, dear. Henry was a bright boy. Always inventing things. I remember he used to talk to me about constructing a pair of wings like this. He had an idea he'd be able to fly, to glide if he could get high enough. It made him happy, I think, to have these experiments to occupy his time. He was lonely, too. I'm sure all the more so when he could no longer even talk to his mother."

"Are you our mother? He said you were dead."

"Maybe that's what those people told him, or maybe he was trying to protect you from the truth. Either way, he didn't want you to meet the same fate, so he helped you escape. To save you. And then you both saved me. I would never have been found if it weren't for the two of you."

"I think he's gone now. I don't feel him anymore. I always used to feel he was with me before. Now there's nothing there."

Margaret gently pulled Lily close. "Maybe he's accomplished what he wanted. Seen us both safe. It's up to us now to take care of each other, for Henry's sake. Do you think we can do that, dear?"

"I… I guess so."

I decided I should take my leave then. Let them start to get used to being a family. I was glad for Lily she wasn't all alone after all, but my heart ached for Victoria, and for me, thinking about a future that might have been.

The rest of our gang had departed back for town in the orphanage's bus, but Victoria was waiting for me in the Caddy. The night had come on and the air was cool, so we put up the top and drove back into town in silence, each cogitating on the whirlwind of events.

We stopped by the hospital to find that Cressley was doing okay, but the docs wanted to keep him overnight for observation. Surprisingly, Livinia insisted on staying with him. I would've thought she'd put her comfort over her devotion, but it only goes to show people got surprising depths sometimes.

Next stop was the vet. They were getting ready to close up shop for the day but let us in to visit the poor fellow. His leg had been too badly mangled to save. Hit by Florrie's car in her hurry to get away with Lily we guessed. The vet had amputated it but assured us Archie could live a full life with three. Victoria cried over him, caressing his soft fur. He did look a pitiful sight, but he was a tough guy. I had no doubt he'd bounce back and be chasing squirrels again in no time.

We arrived back at the cemetery in darkness. I jumped out of the car after we drove through the gates to lock them up tight for the night. We'd had enough of uninvited visitors.

It was cold, but something inside both of us made us want to linger out in the fresh air a little longer, hoping it would help clear away some of the dark things we'd seen that day. I ducked in the cottage and brought out a warm blanket to wrap us both up in as we sat on the bench outside looking up at the stars.

"I feel so sad," she sighed softly.

"It's not what we hoped for, is it? I thought we'd find poor Henry alive and well."

"And Lily. I'm glad for her that she's found her mother. But to lose her brother and even, I guess we'd have to call it a guardian angel. She'll miss him terribly."

"And you'll miss Lily, won't you?"

"Yes, there's no point in denying it. You know me too well. I thought I'd gotten over losing Karolina, but having Lily for these few days and then having her go out of our lives again, it brings it back to me, fresh and heavy."

"Don't cry, honey. Maybe we can visit with Lily when she and her ma are back on their feet."

"Margaret told me she plans to take Lily far away from here. Too many terrible memories for both of them. A fresh start. Sometimes that's the best thing you can do in life."

"A fresh start? Sounds like a smart idea. How about we make a fresh start? You and me?"

"Jim, we've talked about this."

"We have, and you always put me off, and I always let you. But you know, this kind of thing brings it home to me that we don't always have all the time we think we do. Makes me wonder what we're waiting for. Unless you aren't ready to move on. I know Lukasz and Karolina were the world to you. I can't offer you much, but what I've got is all yours. Maybe that ain't enough. If it's not, I wish you'd tell me now. I'd just as soon have my heart torn to pieces sooner than later, if you don't mind."

"I do mind. Very much. I have no intention of tearing your heart to pieces at any time, darling. Oh, look—a shooting star! Did you see it?"

"Yeah, pretty."

"I think it's a sign. I've been looking for one. Something to tell my head to follow my heart." She turned to me then with a shining face. "Let's do it! Let's get married, Jim. Start our life together properly. Whatever comes, whatever blessings or heartache there is to come, let's face it together."

I didn't need no words to let her know what I thought of that idea. It was quite a while later, when the cold got to be too much for us both, that we finally went inside. Neither of us noticed what was left behind on the bench.

Glowing under the starshine lay a single feather, pure and white. A final benediction on earthly friends and lovers from one who had moved beyond such concerns and into the brightest light of them all.

ABOUT THE AUTHOR

Helen Whistberry is an indie author and artist who took up writing after retiring from a long career working in libraries. She is the author of the Jim Malhaven Mysteries series, light noir novels with a cozy mystery feel and a touch of the paranormal that pay loving tribute to the wise guy detectives of the 1940s and '50s; and a Christmas-themed Gothic ghost tale as well as contributing short stories to numerous anthologies. When not writing or drawing, she enjoys exploring the natural world of the Southeastern United States and loves all animals, including her two cats and a rather silly six-pound Chihuahua. She also loves to read and review books by fellow indie authors. You can find out more about her books, art, and book reviews by visiting

www.helenwhistberry.com

Thank you so much for reading *The Avenging Angel*. I hope you enjoyed reading it as much as I enjoyed writing it!